Pra

"Sheila Conn... about apples a... will you get hooked on the mystery, but you will be racing to the kitchen to bake an apple treat!"

—*Cozy Mystery Book Review*

"Fans will enjoy the heroine taking a bite out of crime in this fun regional cozy." —*Genre Go Round Reviews*

"Really well written . . . I was constantly kept guessing. This series is in its stride, and I'm eagerly awaiting the next book in this series." —*Fresh Fiction*

"Meg is a smart, savvy woman who's working hard to fit into her new community—just the kind of protagonist I look for in today's traditional mystery. I look forward to more trips to Granford, Massachusetts!"

—*Meritorious Mysteries*

"An enjoyable and well-written book with some excellent apple recipes at the end." —*Cozy Library*

"A wonderful slice of life in a small town . . . The mystery is intelligent and has an interesting twist . . . *Rotten to the Core* is a fun, quick read with an enjoyable heroine, an interesting hook, and some yummy recipes at the end."

—*The Mystery Reader* (4 stars)

continued . . .

"Full of rich description, historical context, and mystery."
—*The Romance Readers Connection*

"Meg Corey is a very likable protagonist . . . [A] delightful new series."
—*Gumshoe Review*

"An example of everything that is right with the cozy mystery . . . A likable heroine, an attractive small-town setting, a slimy victim, and fascinating side elements . . . There's depth to the characters in this book that isn't always found in crime fiction . . . Sheila Connolly has written a winner for cozy mystery fans."
—*Lesa's Book Critiques*

"A warm, very satisfying read." —*RT Book Reviews* (4 stars)

"The premise and plot are solid, and Meg seems a perfect fit for her role."
—*Publishers Weekly*

"Meg Corey is a fresh and appealing sleuth with a bushel-ful of entertaining problems . . . One crisp, delicious read."
—Claudia Bishop, bestselling author of the Hemlock Falls Mysteries

"A delightful look at small-town New England, with an intriguing puzzle thrown in."
—JoAnna Carl, author of the Chocoholic Mysteries

"Thoroughly enjoyable . . . I can't wait for the next book and a chance to spend more time with Meg and the good people of Granford."
—Sammi Carter, author of the Candy Shop Mysteries

Golden Malicious

Sheila Connolly

BERKLEY PRIME CRIME, NEW YORK

THE BERKLEY PUBLISHING GROUP
Published by the Penguin Group
Penguin Group (USA)
375 Hudson Street, New York, New York 10014, USA

USA | Canada | UK | Ireland | Australia | New Zealand | India | South Africa | China

Penguin Books Ltd., Registered Offices: 80 Strand, London WC2R 0RL, England
For more information about the Penguin Group, visit penguin.com.

GOLDEN MALICIOUS

A Berkley Prime Crime Book / published by arrangement with the author

Berkley Prime Crime Books are published by The Berkley Publishing Group.
BERKLEY® PRIME CRIME and the PRIME CRIME
logo are trademarks of Penguin Group (USA).

For information, address: The Berkley Publishing Group,
a division of Penguin Group (USA),
375 Hudson Street, New York, New York 10014.

ISBN: 978-0-425-25710-4

PUBLISHING HISTORY
Berkley Prime Crime mass-market edition / October 2013

PRINTED IN THE UNITED STATES OF AMERICA

10 9 8 7 6 5 4 3 2

Cover illustration by Mary Ann Lasher.
Cover design by Annette Fiore DeFex.
Interior text design by Laura K. Corless.

ALWAYS LEARNING   PEARSON

Acknowledgments

As always I owe a big thank-you to my agent, Jessica Faust of BookEnds, and my editor, Shannon Jamieson Vazquez. Without their help this book and series would never have seen the light of day.

But for this particular book I also need to thank an unlikely pair of organizations which inspired the story: The Daughters of the American Revolution and the United States Department of Agriculture.

A couple of years ago the Easthampton Colonial building owned by the Betty Allen Chapter of the Massachusetts Daughters of the American Revolution was struck by a fast-moving car, causing significant damage to one corner of the house. Luckily eighteenth-century carpenters knew what they were doing and their building was meant to last, so the damage could be repaired. Restoring a building to historical standards isn't always easy, but the restoration community in western Massachusetts stepped up and contributed materials, labor, and expertise to make sure it was brought back to its original state.

My husband, who is a research entomologist studying the control or elimination of invasive species of insects in this country, has worked for one or another agency of the USDA for much of his career. In the past he studied the Asian longhorned beetle, a threat to forest trees, including those in a part of Massachusetts not far from Granford. I'm familiar with the insect, and now I've found a way to use it in a story, with a twist that surprised even some members of the USDA. How often can a mystery writer claim to have invented a new crime?

To find out how I manage to combine these elements, read on! And to all of the readers who have taken Meg and Seth and the other citizens of Granford into their lives, thank you!

1

Meg Corey awoke before 7 a.m. to the sound of Seth Chapin's cell phone ringing, and she wasn't happy about it. Even though he grabbed it up and answered after the second ring, she had been hoarding the last few minutes of sleep, and now some impatient idiot had stolen them from her. The day hadn't even started, and she was already tired. At the rate things were going in the orchard, she would be tired for the next six months.

Meg could hear the sound of Seth's voice in the hall, where he'd carried the phone. He sounded startled but not upset, so maybe for once an early-morning call wasn't bad news. She decided to lie there and wait for his report, and managed to doze off.

When she opened her eyes again, a fully dressed Seth announced, "Good morning—sorry about that. I made coffee, if that's any consolation."

"Depends," Meg mumbled into the pillow. "What was so important that whoever it was couldn't wait until a civilized hour? It's not even"—she squinted at the digital clock near the bed—"seven o'clock."

Seth sat down on the bed next to her. "It looks like a job, and they need someone fast. Last night some idiot took a curve too fast and ran his car head-on into Donald Butterfield's house. You know—over on the northeast side of town? The driver was a drunken kid. He walked away, but Donald says the house took a big hit."

Meg, still feeling like a newcomer to town after less than two years, did not share native son Seth's encyclopedic knowledge of all the people and houses of Granford. "Do I know Donald?"

"Probably not, but I bet you know the house. It's one of the oldest in town, older even than our two places. Mid-1700s. You must have driven by it, on the way to Amherst."

"Mmm," Meg replied noncommittally. "So what happened?" She accepted that more sleep was out of the question, rolled over, and propped herself up on a couple of pillows. "How bad's the damage?"

"Hard to tell without seeing it," Seth replied cheerfully, "but it's pretty clear that one whole corner is trashed, and more is probably knocked askew. They built houses strong in those days, but they weren't counting on a couple of tons of metal hitting one at high speed."

"If I remember that road, it's kind of hard to go very fast. And how do you go off the road and into a house?" Meg said. "But I can tell you're just drooling to get your hands on the place." Seth's renovation business had been picking up as the economy improved, but his heart lay with restoring the surviving Colonial houses in the area, and this damaged house would give him a prime opportunity to show what he could do.

"Of course. But it gets better. Donald is very proud of the house, because it's been in his family since it was built. So not only does he want it repaired with historically correct materials, I'd guess he's going to want me, or whoever, to use period tools, too, so even the tool marks match."

"Sounds kind of obsessive, don't you think?" Meg said.

"I can understand where he's coming from. Besides, Donald hinted that the kid who was driving the car comes from a family with money, and they're willing to pay whatever it takes to keep Donald Butterfield happy—and keep Junior out of court."

"Do you have to compete for this, or is the job yours for the taking?"

"I'm hoping the latter. I know a couple of other guys I can pull in, who have the right skills, especially in woodworking and replicating antique plaster. And it needs to be done not only right but fast, since the place is wide open, except for some tarps. At least we've got decent weather for it, and a couple of good months to get the work done. If it had happened in winter, Donald would have had to move out—or would have insisted on staying and frozen to death."

"Go!" Meg said, laughing at his enthusiasm. "I give you my blessing."

"We didn't have any plans for today, did we?" Seth asked belatedly.

"Not 'we' as in you and me. Bree and I have plenty of plans." As to exactly what those plans were, though, Meg largely deferred to her young orchard manager and housemate Briona Stewart, who knew far more than novice farmer Meg did about running an apple orchard. "Another round of spraying, since the weird weather this year is throwing off a lot of biological schedules, and some pests have arrived early. Plus irrigating, particularly in the new part of the orchard where the baby trees don't have well-established root systems yet. So the short answer is, a lot of hauling things from place to place, rinse and repeat, at least for the next couple of weeks, if we don't get any rain."

"I should be done in time for dinner. I'll cook tonight."

"You're working, too. I wish Granford had a decent pizza place, one that delivered."

"I'll put it on the town's wish list—one of the perks of being selectman for Granford. Not that it means it will happen. Look, I'd better run. I'll talk to you if plans change. You go back to sleep."

As if. The sun was shining and there was work to be done. A lot of work. Well, she'd asked for it when she took over the orchard. And then expanded it. What was she, a masochist? She wasn't a newbie anymore, and she knew that insects, pests, and water shortages were ordinary parts of raising any crop. She also knew even better that doing anything in the orchard meant doing it herself, alongside Bree, and it was often dirty physical work. So much for the romance of farming. There wouldn't be any other help until harvesttime—and there wouldn't be a harvest unless she got her butt in gear.

She dressed and wandered down to the kitchen, where Bree was already sitting at the table reading some sort of farming journal.

"I saw Seth breeze by—what's his hurry?" Bree asked, munching on a bagel.

"Apparently somebody ran a car into a house at the far end of town, and the owner asked him to work on the

repairs, so he went over to look at it. He seemed very excited about it."

"I can't believe how badly some idiots drive around
here. Was the guy drunk?"

"I love the way you assume it was a guy, like no woman
ever lost control of her car. But yes, Seth said alcohol was
involved, plus stupidity and speed. Seth can fill us in later,"
Meg said as she helped herself to coffee. "He said he'd cook
dinner. So what's on our list for today?"

"There's no rain in the forecast, so we'll be irrigating
again. We're lucky to have the well up there in the orchard."

"I wish I could say it was brilliant planning on my part,
but it came with the place. I agree, though, it's a blessing.
Tell me again why we're doing this by hand?"

"What, you don't like following in the footsteps of your
ancestors?" Bree grinned at her.

"Not if it means heavy lifting. Aren't there easier systems available?"

"Of course there are. Just install drip irrigation. We've
got the water supply."

"But not the money, at least not right now. Why didn't
we do this last summer?"

"Because it rained enough last summer that we didn't
have to irrigate. Lucky us."

Meg sighed. In a way she was grateful that she'd had it
relatively easy in her first year of working with the
orchard—not that it had felt that way at the time!—but part
of her wished she had known that an irrigation system lay
somewhere in her future, so she could budget for it. Ha!
There was no budget. They'd been lucky to do better than
break even last year, and she'd been hoping things would
improve this year, but then she'd laid out money to buy and

plant new trees. Which was a good business move but had
eaten into her cash. "Do we need any more pesticide?"

Bree didn't look up from her magazine. "Not today, but
soon. The trees are stressed enough by the lack of water,
without having critters gnawing on them."

"Global warming?" Meg asked.

Bree shrugged. "Maybe. But I'm not going to worry
about something I can't do anything about. Still, I'd bet our
yield will be down this year, for a number of reasons."

"Gee, thanks. I love starting the day with such cheery
news," Meg said. Fewer apples meant smaller profits, although they wouldn't need as many pickers. But the pickers
were counting on the income from their seasonal employ-
ment, so she couldn't cut back too far there. Ah, well. As
Bree had said, it made more sense to worry only about the
things they could actually control.

"Well, you wanted to be a farmer. Welcome to the real
world."

"I know, I know. Let me finish breakfast and we can get
started."

The day proceeded much as planned, which meant a lot
of hard work. In the absence of a permanently installed irrigation system, Bree and Meg were relying on a tried-and-
true manual system: a tank hauled behind their creaky
tractor. The tank had spray heads on both sides, to water
the trees, but it had to move slowly to provide enough water,
not just a surface sprinkling. Worse, the tank's capacity
was limited, which meant that they had to return to the
wellhead often and refill the tank. It was a time-consuming
process, little changed from nineteenth-century pictures
Meg had seen, except that back then the tank was pulled by
horses. But at least she had the well; without it, she would

have had to depend on municipal water. Another expense she couldn't afford.

So here she was, trucking water around her eighteen acres of apple trees. If her mother or her college classmates could see her now! Meg thought to herself. Sweating and filthy. And worried—to her inexperienced eye, there weren't as many baby apples as there should be, or as there had been the year before. She knew she'd been lucky with her first crop, but it made it hard to accept less this year. Was the weather going to improve anytime soon? Bree didn't seem optimistic. What constituted an official drought? Was this one? Was it only last winter that she had yearned for sun and warmth? Well, she'd gotten it, and then some. Temperatures hadn't gone much below eighty for a couple of weeks, even at night.

It was after five when Meg walked slowly down the hill, glad to see Seth's car in the drive, and hoping he had remembered his promise to make dinner. She let herself in by the back door and found Seth absorbed in reading one of her cookbooks.

"All you need now is an apron, and this would be the perfect picture," Meg said with a smile when he noticed her.

"Glad to be of service. You look beat. Where's Bree?"

"Bringing the tractor back down the hill for the night. It's not much, but I'd hate to lose it. There are probably other farmers worse off than I am who might decide to drive off with it. And I am beat. I think I'll claim executive privilege and grab a shower before she gets here."

"Go for it. Dinner should be ready soon."

"Sounds good." *Especially since I don't even have to cook it.* Meg trudged up the stairs, feeling every muscle. Twenty minutes later, minus a layer of dirt, she passed Bree coming up the stairs as she went down. "It's all yours," Meg said. Bree grunted in return and kept going. Meg ran her fingers through her hair, almost dry already, even though she'd been out of the shower for only a few minutes.

Back in the kitchen, Meg dropped into a chair, and Seth handed her a glass of chilled wine, a thin sheen of moisture beading the outside. Meg accepted it gratefully and took a long sip. "Oh, that's good. So, how was your day?"

"Interesting. I saw the house and went over it with Donald and his insurance assessor. The car did a real number on it—took out the corner altogether, so we have to shore that up so the second story doesn't collapse. An original eighteenth-century corner cupboard is now in splinters, and a lot of the wainscoting is beyond salvage. A number of windows are gone. Donald is in mourning for every fragment."

"I assume you got the job?"

"Yes. Donald knows my work and trusts me."

"How much can be repaired or replaced?" Meg asked, feeling pleasantly buzzed by the wine.

"All of it, for a price, but that doesn't seem to be a problem. I'll check out some of the salvage places locally—you remember Eric, over in Hadley?—and see if there are any windows of the right size. But most likely we'll have to reconstruct them. Matching the boards for the wainscoting is going to be a bigger problem, since they've got to be eighteen inches wide, like yours."

"Is that kind of stuff still available?"

"Not at your local box stores, but there's an old family-owned sawmill not far from here that can probably help us out."

"There used to be a sawmill at the back of this property,"

Meg said. "I remember seeing a picture at the historical society in town."

Seth sat down across the table from her, with a bottle of beer. "Back in those days it didn't take anything fancy, and you weren't supplying more than your own needs and maybe a couple of neighbors. Once the insurance comes up with a figure, I need to go back and get some measurements so I can give Donald estimates for materials, and since he's got the budget for it, I may call in a professional cleanup team, although I'll have to keep an eye on them to make sure they don't take away any of the good stuff that can be reused. Even if it's only a piece of board, it can be recycled somewhere in the house. Did you ever notice that some of the timbers in this house in the attic were recycled?"

"No, sir, I did not. How can you tell?"

"A few of the long beams have mortises that don't match any timbers with tenons. And they're pretty major beams. Why waste a perfectly good piece of lumber? Especially one that nobody was ever going to see?"

"Why is it that you know more about my house than I do?"

"You know plenty. I just have an eye for construction."

Bree came loudly down the stairs from her room, her hair wet. "Something smells great. Are we ready to eat?"

"Sit and I'll dish up," Seth said.

He looks so cheerful, Meg thought. *It can't be because he likes cooking so much, so it has to be the new project.* "You look like a kid with a new toy," she told Seth.

He distributed filled plates and sat down. "I feel like that. Historic renovation and reconstruction really are what I like to do best, and I don't get many opportunities. Hey, you should come see the place, while its bones are bared. Bree, can you spare her for a few hours?"

"Tomorrow's okay," Bree said, her mouth full. "We've just started irrigating, and I've got to measure the soil moisture. We probably didn't give it enough today, but I've never tried it in this orchard and I didn't want to waste water. I'll check it in the morning, but let's assume it'll be every other day for the moment."

"If your boss is going to give you the time off, Meg"— Seth smiled at Bree—"figure on most of the day tomorrow. That way I can take you to see the sawmill, too."

Meg sat back and watched the two of them plan her week for her, but she had no objections. She enjoyed learning about old houses like her own, and she loved sharing Seth's enthusiasm. For him, his job was the perfect blend of work and pleasure—and how many people could say that?

"Let me know when you've figured out my schedule," she said with a smile, then dug into her dinner.

2

Since Bree had graciously granted her a day off, the next morning Meg enjoyed some cherished moments of leisure, and a second cup of coffee. Her cat Lolly was sitting on the windowsill in the sun, diligently washing her face with a paw, and Meg had actually managed to finish reading the newspaper by the time Seth let himself in the back door.

"Hey, is there any more of that?" He pointed to Meg's cup.

"Help yourself. I'm too lazy to get up."

He poured himself a cup and sat down across from her. "You still up for seeing the house?"

"Sure. I can't imagine losing an entire corner of my house. What's going on there now?"

"Donald insists he's going to stay there twenty-four-seven with a shotgun in hand, if need be, to drive away any snoops. Or looters. Yesterday I followed the insurance

assessor around while he checked it out. He's a good guy.
I've worked with him before. Of course, the problem is that
anything new that goes in will not only have to meet Donald's standards but also current code requirements, which
is going to make things complicated."

"Do you have to bring the rest of the systems up to that
standard? Like plumbing and wiring?"

"Probably, at the least for the repairs. Frankly, if the
walls are open it makes sense to upgrade the rest, if I can
persuade Donald. I'm still looking into what's required."

"I assume he wants you to get this done fast?"

"Within reason. I told Donald it might take some time to
pull together all the historically correct materials, but I'm
already working on it. I think the bottom line is, he'd rather
have it done right than done quickly. You ready to go?"

Meg drained the last of her coffee. "I guess so."

"Don't sound so excited! I thought you'd enjoy it, but if
you'd rather take a nap and do your laundry, I'll understand."

He would, too, Meg knew. But this was something she
could share with him, and it would help her to understand
her own house, and she had the time free, and the sun was
shining . . . She had no excuses. "Let's go."

Meg's house lay close to the south end of Granford, but
the whole town extended no more than a few miles to its
farthest point. To the north lay Amherst, with a large hill,
locally called a mountain, in between. Donald Butterfield's
house lay in the northeast corner of Granford, along the
main road heading north. It sat close to the road, typical of
the Colonial houses in the area, and as they approached,
Meg could see the damaged corner on the near side, draped
in billowing blue plastic tarps.

"Wow. That kid must have been going pretty fast to do

so much damage! The house was in generally good shape before, wasn't it? I mean, no termites or rot?"

"I don't know what the police report will say, but yeah, he had to be going close to eighty, way above the speed limit along here. The house was in as good shape as any house this age can be. Does it look familiar?"

"You mean, does it look like your house and my house?" Seth's house, as well as his mother Lydia's, lay just over the hill from Meg's, no more than a mile or so away, although out of sight. "Pretty much. I've already figured out that most Colonials follow the same general pattern, and yours and mine were built about the same time, maybe 1760, right?"

Seth nodded. "And probably by the same people—neighbors helped each other out."

"Nice," Meg said. "Except I've got two windows on the sides, and Donald has only one. And this has only one chimney instead of my two."

"Yours had only the big central one originally, re-member?"

"True. So this is like mine, only a little older and a little smaller. The parts the car didn't take out look to be in decent shape. It's been painted recently?" Meg was still trying to figure out where she'd find the money to paint her own house, but she had to replace the roof first. She felt a pang of jealousy, looking at the obviously well-tended house in front of her. But at least no car had run into hers.

"A few years ago. The chimney's been repointed, too."

"Don't tell me that's something else I have to worry about," Meg protested.

"You can do it when you take care of the roof. Let me show you the rest of the building." Seth got out of the car and waved at a man who had come out the front door. He was slight, with thinning hair, and appeared to be in his sixties. "Hi, Donald. I brought Meg Corey along to see your place. She lives in the Colonial—"

"On the Ludlow road—I know the place," Donald said promptly. "It's the old Warren house. Welcome, Meg." He offered his hand and Meg shook it. "I'm sorry we're not looking our best at the moment. Damn kids."

We? He seems to have personalized his house, Meg thought with amusement. "Even with the damage, I can tell you've taken good care of the place."

"I consider it a privilege to be custodian of a piece of our past, Meg."

"Did the appraiser drop off his report, Donald?" Seth asked.

"He did, and he left a whole stack of papers. I thought for sure Ben Lathrop was going to make me evacuate, but I told him that our forefathers got by just fine without indoor plumbing and electricity, and I didn't need heat, this time of year."

"And he bought that?" Seth asked.

"Sure did."

"Good for him," Seth said. "I don't know if you've met Ben yet, Meg. He's our town safety inspector, and he's been known to be a stickler for regulations."

"I had to promise him to have this closed up and back together by the end of the month, Seth," Donald said. "I know it's a tight schedule, but he wouldn't budge. Can you make that work?"

Seth considered before answering. "If I postpone a couple of other projects I've been working on and can get the right people on board, then yes. Problem is, I know you want to keep this authentic, which means it might take longer than usual."

"If it's any help to you, that idiot kid's father gave me a fat check to get started, and I took it straight to the bank. So if it's a matter of cost, don't worry."

"That's not the issue, Donald. Getting the right materials is. But Meg and I are heading over to Nash's Sawmill from here, and we'll see what they've got in stock, or can get easily."

"Good people there," Donald said. "I like the way they take care of the forest properties they own."

"I agree," Seth said. "They've got a solid long-range plan. The problem is, they're finding it hard with a small sawmill operation to compete with the big chains. Specialty moldings are not enough to keep a business going. But for now, I throw them whatever work I can."

"Let me know what you find, Seth," Donald said.

"Don't worry, I will."

"Nice to meet you, Donald," Meg said. "I look forward to seeing the progress on your house repairs. It'll make mine look less overwhelming."

"Good to meet you, too, Meg. Maybe sometime I could take the tour of your place? I hear tell you've got a well in the basement."

Meg laughed. "I do, and there's still water there. If I'm ever under siege by angry natives, I'm prepared. I'd love to show it to you. Just let me know when you want to stop by—I'm out in the orchard a lot."

Donald waved farewell as they pulled away, and when Meg looked last, he was pacing around the broken corner of his house and shaking his head.

"Poor guy," she said. "He really loves that house. Does he have any family?"

"The kids are grown, and his wife left him a few years ago. People in town used to joke that she felt she couldn't compete with the house. Anyway, Donald's alone there now. He's retired, so he doesn't have much else to do than worry about the place."

"I can sympathize up to a point, but I've got enough other things going on to keep me from becoming monomaniacal about my house. Of course, I'd have to win a lottery to do all the things I should or I'd like to."

"One step at a time, Meg."

"I know, I know. Roof first, then paint. But my fondest dream is to have another bathroom. Of course, I can't pay much, but I might be able to offer some other considerations to a handsome local contractor . . ."

Seth sneaked a quick glance at her. "I'm not sure how the bookkeeping for that would work. But I'll keep it in mind," he said, smiling.

"You do that," said Meg. "Okay, so about this sawmill. What were you and Donald talking about, when you said you admired their land management policies?"

"It's an interesting story, but I kind of have to go back to the beginning to explain it. Nash's Sawmill has been in business since the 1740s, and they own a lot of timberland, not just in Granford, but in over twenty other towns in a couple of counties. Massachusetts has what is called Chapter 61, a ten-year management plan for conserving forestland, and Nash's sticks very closely to it. What that means is that their forests are harvested only periodically and carefully, and they work hard to maintain conservation of soil, water, and wildlife. They even keep the land open for some recreational uses. They plan to hold the timberland for the long term, and even expand it for Chapter 61 conservation. The mill itself is only a small portion of the operation."

"That's impressive," Meg commented. "Do you know the family?"

"Some of them. It's one of the oldest family-run businesses in the country, and it takes more than one generation to manage it. I know some of the younger ones, though unfortunately they may be the last generation to play a role in the company. Over the last few years the sawmill has been mostly a tourist attraction, and it loses money. I have to say I'm tempted to invest in some of their less available woods and stockpile a supply for projects like this, before it's too late."

"So in an odd way, it's good that car hit Donald's house now, rather than next year?" Meg asked.

"You could look at it that way, if you're a Pollyanna. Not a bad thing to be." Seth turned into a wide but mostly empty parking lot in front of a long, low building, its axis parallel to the road. "Hang on a sec—I want to see if Jonas is here," Seth said. "He said he'd be in and out this afternoon."

Meg waited while Seth climbed the wooden steps of the building. He returned only a minute or two later. "He's not around?"

"Not in the mill," Seth said, climbing back in the car, "but one of the guys said he's over at one of his local woodlots, only a few minutes from here. You game to head over?"

"Hey, I'm enjoying a day when I not only don't have to do any work, I don't even have to decide where to drive. It's fine with me. Do I know this place?"

"You've probably driven by it without noticing. You haven't been taking many picnics in the park lately, have you?"

"Who has time? I didn't even know there are picnic areas around here."

"Several. I should show you the map of Granford. We've got state-owned land, town-owned land, and privately held land, and most of those properties include some recreational areas. The ones you might have noticed lie along Route 202. That's where the town's ball fields are."

"I guess I haven't been paying attention, but if I wanted to picnic I'd be more likely to do it on my own property. Doesn't all this land with different owners make life complicated for Granford to manage?" The problem had never occurred to Meg when she lived in Boston.

"It does. It takes a certain amount of cooperation, and a lot of paperwork, but we do have a green space plan in place. Now, Nash's land is one of those multiuse examples I told you about. There are a few fire pits and some tables and benches. The sad thing is, people can be careless with their fires, and sometimes local kids go out and trash the place because they know no one can see them. But Jonas believes in keeping the land open to the public, even if that means he has to pay for cleanup now and then. And that's above and beyond logging the forest."

Jonas sounded a lot like Seth, putting the needs of the community before his own, or at least before his own financial benefit. No wonder Seth liked working with him; they were a rare breed.

Another five minutes brought them to a marginally paved road, marked by a discreet sign indicating that picnic facilities were available, though none were visible from the road. Seth turned with the ease of familiarity and followed the lane to where it opened out into a roughly marked parking area, where there were already two other vehicles parked. Seth pulled over to one side and parked. "This is it. That's Jonas's truck over there. From here we walk."

"Sounds good to me," Meg said, climbing out of her side. "How do you expect to find him here?"

"He'll be looking at the older growth trees—you can tell which ones they are if you look. They're bigger, and there'll be a bunch of trees, together but not too close. Jonas likes to keep an eye on the foresting operation."

"Hey, my expertise so far is limited to apple trees."

"That way," Seth pointed, and he started walking.

Meg had to hurry to keep up. Obviously Seth knew where he was going, but then, he'd grown up around here and probably knew most of the parks and recreation areas. It was nice having green space, Meg admitted; a benefit to the town, and to others who did not have as much land as she did. Even though she'd been raised largely in suburbs with sidewalks, she had learned to enjoy open space and plants and trees and the occasional animal that wandered through her yard. Most of the time.

Ouch. She hadn't worn shoes suitable for hiking, and somehow a pebble had worked its way inside one shoe. "Seth?" she called out. "I'm going to sit for a moment and get this rock out of my shoe. Don't go too far, okay?"

He stopped for a moment to look back at her. "You all right?"

"Of course I am. It's just something in my shoe. I'll only be a minute. You go ahead."

"Okay—I won't be far. You'll hear us talking from here." He turned and followed the faint path at a faster clip.

Meg looked around to find somewhere to sit—a handy

log or flat rock. There was nothing near the path, but maybe ten feet away the land rose slightly, and a dead tree had fallen along the ridge. She made her way up to it and sat down with relief, untying and pulling off her shoe and shaking out a small piece of gravel, before replacing the shoe and tying the laces tightly. Then she leaned back, her hands on either side, and listened. Birds. Distant voices, male—Seth and Jonas, most likely. She couldn't see them from where she sat, but she wasn't concerned. She was only a couple of miles from home, not lost in a primeval forest.

As she sat, she noticed a large insect a few feet away, lying on the log with its feet in the air. Dead, obviously. It wasn't anything she recognized, and she would have remembered. It was unusual looking; it had to be two inches long, mottled black and white, with antennae as long at its body. She shifted a couple of feet farther away—irrational, she knew, since the creature was clearly dead.

What was that smell? It smelled like something had died. *Well, it's the woods—what do you expect, Meg?* There were coyotes around here, and hawks, and probably other predators she couldn't name. She was pretty sure they killed smaller animals. Hadn't someone seen bears in the county? She wouldn't welcome meeting one of them out here.

The odor managed to interfere with her enjoyment of nature. Meg stood up and dusted off the seat of her pants, taking a last look around. The odor was definitely coming from the far side of the low ridge, away from the path, and it was clearly something rotting. She scanned the ground, through the thick underbrush.

Nothing to be seen . . . except a human hand, protruding from the brush.

Whoever was attached to it was obviously dead. Meg sat back down heavily on the log, since her legs didn't seem to be holding her.

Not again.

3

The woods were as still and lovely as they had been the minute before, but Meg was not fooled. Now there was a body. She was not going to look any more closely; there was no need to make sure whoever it had been was dead. The mottled discoloration of the fingers, not to mention the ragged patches where something had nibbled on the unexpected treat, took care of that question.

It depressed her that she knew the right procedures. The basics: don't disturb the scene, and notify someone in authority as soon as possible. Well, the first one she'd follow, but she couldn't bring herself to deal with the second. Instead, Meg chose to sit, facing away from whoever it was. This was not her body. It had nothing to do with her. Seth would come back any minute—let him handle it. Thank goodness he hadn't decided to bring his Golden Retriever Max along. Max would have been thrilled by Meg's find, and probably would have wallowed in it. How do you rid a dog of the odor of decomp? Tomato juice? Or did that work only for skunk odor? Her mind was jumping all over the place.

After a few more minutes Seth did indeed appear, followed by a man about his age who must be Jonas Nash. When Seth came within a few feet of her, he said quickly, "What's wrong?"

Meg felt a hysterical urge to make him guess, but that would simply delay the inevitable. "There's a body. Back there." She pointed behind her without turning.

Seth gave her a searching look, then peered past her. "Damn, you're right."

"Who is it?" Jonas shoved his way past Seth to get a better view. Seth blocked him from going closer with an arm across his chest.

"No way to tell from here." He glanced at Meg. "Would you believe I have the state police on speed dial?"

Meg smiled faintly but said nothing.

"Are you all right, Meg?" When she nodded, Seth laid a hand on her shoulder briefly, without saying anything more, then walked away a few paces to make the phone call that had to be made.

That left Meg alone with Jonas Nash. She stood up and held out her hand. "Hi. I'm Meg Corey, if Seth hasn't told you, and I assume you're Jonas Nash and these are your woods?"

Jonas shook, with a rueful smile. "Correct on both counts. It's nice to meet you, although the circumstances could be better."

"Are you missing anyone? Like an employee or a relative?" Meg asked.

"I don't think so. For my own sake, I'm hoping this is a stranger who wandered into the park and happened to die of natural causes—heart attack, stroke, who knows? It would still be a terrible shame, of course, but I hope it's not much more complicated than that."

Meg nodded. "Me too."

Seth returned, stuffing his cell phone in his shirt pocket. "The state police are on their way. Maybe we should meet them at the parking area?"

"You mean, get away from here? Good idea," Jonas said heartily. "We can head off anyone else who shows up looking for a good picnic spot."

"You go ahead. We'll be along in a minute," Seth said.

Jonas looked at them for a moment, then said, "Right." He turned and strode off the way they had come.

Seth offered Meg a hand, then pulled her up into his arms. "I'm so sorry."

"You don't need to apologize. Neither of us had anything to do with this. This is just our usual bad karma following us around. But thank you for worrying." Reluctant to withdraw from Seth's reassuring embrace, Meg reflected that it was nice to have someone who worried about how she felt. She was still getting used to that.

"We should go join Jonas. It shouldn't take Detective Marcus more than twenty minutes to get here."

"Seems long to me, although I'll be happy to get away from the body. Him. Funny how a person goes from being human to being a thing when he's dead," Meg mused. "You don't think Jonas had anything to do with this?"

"I can't see why he would. I don't know him well, but he's always seemed like a good guy. But you know as well as I do that we've both been wrong about things like that in the past. It is Nash land, after all—although if he'd wanted to hide a body, no doubt he knows of much better places to do it, where it wouldn't be found for a long time."

"Maybe he wanted it to be found. It's not that far off the path."

"Hey, let's not get ahead of ourselves. Right now the only fact we have is that there is a body lying maybe twenty feet from where we stand."

Meg backed away and brushed down her shorts. "We'd better go face the music. I hope this doesn't spill over into tomorrow, or Bree will be seriously annoyed."

In the parking area they all waited silently until Detective William Marcus's state police car arrived from Northampton. He parked at the end of the lot, closest to where the access lane entered, and climbed out. Another officer emerged from the passenger seat. Marcus surveyed the scene and finally focused on Meg, Seth, and Jonas Nash. He shook his head.

"Why am I not surprised?" he said, when he was in earshot.

"Hello, Detective," Meg said, her tone resigned. "Maybe you should simply hire me as a bloodhound for homicides in your jurisdiction. I seem to have a knack for finding bodies."

"Meg, Seth," said Detective Marcus by way of a greeting. "And this is?" He looked at Jonas.

Jonas stepped forward and extended his hand. "I'm Jonas Nash—I run Nash Lumber. My family owns this property."

"I thought the name sounded familiar. Meg, you found the body?" When Meg nodded, Marcus went on, "Before we go take a look, tell me what happened."

Meg recited what little there was to tell. She had arrived, followed Seth and Jonas, stopped to remove the stone from her shoe, then smelled the rotting body. No, she had not gone any closer, much less disturbed the body. To be strictly accurate, she didn't know if there actually was a body; all she had seen was the hand.

Marcus nodded without comment. "So you have no idea who it is or how this person died. Seth, you didn't notice anything?"

"Nope, I was looking for Jonas. We'd planned to meet this morning, and one of his employees at the sawmill said he was here."

"What about you, Nash?"

"No. But if it was downwind, I wouldn't have smelled anything. I certainly didn't see anything on my way in."

Marcus checked his watch. "The forensic team said they'd be here as soon as possible, and we've got a few hours of light left. Show me where he is. I suppose there's no point in keeping off the path?"

"You mean, in terms of preserving evidence?" Jonas asked, surprised. "Probably not. Plenty of people come this way. Animals, too, like deer."

"Figures," Marcus said. "Show us the way."

Meg let Jonas lead the way. After all, it was his property. When they reached the point closest to the log where Meg had sat, she pointed. "If you go stand by that log there, you'll see the hand."

"Stay here," Marcus ordered. He studied the scene for a moment, then walked off at an angle so he could approach the body obliquely. He was out of sight beyond the ridge for a few minutes, then returned with a wallet in his latex-gloved hand. "Name's David Clapp, from Easthamp-ton. That ring any bells?"

Meg and Seth looked at each other, and they all came up blank. "Doesn't mean anything to me," Seth said, "but I didn't look at his face." Meg felt obscurely relieved that it wasn't a neighbor.

Marcus turned to Jonas. "Nash, what about you? Is he an employee?"

Jonas looked shaken. "Not at the moment, but he used to be, until a year or two ago. Nowadays we contract out for the lumbering, unless we're harvesting trees specifically for the sawmill. He's from one of the logging teams. I've seen him now and then, since he left the sawmill."

"You two part on good terms?" Marcus asked.

"Well, he wasn't happy to be let go, but he understood why—we just couldn't afford to keep all the staff on. It made more sense to bring in a crew on an as-needed basis. No hard feelings."

"Get me the name of your logging contractor, and I'll check with him," Marcus said.

"No problem," Jonas answered.

From where they stood they could hear the sound of another vehicle arriving, and then the sound of multiple voices. Marcus led them back to the parking area and greeted the forensic team, pointing down the path. Then he said, "I'll take it from here. Nash, I want you to stay, since you know the property. Seth, Meg—you might as well go on home. I know where to find you."

"Thanks," Seth said. "Jonas, I'll call you tomorrow about that lumber."

Jonas nodded, then turned and followed Marcus and his

crew back into the woods, leaving Meg and Seth standing alone in the parking lot. "Home?" Meg asked hopefully.

"I guess," Seth said. "It doesn't look like I'm going to get much more done for Donald's house today. Sorry I dragged you into this."

"Seth, you are not responsible for every corpse in Granford, and neither am I. You were here on legitimate business, and you wanted to show me the sawmill. We didn't know this guy, but I'm sure Detective Marcus will figure something out, and it won't involve us. So let's go home and sit and contemplate our mortality—or our lousy luck—and then I'll make you dinner. That work for you?"

Seth smiled reluctantly. "This was supposed to be your day off. You want to cook?"

"Yes, I do," Meg said firmly. "I find it relaxing. If you insist on feeling guilty, then you can peel or chop—or better yet, wash the dishes. We can eat outside, since it's so nice. You can go get Max and bring him over. I'll talk to the goats. And we can pretend it's just an ordinary day, okay?"

They drove home quietly, as Meg mentally reviewed the contents of her refrigerator. Why was it she never found time to go to the market? If it weren't for needing cat food, she would probably subsist on dry cereal. But an apple orchard was a demanding creature, and it refused to wait for ordinary human things.

Bree's car was still in the driveway when they arrived at Meg's house, but Bree was coming out the kitchen door when they pulled in. "There you are!" Bree called out. "I left you a note in the kitchen—I'm headed over to Michael's." As she came closer, Bree noticed Meg and Seth's shared expression. "What? Something happen? You two all right?"

"I found another body," Meg said.

"You're kidding me!" Bree's glance shifted between Meg and Seth. "You're not? Jeez, Meg, what is it with you and bodies?"

"Bree, it seems that the only way I can avoid it is to never leave the house. Sorry," Meg said, laughing ruefully.

"Right. Maybe I shouldn't spend so much time near you—it could be dangerous. What happened?"

"We don't know yet," Seth answered her. "We know the man's name, but Meg didn't recognize it. It sounds kind of familiar to me—he's from Easthampton, but maybe he's been involved in some Granford activities. Jonas Nash is the guy who owns the property where the body was found, and he said the guy used to work for him, but not currently. And that is all we know for the moment."

"Huh. Well, I'm off now. Don't wait up." With that, Bree headed for her car, and a minute later she pulled out of the driveway, leaving Meg and Seth standing indecisively in the driveway.

"Are you going to go get Max?" Meg asked.

"I guess. Can I bring back anything?"

"Don't go out of your way. If something in your fridge is calling to you, bring it along."

"Will do." Seth set off on foot up the hill toward his own house.

Meg let herself in the back door. Lolly appeared from the front of the house, anticipating dinner. "You could at least suck up to me a little, cat," Meg said, as she dished canned food onto a plate. That task accomplished, she turned her attention to people food and tried to push thoughts of her grisly discovery in the woods out of her head. It was a sad coincidence that she had found the body, but she had no responsibility to do anything about this death. Let the professionals handle it.

So here she was, with an evening free to spend alone with Seth. Funny, that was happening more and more often, usually here at her place, while Bree spent time with her sometime boyfriend Michael in Amherst. Of course, since Seth's business office was behind her house, it was easy for him to come over after he was done for the day. Now that the weather was dependable and the days were long, he was busy, in and out most of the days. When he was working from his office he often brought Max with him, and taking the energetic dog across the fields for a walk was a nice break for both of them.

It had been interesting to see the "bones" of Donald's house. It was like seeing an x-ray version of her own home—the skeleton beneath the skin. Of course, it was painful to see the damage to a building that had survived over two hundred years of New England winters and witnessed much of Granford's history, but builders then had put up sturdy houses, and Seth had said there was nothing that couldn't be fixed. And he was so excited about being a part of the restoration.

A few minutes later, as Meg was washing lettuce, Max appeared in the driveway, dragging Seth after him. Meg went to the door to let them in. "Lolly's already had her dinner, so Max can join us for a bit. What's that?" She pointed to a bag that Seth was carrying.

"It's a whole chicken I forgot I had. I thought maybe we could grill it outside?"

"Brilliant! I love the way you return bearing meat, er, poultry. Hand it over."

He did, and Meg pulled it out and washed it, split it

down the back, then threw together a quick marinade and stuck the spatchcocked chicken and the marinade into a plastic bag. As she was washing her hands Seth grabbed her from behind and turned her to face him.

"You sure you're all right?" he asked.

"Oh, Seth, it's sweet of you to ask, but I'm not a fragile flower of womanhood. I've handled worse, as you well know. Are you suggesting that I *should* be a fragile flower?"

"Heaven forbid. I'll take you just the way you are." He grinned.

"Dinner can wait. I'm all yours."

4

At seven the next morning, Bree stumbled down the back stairs to the kitchen.

"I didn't hear you come in last night," Meg said. "We left some coffee for you."

"You might have been kind of busy when I got back." Bree helped herself to coffee. Meg and Seth exchanged a smile. "Did I imagine it, or did you really say you found another body yesterday?"

"Sad to say, yes," Meg answered. "I think I told Detective Marcus he should hire me to find all the bodies in his jurisdiction."

"Did you at least get a smile out of him?"

"I don't think so. He was pretty focused." Which was normal for him, Meg reflected. Detective Marcus never smiled much.

"He won't be coming by here, will he?" Bree asked darkly.

"I don't know why he would. We told him everything we knew, which wasn't a lot." Meg turned to Seth. "Are you going back to the sawmill today?"

"Unless Jonas is tied up with the police. I can't get started on Donald's house until I know what lumber I've got to work with."

"What kind of wood did they use in Colonial construction? I never thought to ask."

"It depends on where you are, of course. Around here the original forests were pretty diverse: hemlock, beech, oak, birch, pine, hickory. When people settled in Granford in the eighteenth century, they used mainly pine, oak, and chestnut for timber frame construction, and other woods for fuel or fencing. Sometimes they used the trunks of whole trees—you've seen that in your basement and attic. It saved work, and why pretty up something most people would never see? How much do you know about the history of New England forests?"

Meg smiled at his enthusiasm. "I know something about apple trees, and that's about it. Are you going to enlighten me?"

"I can give you the short version. First stage: natural forest when the settlers arrived, and they cut down most of it to make open fields for crops and to heat their homes. The peak deforestation took place in the mid-nineteenth century. Then in the second stage, people either moved to the cities where the jobs and money were or moved west for the same reasons, and the farms went back to nature again. That is, trees came back, but not always the same trees. Third stage: much of the state is now forest again—about three million acres, which is about sixty percent and puts it in the top ten in the country. Most of the forestland is privately held by people like Jonas. Most of the trees now are white pine, red maple, northern red oak, and hemlock."

"Is there anything you don't know?"

"Quantum physics," he answered quickly. "How to knit. You want more?"

By now Meg was laughing. "No, that's fine. What kind of wood do you need to repair Donald's house?"

"Probably oak beams. For the clapboards, pine would be easiest, but it doesn't last as well as cedar. Cedar grows around here, so it's historically correct."

Seth was interrupted by a knock at the door, and Meg got up to let in Art Preston, Granford's chief of police. "Hey, Art. I can guess why you're here. Want some coffee?"

"Hi Meg, Seth, Bree. Sure, I'll take some coffee. Although I have to say I'm not happy that you two find a body in my town and you don't even call me."

"Sorry, Art," Seth said. "I didn't even consider *not* calling Detective Marcus for a suspicious, unattended death, so I guess I kind of skipped right over you. Of course, we're hoping it was natural causes."

"Fair enough. Did Marcus find out who it was?"

"He got an ID from the guy's driver's license," Seth replied. "Name of David Clapp, from Easthampton. He used to work for Jonas Nash, but more recently he was working for the logging company that Nash uses. He was found on Nash's land."

"And before you ask," Meg said, "we didn't get close enough to see how he died. Although I think it's safe to say that a tree didn't fall on him. I probably would have noticed that. Sorry we left you out of the loop."

"I'll survive." Art sighed histrionically. "At least I got a decent cup of coffee out of it. What were you two doing out there at all?"

"Looking for lumber for Donald Butterfield's house," Seth explained. "He's asked me to handle the repairs."

"I should have known. That kid who was driving—what an idiot. The car was totaled. He's lucky he survived."

"Is the boy going to be charged with anything?" Meg asked. "Was he drinking?"

"That's what everybody assumed, but no, basically he was joyriding with some pals and things got out of hand. I've slapped him with a healthy fine, but since his folks said they'd pay for all damages, he probably won't care. Kids!"

"Maybe he's learned something?" Seth added hopefully. "Anyway, Donald wants the restoration to be historically correct, and to do it right I'll need wide boards, which are getting harder and harder to find. Nash's was the best bet."

"Got it. Well, that's all I wanted to know. How's the orchard doing, Meg?"

"Too dry, or maybe dry at the wrong times. We're having to irrigate, and that means hauling water and hoses around a lot."

"Speaking of which, Meg," Bree interrupted, "we've got work to do. And I asked Christopher to come by whenever he can and make sure we've got it right, and tell us if there's anything else we need to be doing. Whatever we did right last year isn't enough under this year's conditions."

"I haven't seen Christopher for a while," Meg said. Christopher Ramsdell was a charming agriculture professor at the nearby university, and long before Meg came along, he'd managed her orchard for years. He was still a mentor to Bree, who had studied with him, and now Meg also considered him a friend. "And I'll be happy to have his advice. When will he be here?"

"He said maybe around lunchtime. He's really busy these days, since not only is it peak agriculture season, but he's involved with the construction of that new center, so he couldn't be sure."

"Well, he'll know where to look for us."

Seth stood up and carried his dishes to the sink. "I guess I'd better get moving, too. Walk you out, Art?"

Art drained his coffee and stood up. "Nice to see you, Meg, but I wish you'd stop finding corpses."

Meg laughed. "Believe me, Art, so do I!"

They all left together, parting ways in the driveway— Art back to the center of town, Seth into his office at the end of the drive, and Meg and Bree up the hill to the orchard.

Meg knew she was lucky to have the natural spring that emerged halfway up the hill. Still, she and Bree were spending an awful lot of time hauling water around the orchard to reach all the trees, especially the vulnerable new ones they'd added in the spring. The new ones most needed water, in order to establish a strong root system, but they were also the farthest from the water source. It was an ongoing balancing act: under-watering would result in drought stress and poorer fruit quality; too much water and the roots would stop growing, and some essential nutrients would be leached out of the soil. Meg had to leave most of the calculations to Bree, since she wasn't even sure what "drought stress" would look like. "Have you checked out permanent irrigation systems, Bree?" Meg said, panting, as she came up behind her manager.

"Of course I've looked at them," she said testily. "Think

I like all this watering? Drip irrigation for fifteen or twenty acres would set us back maybe fifteen thou just to purchase and install. You got that much sitting in your bank account? And that's just to install it—using it would probably cost us a couple of thousand dollars a year, per acre, more for the high density planting of the new trees."

"We could take out a loan," Meg said dubiously. "We've already got the water source in place."

"And we've already got a delivery system in place—us," Bree shot back. "Look, I can do a cost-benefit analysis for you, if it'll make you happy, but for most farmers they're kind of guessing anyway. And you won't see a return on your investment for a couple of years at best."

Meg had to smile. "Listen to you! You're taking me back to my financial analyst days in Boston. So you're saying stick to what we're doing now?"

"That's about it. Why? You getting tired already?"

"I'll manage. But you don't mind if I pray for rain, do you?"

"Knock yourself out!"

They worked companionably for a few hours, and then Meg saw Christopher's car pull into her driveway below. She waved and waited for him to climb the hill, because she knew he'd want to see the orchard. Thinking back, she realized he hadn't visited since they planted the new section a couple of months earlier.

"Hey, Christopher! It's great to see you!" Meg gave him an enthusiastic hug when he arrived. Despite the fact that he was in his sixties, he didn't seem to be the least winded from his climb.

"My apologies to have been away so long! This new De-BroCo research building on campus is eating up all my free

time, especially atop my teaching and research responsibilities. But I'm delighted to have a chance to get out,
and of course, to see you and Briona. How fares your
orchard?"

"You'll have to ask Bree—I seem to be the labor side.
But I do have concerns about our water supply and our distribution system."

"Then let's walk together and discuss your issues." They
set off along the grassy alleys between rows of established
apple trees. Meg could tell that Christopher was assessing
their condition even as he expounded on the alternatives for
irrigation. They had covered most of the acreage when he
arrived at a final point. "Have you considered fertigation?"

Meg looked blank, and Bree volunteered, "You mean,
like fertilizing at the same time we water? I've been reading about that."

"Precisely. Of course, the original investment costs are
high, although the long-term application costs are less."

"That could be a problem," Meg said, "although I like
the sound of combining two tasks into one. But we're kind
of cash poor up front."

"From what I've seen today, my dear, you're managing
well under the status quo. I know it's hard work, but I think
you can get a couple of harvests under your belt, if I may
muddle a metaphor, before you have to decide whether to
install a new system."

Meg briefly contemplated another two years of hauling
irrigation hoses around and resolved to take a hard look at
the numbers. "The trees don't look stressed yet, do they?"

"No, they're fine so far, but I'm sure Bree is keeping a
sharp eye on them."

"Of course I am," Bree said promptly.

"What about insects?" Meg asked. "We've been doing limited spraying. Isn't there some new apple pest?"

"Are you referring to *Epiphyas postvittana*?"

Meg grinned at Christopher. "I don't know—am I?"

"The light brown apple moth, native to Australia, now established in New Zealand, the United Kingdom, and Ireland. It has recently been found in California, but so far it is limited to that state. Rest assured I shall alert you should it venture farther eastward."

"One less thing I have to worry about!" Meg said. "Speaking of insects, yesterday I saw one I'd never noticed before." She could excuse herself for forgetting about that critter, since it had been only moments later she had become aware of the body—something she didn't feel compelled to explain to Christopher. Still, it was large and memorable enough to have made an impression on her.

"Can you describe it?" Christopher asked.

"About two inches long, black and white—oh, and its antennae were as long as it was."

Christopher's cheerful expression faded rapidly. He pulled out his cell phone, tapped on the screen several times, then handed her the phone. "Is this what you saw?"

Meg took the phone and looked at the image he had called up. "Yes, that's it. You know what it is?"

"I'm afraid I do. It looks like an Asian longhorned beetle, an invasive species that enjoys a wide range of hosts. There's no known treatment, other than eradication."

"What do you mean by that?"

"Cutting down all infested and potential host trees in the area where it was found, and a wide margin beyond that. Surely you've read of the problems that have emerged with this pest in and around the city of Worcester?"

Meg shook her head. "I haven't had a lot of time for reading the paper lately."

"Oh, my dear, this has been going on for several years, even before your arrival in Granford. Already they've cut down something like twenty-five thousand trees in the central part of the state, and there's no guarantee that it's under control even now."

"That sounds serious," Meg said.

"I promise you, it is. Where did you come upon this insect?"

"In Jonas Nash's forest plot on the north side of town, toward Amherst."

"Where the dead man was found?" Christopher asked.

"How did you hear about that?" Meg asked with surprise.

"It was on the news. No one mentioned that you were there, my dear, only that a body had been discovered and that the police were investigating. So that is indeed the same place?"

"Yes, it is. In fact, the insect was only a few feet away."

"I'm sorry that you were there, Meg. But now I'm afraid I shall need to speak with Jonas Nash," Christopher said somberly.

5

Christopher, clearly troubled, had left without any further explanations. Before leaving he had shared the picture on his phone with Bree, whose reaction was nearly as quick as Christopher's had been.

"Wow, that's bad news! There haven't been any other sightings around here, have there?" she had asked.

"Not yet, but there aren't enough eyes to check every potential site," Christopher had replied. "Meg, can you show me where you saw this?"

"Sure." Unless it was still a crime scene, she amended to herself. "If you think it's important. When would you like to go?"

Christopher tapped at his phone some more and pulled up a calendar. "Would tomorrow afternoon suit you?"

Meg looked at Bree, who shrugged and said, "It's okay.

We're only watering every other day at the moment, and from what you've told me, that's working for now."

"I believe it is, my dear, although with no rain in sight I'd keep a close eye on your water levels," Christopher said. Meg explained to him where the forest plot was, and they arranged to meet at the site, then said their good-byes.

After watching Christopher head down the hill, Meg turned to Bree. "Why are you and Christopher so concerned about this bug?"

"It could be nothing, but what you saw looks like an Asian longhorned beetle. It's an invasive species, probably carried into this country through wooden packing crates at a variety of ports. It eats a whole lot of tree species, and the only way anyone has come up with to stop them is to cut down all the infested trees and grind them up. Left alone, they kill the tree in a couple of years, or at least seriously weaken it. What's worse, while they're big and easy to see out in the open, they usually spend most of their life cycle inside a tree, mainly up at the crown level, so they're hard to spot. Most of the infested areas have been identified because one of the beetles showed up in an ornamental tree in someone's suburban yard. Like Christopher said, Worcester's been hit hard, and they're still finding new outbreaks there and in the surrounding communities. They just cut down another ten thousand trees in Shrewsbury. It's pretty likely that if there were more people looking, they'd find a lot more."

"You're certainly well informed." Meg digested what Bree had told her. "So if it's identified on the Nash property, what happens next?"

"Well, first there's an official identification process—there's a government office that does that. If it's confirmed, then the USDA gets involved, and the UMass extension service. And then basically crews go out and chop down a whole lot of trees."

"Which wouldn't make Jonas Nash and his company very happy."

"Exactly. And it would be a shame, because they've been good about maintaining their land responsibly. I read about them as a case study when I was at school."

"Maybe it's just a single beetle that flew in from somewhere else?"

Bree shook her head. "Those suckers don't fly very far or very fast. So if you see one, there are probably others nearby." She made a quick scan around her. "I think we're pretty much done for the day. You have plans for tonight?"

"You mean with Seth? I don't even know. Were you volunteering to cook dinner?" Meg ended hopefully.

"If you insist." Bree gave an exaggerated sigh. "I guess it's my turn."

They ambled down the hill, and Bree peeled off for the kitchen door. Meg saw both Seth's car and his van parked in the driveway, so she figured he was in his office, which was located in the old carpenter's shop behind her house. She climbed the stairs up to his office space and rapped on the half-open door.

Seth looked up and smiled. "Hi. Have I missed a meal or something?"

Meg came in and dropped into a battered chair in front of his desk. "Not yet, unless you're talking about lunch. Where's Max?"

"I left him over at Mom's—she's got an old dog run there, from when we were kids. I'm working on adding one at my place, but it's not finished yet."

"Poor baby. Doesn't he get lonely without you? Anyway, I wanted to talk to you about something Christopher just told me."

"Okay. Shoot." Seth stretched and leaned back in his chair.

"Let me back up and start from the beginning. Remember when I sat down to get that rock out of my shoe yesterday?" Seth nodded, so Meg went on, "There was this big insect on the log. Yeah, I know, woods, nature, et cetera, but this was a big, showy one—black and white, with long antennae. Did you notice anything like that?"

He shook his head. "No, but I wasn't looking, and then we got kind of distracted by the body. Why does it matter?"

"Because I described it to Christopher today, and he knew exactly what it was: something called an Asian longhorned beetle. From what he and Bree have told me, it's a nasty pest."

"And?"

"If there's an infestation on Jonas's land, I gather that kicks in a whole official process that goes all the way up to the federal government. And the only way to deal with the insect is to cut down all the trees it likes to eat."

Seth's expression turned serious. "Ah. I see the problem. If—it is still 'if,' isn't it?—there is an infestation, then Jonas stands to lose a whole lot of trees."

"Exactly."

Seth thought for a moment, then said, "Jonas told me in confidence that the sawmill is losing money. He said he might even have to sell. So losing some of his lumber would hit him hard. What does Christopher say the next step should be?"

"Well, there would have to be confirmation, for a start. He wants me to show him where I saw the beetle."

"Do you want me to come along?" Seth offered.

Meg smiled at him. "No, you don't have to. The thing is, I forgot to ask Christopher who should tell Jonas about this. I don't think he will, until he has confirmed the sighting. But from what Bree said, I gather that if you see one beetle, there are probably a lot more hiding in the trees. Did you get a chance to talk with Jonas today?"

Seth shook his head. "No, I was thinking about talking to him tomorrow. What time are you meeting Christopher?"

"Mid-afternoon tomorrow, at the forest site."

"How about this: you and I can go to the sawmill before that and talk to Jonas, and then I'll drive you over to the woodlot to meet Christopher."

"That sounds good to me. Are you coming by for dinner tonight? I think Bree's cooking."

"No, I promised my mother I'd eat with her. Tomorrow night?"

"That's fine."

When Meg arrived at her kitchen, Bree was banging pots around and something smelled like onions and spices. Meg sat down at the kitchen table.

"Why do you know so much about this beetle thing?" Meg asked.

"Hey, I haven't been out of school all that long. Christopher actually oversees some kind of research lab on campus, and I think I remember taking a tour of it once. But I was never much interested in the lab research side of things. Anyway, it's my business to keep track of anything that might affect what we do here, isn't it? This critter has set up housekeeping not all that far away."

"You mean in Worcester. But it doesn't go after apple trees, does it?"

"No, but you've got to look at the bigger ecological picture. Left uncontrolled, this thing can really change the makeup of our forests, and that affects all of us. Maybe it'll take a while. Heck, maybe it's already been here for a while and nobody happened to notice. But in the end, it can do a lot of damage."

"Christopher certainly took it seriously."

"Of course he did. It *is* serious. Something like this has to be reported officially. If he knew and didn't act on it and somebody else found out, his professional credibility would be on the line."

"Ah, I see. Well, Seth and I are going to go over to the Nash sawmill tomorrow, and then I'll go meet Christopher. I'll show him where I found the insect and we'll see what happens."

"Speaking of you and Seth, you two sure do spend a lot of time together these days. You planning to do anything official about it anytime soon?"

Meg was surprised that Bree had even asked. "We haven't discussed it. We both have our own lives, you know. We seem to be muddling along well enough."

"Hey, as long as it works for you. And before you ask, Michael and I are status quo, too, and happy with that. Quite the independent women, you and me, huh?"

Seth came by the next day after lunch. "Ready go to?"

"I am. Listen, I've been thinking. It sounds as though Jonas has enough to worry about without dumping this possible beetle problem in his lap. Maybe we should wait until we know for sure what's going on before we say anything. What if we don't find any more? Does Christopher still have to report it? I mean, I saw one dead beetle, and it might not even be what we think it is. I didn't stick it in my pocket or take a picture of it. I could have been wrong about it."

Seth laughed. "Meg, slow down. You don't have to say anything. You did the right thing to report it to Christopher, but that's where your responsibility ends. You show him the place, and either he finds more or he doesn't, but he's the one who has to take the next step."

"Fine. I'd be happy not to worry about it. So, how are you today? How's Donald's project going? How's your mother?"

"I'm fine, she's fine, the world's a great place. Donald is less than one hundred percent happy because he wants everything done yesterday, but I calmed him down. And you're going to get to see how our ancestors cut the wood that went into building our houses."

"That part I'm looking forward to."

It didn't take long to reach the sawmill, and as Meg stepped out of the car she inhaled the scent of freshly cut wood. Could someone who handled different woods regularly learn to distinguish each by scent? She could tell the odor of pine from most other woods, but her expertise stopped there. But why was the smell so appealing?

Jonas came out to greet them. "Hey, Seth, Meg. Seth, you're still looking for wood for Donald, right? I set aside some boards for you—you can take a look."

"Thanks. Donald's been on my back about getting started. And if you have time, I promised that Meg could see how a real sawmill works."

Jonas smiled. "Of course. We're really proud of the place."

"Good," Meg said. "You can start by telling me how different this is from the way it used to be done."

"Actually, not very, and that's been our choice. We get school groups coming by a few times a year, so they can see how it was done in the old days. Our machines are power driven, but there are people managing them all, not computers. Most mills are a lot more automated than this, but it makes no sense for an operation of this size." Jonas smiled again. "I love to show this one off."

"And I'd love to see it, Jonas," Meg said. "Lead me to it."

"All right!" Jonas pointed to a stack of logs at one end of the long building. "Here's where we start. Those are mixed hardwoods, and they come from a variety of sites. They're scaled and graded—you want the details?"

"No, I think the general outline is enough for me," Meg replied.

"Got it. From there we strip the bark off and move the logs to the mill. First they go through the headsaw, which makes the round log into a square. The result is called the 'cant.'" The stuff that's cut away goes to a chipper, and the cants go to the cant deck, where they're run through the resaw—that's what actually cuts the boards."

Meg stared, fascinated. It was a noisy, messy process, but the basics were simple: logs went in one end and came out as boards on the other, all within one building—depositing coarse sawdust like snowdrifts on every surface.

Jonas was still talking. "One reason I've got real people running things is because there are decisions about individual cants that a computer just can't make, or not as well." They walked farther down the line. "So, next is the edger, then the grader. The USDA has grading rules for logs, but at our end we have a trained grader who inspects the boards. He has to grade each board and decide whether it needs more trimming or edging. Only when he's approved it does it go to the dry kilns. You have to dry the boards under controlled conditions for temperature, moisture, and air circulation. Had enough yet?"

Meg smiled at him. "I'm overwhelmed. Is there more you have to do, before you can actually use the wood?"

"That's where I come in," Seth said. "Depending on how I want to use it, I may need to surface-plane it, to smooth it off. And I do some of my own trimming, particularly for these old houses, where what's there may be out of true, so I have to match up the boards. Speaking of which, let's take a look at those boards. You coming, Meg?"

"No, I think I'll stay here and admire this process awhile longer. You won't be long, will you?"

"Fifteen minutes, tops."

Meg turned back to Jonas. "Thank you for the tour, Jonas. I'll definitely look at the wood in my house in a different way from now on."

"Happy to share it with you, Meg," Jonas said. "This way, Seth."

For a couple of moments Meg watched them walking away: Seth compact, fair in complexion; Jonas taller and rangier and darker. But physical differences aside, both cared about the materials they were using and the history they were preserving, even sometimes in the face of common sense and expense. She could sympathize. No way would she repair her own house with modern plywood, even where no one would see. It would be like a bad graft, and she had the irrational feeling that her house would reject the unfamiliar patch. She found an upended stump and sat, watching the men who were operating the machines come and go. It didn't take a large staff to run this operation; she'd counted fewer than ten men.

Seth and Jonas came round the building maybe ten minutes later, still talking.

"Can you deliver the larger pieces to Donald's house?" Seth was asking.

"Sure, no problem. Tomorrow?"

"That'll work. And when you're there I can give you a sample of the clapboards, so you can match them. Bring an invoice along, will you? Cost isn't a major issue on this project, but it's nice to keep ahead of the paperwork."

Jonas laughed. "I hear you. Tomorrow, then." He waved at Meg, then turned back to the sawmill.

Meg stood up and brushed sawdust off her pants. "All set?"

"We're good. Let's go meet Christopher."

6

"Did you talk about . . ." Meg began, when they'd gotten into Seth's van.

"David Clapp?" Seth completed the question for her. "No. This was business, and you and I don't know any more than we did. Shoot, I forgot to ask Art if he knew him."

"Clapp didn't live in Granford. Why would Art have known him?"

"Easthampton's not far away. Granford plays Easthampton in various sports, so if Clapp had kids of the right age, he might have been around here a lot."

"Where are the sports fields?"

"I think I told you—near the high school, of course, on the other side of town, and there are a couple in the town parks. Why?"

"I'm just wondering how well David Clapp knew the town, that's all." Meg turned in her seat to face Seth. "Tell me, am I crazy to be wondering whether it's no accident that that insect was found so close to the body?"

Seth shook his head slightly. "I don't know what you're getting at."

"Well, if Clapp was a professional forester, he should have recognized the bug for what it was, right?"

"Probably. So?"

"If he found something like this, theoretically he'd have had to report it to someone, right? Look, I never knew him and I don't want to speak ill of the dead, but what if Clapp first decided to tell Jonas Nash about the bug he found, before he went to any officials? Say, to make the problem go away? Both Bree and Christopher have said that unless you really look for this thing, it's hard to find. You said Jonas told you he's having financial problems, right?"

"Yes. He told me today he's been talking to a few developers who have showed an interest in the property. Why do you ask?"

"Because Clapp would know that Nash's Sawmill was in financial trouble, since he had been let go, and that losing a bunch of trees would hurt them."

"I think I see where you're going with this," Seth said slowly. "So he might have told Jonas Nash that he was going to keep quiet about it, as a favor to a friend?"

"Or in return for something. Like a bribe, or maybe his job back, or a good reference. Maybe he's not happy working where he is and wants out."

"Meg, I think you're building a house of cards. I don't know anything about David Clapp's character, but I'm not going to leap to the assumption that he's a blackmailer. Or the implication that Jonas had a reason to kill him. I do know Jonas, and I'm not going to believe that. Besides, we still don't know if Clapp's death was even suspicious."

"Is Marcus going to tell us? Or Art? I'm just throwing out ideas. I don't know any of these people personally. Did you tell Jonas where we were going?" Meg asked, as they rode toward the forest plot.

"No. I thought we'd decided to hold off on that until we talked with Christopher," Seth answered. "It could be a false alarm. What if he can't find another one there?"

"I don't know. I'm not even sure what I'm hoping for. If we don't find another insect, I may look like an idiot, but only you and Christopher and Bree will know. If we do, Jonas may be in for a whole lot of trouble, and it's not even his fault. I guess I'd rather find out I was hallucinating than that I set a massive government tree-cutting program in motion."

"One step at a time, Meg," Seth countered.

"I hope Detective Marcus has cleared the scene. I can't imagine doing forensics out there in the open. How do you know which bits are important? How deep do you go? If you believe the television shows, someone can look at a maggot on a body and announce that the person was killed on Tuesday at 7:14 a.m. Is that really all it takes?"

Seth smiled, watching the road ahead. "Why are you asking me? I've had just about exactly as much experience with this as you have. Besides, there are other factors in determining when David Clapp died. For example, if he had a family, they must know when he went missing. Or if he was working with a logging team, they might have noticed if he disappeared while they were there, or if he didn't leave with them."

"True," Meg admitted.

"Here we are." Seth entered the parking area they'd visited the day before yesterday.

Christopher greeted them with his usual enthusiasm. "Ah, good, I see I've found the right place. Seth, nice to see you again. How is your charming mother?"

"She's fine. I hope you don't mind me trailing along today."

"Of course not. The more eyes, the better. Meg, lead on!"

"Of course. We take that path." Meg led the way and stopped when she came to the rise with the log at the top. There was no sign of any police activity, save for the trampled appearance of the dead leaves and low vegetation, so the area was clearly no longer considered a crime scene. "That's where I sat down." She pointed.

"And the insect was lying upon the log?" Christopher asked.

"Yes. I could see that it was dead when I sat down, but I didn't want to sit too close to it so I scooched down to the other end."

"You're not alone in that, Meg. Many people are repelled by insects, and this one was particularly large, I assume?"

"Well, it looked large to me. Otherwise I probably wouldn't have noticed it. I'm not usually squeamish about things like that."

Christopher's attention had turned to the tree canopy, and he was talking to himself. "Mixed forest, both hardwoods and softwoods. A scattering of maples, right." He turned back to Meg and Seth. "And you say that this has been logged regularly?"

Seth answered. "I don't know how often—you'd have to

talk to Jonas Nash about that. By the way, I didn't say anything about this to him. Didn't want to worry him if it
turned out to be nothing."

"Of course, of course," Christopher said absently. He
stepped carefully up the slight slope and stopped at the top,
taking another 360-degree survey. Then he looked carefully at the log where Meg had sat, then on both sides of it,
kneeling in the leaves. "I assume the state police have done
whatever it is they do here. I don't see the creature—no,
wait." He reached under the log and emerged with something in his hand. Then he stood up, brushed off his knees,
and returned to where Meg and Seth were standing. "At the
risk of making a poor joke, here is your corpse."

"And is it . . . ?" Meg asked.

"I'm afraid so," Christopher replied.

The three of them silently contemplated the dead insect
lying on Christopher's palm for several seconds.

"It may have been brushed off and swept under the log
by the investigators."

"I'm surprised they didn't collect it as evidence,"
Meg said.

"It seems unlikely. This beetle is not a flesh eater, but of
course the investigators could not be expected to know that.
Either they failed to see it or they dismissed it as unimport-
ant," Christopher said.

"What happens now?" Seth asked.

Christopher sighed. "There is a rather convoluted chain
of events that must take place if we are to declare this an
official problem. I'd like to take a few minutes to look for
additional evidence—perhaps more insects, although the
odds of finding another dead one are small, for the reasons
I outlined. If they're here, it's more likely we'd see their exit

holes in the trees themselves. As you noted, Meg, this is a large insect, so the holes where they emerge from the tree trunks are correspondingly large, perhaps a half-inch across, and perfectly circular. Let's see if we can spot any of those. There are binoculars in my car, which may help."

"I can get those for you, if the car's unlocked," Seth said.

"Thank you, I'd appreciate that."

As Seth headed down the path to the parking area, Meg asked, "Bree filled me in a little, but I still feel ignorant. What more can you tell me about these beetles?"

"I assume Bree explained to you the ecological impact?" When Meg nodded, Christopher went on, "That doesn't begin to take into account the potential economic impact. Thus far, people have become aware of the ALB when the insects turn up in heavily populated urban or suburban areas, where they're more of a nuisance that anything else. People don't like to lose their shade trees in such settings. But there may be far more in our forests, where no one has yet looked for them. If the forests are affected, which I regret to say is quite likely, then we face a much bigger problem."

"Is there anything we can do about it?"

"Despite the best efforts of a range of scientists over the past decade and more, the short answer is, not much. To date we have not found any chemical or biological method for controlling them, although the research is ongoing, even at the university here."

"Bree mentioned visiting a lab on campus."

"Yes, there is one, and I'm responsible for it. Of course, the ALB is not our only area of research. In any case, unfortunately, the only solution available to us at the moment is complete eradication, which means sacrificing a massive number of trees, which must be reduced to chips."

"They can't be treated and used for something else?"

Christopher shook his head. "Not at this time. It is a tragic waste."

"So hypothetically, say Jonas Nash came strolling along this path and noticed one of the beetles. He would have a reason to pick it up and take it away, without telling anyone?"

Christopher stared at her, his expression troubled. "Assuming he recognized it for what it was, and he had read our public information outreach materials, which as a responsible forester he should have done, then I suppose the answer is yes, it's conceivable that he might do that, to protect his own interests."

Seth returned and held out the cluster of binoculars he was carrying. "Here you go. Now what?"

"I want you to look at the upper portions of the trunks for the round holes I described. When we mount a full survey, we get either tree climbers in or use a bucket truck, to get closer. It's difficult, especially if you don't know what you're looking for, so I won't hold it against you if you fail to find anything."

"But if we rank amateurs do find something, we've got a real problem?" Meg offered.

"I'm afraid you're right, Meg. Happy hunting. Or not."

They split up. Meg made a good-faith effort to see through the canopy to the central tree trunks, but there were simply too many leaves in the way to spot a half-inch hole. It had been near miraculous that she had found that one insect at all. Perhaps a bird, startled by people walking around, had dropped it just after killing it?

After half an hour Meg gave up looking and wandered back toward the parking area. Passing through the trees was not difficult—someone had kept the underbrush cut down, maybe to reduce the fire hazard. The logging crew? Was that part of their job? She had no idea how far the woods extended, in any direction. Had David Clapp known this particular site? Had he been here with a team, or had he been sent ahead to scout out trees? How did anyone decide which trees to cut? And who decided? Jonas? The logging company? Was it supply and demand? Good forest maintenance, to eliminate the big, old trees so that younger ones had a chance? There was so much she didn't know.

She was first to arrive back at their cars, but Seth and Christopher also emerged from different directions within a few minutes. "Anything?" she called out when she saw them.

Christopher nodded. "I found exit holes, although no further insects. You, Seth?"

"I can't be sure."

"Well, I thank you for your efforts. Sadly, what I've found is enough for it to be incumbent upon me to set the wheels in motion and report this find."

"And then what?" Meg asked.

"Various government agencies will step in. I'll keep you informed, should anything else turn up."

"Thanks, and thanks for the advice on my orchard yesterday."

"My pleasure, my dear. Your orchard is in good hands. Seth, good to see you again." He raised a hand in farewell, then got into his car and drove off, leaving Meg and Seth alone in the parking area.

"Well, that was an interesting way to spend an afternoon—looking for tiny holes in the tops of trees," Meg said wryly. "At least we were out of the hot sun. Who would have thought?"

"Life is full of surprises. Shall we head back?"

When they were on the road again, Meg said, "You know, the way Christopher describes it, a lot of this insect program—what do I call it? An insect watch?—seems based on the goodwill of the community. And that assumes the community is aware at all. I mean, almost any one of us could see something and never give it a second thought, and yet it could be a pest that could bring down a whole sector of the agricultural market or local forests. I didn't know, and I'm in the business! What about your ordinary Joe or Jane Citizen, who is clueless and doesn't much like creepy-crawlies anyway?"

"You've got a point there, Meg. I know about the kind of pests that affect buildings, like carpenter ants or powder-post beetles, and of course termites, but I couldn't identify a vegetable pest even if I bit into it."

"Exactly. And even if you do find something you think is suspicious, who do you tell? Do you try to capture the insect? Is a picture good enough?"

"I have no idea. I guess we'll have to see what Christopher tells us."

7

When Meg and Seth pulled into Meg's driveway, Art Preston was leaning against the fence talking to Meg's goats, Dorcas and Isabel, and his car was parked in the drive. Meg climbed out and gathered up several bags of vegetables. They'd stopped off at the farmer's market on their way back.

"Hi, Art," she called out. "Getting your goat fix?"

He gave Dorcas and Isabel one last pat each, then strolled over. "I was having an intelligent conversation. They're good listeners."

"More likely they're hungry and they were hoping you were hiding something tasty. What brings you here?"

"Marcus was kind enough to share reports on your late logger, and I thought I'd drop off copies on the way home."

"He's not *my* logger, thank goodness. I'm surprised Marcus was willing to part with the information so easily."

"I guess he figured there was nothing controversial in them."

Meg concurred. "You want to stay for dinner? We're throwing together something that involves vegetables, although we haven't decided what yet."

"Sure, why not? My wife's visiting her sister on Cape Cod."

"Then come on in. I think I've got beer." Meg pulled open the screen door and wrestled her full bags through. "Bree?" she called out.

"Yo," came the answer from somewhere upstairs, and then Bree came pounding down the stairs. "Hey, hi, Art. Something new happen?"

"Hey, Bree. No, nothing important. I'm just delivering some reports, and Meg asked me to stay for dinner."

"Are you going to be around, Bree?" Meg asked. "I think it's something vegetarian, although I'm not sure what. I couldn't make up my mind what to get at the food stand, so I got a couple of everything, and it's all better eaten fresh."

"Curry?" Bree suggested.

"Veggie curry? Sure, but you'll have to show me how to make it."

"Where do you want this stuff?" Seth asked, coming inside with several more bags.

"On the kitchen table. Let's see what we've got."

As both Meg and Seth unpacked their haul, the table began to overflow with bright summer colors: a variety of lettuces, fresh herbs, small peppers, tomatoes, and more. "I should take a picture of this," Meg said. "Bree, you sure we shouldn't put in our own vegetable garden?"

"When you've got good stuff like this available from that organic farm only a mile or two away? Let them do it—looks like they're doing a great job. Hey, you guys, why don't you do the chopping? You can talk and chop at the same time, can't you?" Bree grinned at Seth and Art, then handed them knives and cutting boards. She washed a batch of the vegetables in a colander, shook off the water, and put them on the table between Seth and Art, then set out a couple of large knives. "Go!"

Meg handed out beers all around, then sat down to admire the men's efforts. "Anything jump out at you from the reports Marcus sent, Art?"

"I only glanced at them. The guy arrived under his own steam—his car was in the parking area. Cause of death was blunt force trauma to the head, specifically the back, and nobody's committing to anything. Could be somebody hit him from behind with something. Or, could be he tripped and fell backward and hit his head, although for someone used to forests it's hard to see that. Still, accidents happen."

"If he fell, why was he found under some bushes off the path?" Seth asked.

"Playing devil's advocate, are you? But it's a fair question, and there are several possible answers. For one, blows to the head are notoriously tricky. Clapp might not have been rendered unconscious immediately and might have tried to get help but ended up going the wrong direction because he was disoriented by the blow. Or he might have been knocked out at first, then woke up and started crawling, likewise the wrong way."

"He could have been trying to hide from whoever hit him," Bree volunteered, as she chopped large quantities of basil, whose pungent odor quickly filled the kitchen.

"That would work—*if* there was someone else involved. Or the final possibility: somebody knocked him out, killing him, accidentally or on purpose, and then dragged him into the bushes to hide him. But there's no evidence that anyone else was there. Or rather, there's lots of evidence that many people were there, like hikers, but nothing that points to any individual."

"He wasn't dragged by a bear or anything like that, was he?" Meg asked, suppressing a shudder at the thought.

"No marks on the body to suggest that, per the report," Art said.

"You said the blow came from behind?" Seth asked, slicing peppers.

"Yeah," Art said, "by someone right-handed. Unless he fell."

"Defensive wounds? Signs of a struggle?"

"Jeez, people—listen to yourselves," Bree said, laughing. "Who's playing Sherlock Holmes now?"

"I'm trying for Columbo," Art said with a smile. "Make people think I'm harmless and then I zap them with the right question."

"Bree, we're just trying to work out how it happened," Meg protested. "Was there blood, Art?"

"Oh, ick, you all—we're making dinner here," Bree said.

"No blood. You want me to cover putrefaction next, Bree?" Art asked.

To forestall that subject, Meg jumped in. "Have they figured out *when* he died?"

"Best guess, maybe twenty-four hours before you found him, which would make it Sunday sometime. Now, Marcus did confirm that Clapp was working for the logging company that Nash uses, but nobody there sent him out on a Sunday. Although his crew said their next cut was scheduled for the end of the month, so Clapp could have been out there tagging trees for that. He lived close enough that he might have stopped by to get ahead of the game."

"So let me get this straight," Seth said slowly. "David Clapp, who was familiar with the site, goes out to check out the trees and tag for the next cut. Either he falls over backward, hits his head, and crawls away from the path, or somebody comes up behind him and whacks him in the head, then hides the body?"

"Maybe. If that's what happened, the attacker didn't do a very good job of hiding Clapp's body. It was out of sight, but not all that far from a path that's used regularly. Even Meg noticed the, uh, evidence. On the other hand, could be Clapp tripped over a root and fell over backward, hitting his head, then got up again and stumbled his way under a bush," Art said amiably.

"Come on, Art—what's your guess?" Seth challenged.

Art sighed. "I don't think he fell," he said carefully, "but it's not ruled out. And that, I'm sorry to say, was Marcus's conclusion. He hasn't exactly closed the file, but he has no reason to suspect anyone else was involved, and no evidence to work with."

"I don't know whether to be relieved or disappointed," Meg said. "We already knew he wasn't robbed, because Marcus retrieved his wallet while we were there. Has he looked into why on earth anyone would want him dead? Any enemies? What do we know about David Clapp?"

"The state police are still interviewing his colleagues, family, friends," Art said. "There's nobody obvious, like an ex-wife or a jealous workmate. Good family man, couple of sons. If you're wondering why nobody was looking for him, sometimes he spent a couple of days in different areas in this part of the state planning for the next cuttings, so he wasn't always home at night. He hadn't been where you found him for long, Meg. You'd be surprised how fast decomp sets in, especially in weather like this. Anyway, he had no debt beyond his mortgage. No criminal record—not even a speeding ticket. Most people said they liked him, and he pulled his own weight on the crew. Model citizen all around."

"What if he stumbled onto something he wasn't supposed to see?" Bree chipped in, mixing herbs and spices in a food processor.

"Out in the woods? Like what? A Druid coven performing human sacrifice? There's nothing there but trees. No rare, exotic flowers or birds or snakes that would interfere with their harvesting trees. Just woods."

"No buildings on the property?" Seth asked.

"Nope. There's a portable john for picnickers near the parking area, and that's it."

"You people are ridiculous—why do you *want* to think it was anything more than an accident? He was a good guy and it's too bad he died, but that's all there is. And you chop way too slowly. Hand it over—I want to start cooking," Bree demanded.

"So where does that leave us?" Meg asked. "An ordinary guy going about his business dies or is killed—by accident or by someone unknown—for no apparent reason?"

"There's almost always a reason when someone is killed, but in this case nobody's found it yet," Art reminded her. "And we have no reason to think he was killed. Look, the simplest answer, and without any other evidence, the one Marcus is most likely to choose, is that the guy tripped, hit his head, crawled in the wrong direction, and died.

There's nothing in the file or from the autopsy that contradicts that solution. I'd bet Marcus is going to close this case quickly."

"I'm starting the rice," Bree broke in. "Dinner in fifteen. And I agree with Art—the simplest solution is the most logical one here. You don't really have to find evil plots *all* the time, Meg."

Meg held up her hands. "Okay, I surrender! Another beer, guys?"

The talk turned to other things over dinner, followed by ice cream. Art went home shortly afterward, leaving the folder of photocopies with them. Bree excused herself and headed up to her room.

"You want to sit outside for a while?" Seth asked Meg.

"If I've still got bug repellent," Meg answered.

"Water's down in the Great Meadow, you know," Seth replied. "That means fewer mosquitoes."

"The one good part of this drought I keep trying to forget about, I guess. Sure, let's go watch the bats come out of the barn."

They made their way through the gathering dusk to the pair of Adirondack chairs overlooking the Meadow that lay behind Meg's old barn. Meg dropped into one with a sigh. "I don't know why I should be tired. I didn't do any manual labor today. Maybe I'm just frustrated."

"Why?" Seth asked, settling in the chair beside hers.

"The usual. The house needs some serious repairs that I can't afford. The orchard needs a permanent irrigation system, which I also can't afford. Finding that nasty beetle. Not to mention poor David Clapp's dead body. Sorry, I've got that backward: finding David Clapp should be more important than finding the beetle. Or maybe they're linked.

I notice that neither one of us mentioned the beetle angle to Art."

"Because there's no evidence that it's connected," Seth replied. "What's the point?"

"None, I guess," Meg said, but she was still troubled. She decided not to pursue it any further—for now. "How about you? Any unpleasant surprises at Donald's house?"

"You mean, like bodies falling out of the walls? Nope, it's pretty straightforward. I may need to get some heavy equipment in to square up the walls again in the corner, but otherwise it's structurally sound. I love working with the wood, and Jonas puts out a good product. Sometimes sawmills cut corners, like not drying their lumber long enough, and then people like me have problems with it twisting and warping, and the homeowner blames us for the shoddy work. But I can count on Jonas's wood."

"I assume it costs more than if you ordered lumber from the big box stores?" Meg asked, feeling the tension seeping out of her body as she relaxed in the dusk.

"Yes, and sometimes customers balk at the extra expense, but not people like Donald, thank goodness. He loves that house."

Meg could understand that, but she didn't want to dwell on all the repairs she should be doing on her own house, authentically or otherwise. Looking out over the darkening meadow, she asked, "Do you think this view has changed much since my house was built?"

"Probably not. I think you showed me the documents about grazing rights on the Meadow there, back in the eighteenth century—some years it was simply too wet for cattle. So it's been wetlands from the beginning. Back in the day the term 'meadow' and 'swamp' were more or less the same, in some cases. As for the forest beyond? I'd have to look more closely. It's likely that it was cleared and what you're looking at is regrowth, but even that's old now. Why, are you thinking of selling lumber?"

"I never even thought of that. I guess I could have some of the trees cut and made into boards, and hold them until or in case I need them for the house. I like the idea of continuing an old tradition like that."

"Agreed. Definitely an idea—I can ask Jonas what it would cost. And I—"

"Could probably get a good deal for me," Meg finished his sentence, laughing. "Put it on the to-do list, page thirty-seven." Meg reached out a hand, and Seth took it. They sat in peaceful silence, hands linked. Bats emerged from the barn and swooped through the dusk, eliminating their share of mosquitoes.

"I should go in," Meg said, reluctant to move. "Are you staying?"

Seth's hand tightened on hers, and then he stood up and pulled her to her feet. "Anytime you want."

8

"More coffee, anyone?" Meg waved the pot at Seth and Bree, each reading a section of the paper at the kitchen table the next morning. They mumbled what Meg interpreted as a "no," so she refilled her own cup and sat down. "Bree, what's next on the schedule?"

"I'm going to run some soil moisture tests today, but I think we can wait for tomorrow to water again. Although if it's going to stay hot for a while, we may need to go to a daily schedule. You got some other project you want to jump into? A short one, anyway?"

Meg sat back. "Let's see—I could put on a new roof, repaint the entire house, build a chicken coop, maybe take up weaving so I could do something useful on those long, cold winter nights. That would mean I'd have to get some sheep, although I suppose I could try spinning goat hair." Meg stopped when she realized that both Bree and Seth were staring at her as though she had lost her mind. She held up both hands. "Hey, just kidding, guys. But you must have figured out by now that I don't like to just sit around, especially when the weather is good."

"You want to come along to Donald's?" Seth suggested. "Most of the damaged stuff has been cleared away, so I'm about ready to start rebuilding. You could get a good look at eighteenth-century construction, up close. Maybe I could teach you how to plaster, the old-fashioned way."

"Doesn't that involve horsehair?" Meg asked.

"No problem—I know—"

"A man with a horse," Meg completed his sentence. "Sure, sounds like fun. Will Donald mind?"

"As long as you don't try to suggest modern improvements, he's happy to have visitors—he loves to talk about his house. And you can learn a lot from him."

"Sounds good. Oh, and let's invite your mother to dinner, and maybe Rachel and her clan, since I might have time to cook something nice. Over the weekend, maybe?"

"I'm sure Mom would love to see you," Seth said amiably.

"Bree, you want to ask Michael to come over, if we do a cookout or something?"

"Maybe." Her tone was not exactly enthusiastic.

Meg and Seth exchanged a glance. If Bree and Michael were having problems, Bree wasn't about to confide in her. It was hard enough living with a full-time roommate—with only one bathroom—and Meg tried to give Bree some privacy. Of course, since Seth was around so much, that made it all the more difficult. Meg decided to take the coward's route and change the subject. "So, Seth, if we're going to Donald's, can I be your apprentice? Maybe we could draw up an indenture, or whatever they're called."

"I'll take it under advisement. How do you feel about tools?"

"Power tools that cut, like circular saws, scare me. Drills I can manage."

"Well, that's a start. I can show you manual tools that do the same thing, only a lot more slowly. But they build up your muscles."

"I've got plenty of muscles these days from the orchard. You should know."

"Believe me, I do."

They smiled at each other, which led Bree to snort. "I'm leaving, so you two can be alone to talk about, uh, tools and stuff."

"Have a good day," Meg chirped, with only a hint of sarcasm.

"Ha!" Bree said, and she vanished up the stairs to her room.

Meg turned back to Seth. "Seriously, I'd love to come. Maybe I can carry your toolbox."

"Works for me," Seth replied. "Wear something you don't mind getting dirty."

Meg wondered if she owned anything that *didn't* fit that category. Farmwork required clothing with only a few primary characteristics: primarily, durability, and washability.

Fifteen minutes later they were pulling up in front of Donald's house. He was waiting for them—poor man, did he never dare leave his property these days? There seemed to be no one else to watch it for him.

"Hey, Donald!" Seth called out. "I brought Meg along—hope you don't mind."

"No problem, as long as she doesn't slow you down. Hello, Meg, nice to see you again."

"And you, Donald. Things are looking neater now."

"They are, although I hated to part with any of the old wood. You can see all the tool marks on the beams—you know just how each one was shaped and fitted. And in my case—and yours, too, I hear—you even know whose hands did the work."

"True. It does make the building more personal," Meg agreed.

"Nash's just delivered the wood, Seth," said Donald, pointing to a stack of lumber off to the side, covered with a tarp. "Looks good. Where do we start today?"

"Now that the debris is out of the way, I want to show you exactly what I'm planning, if you don't mind."

"Sounds good to me," Donald said.

Meg trailed after them, listening. It was an unexpected pleasure hearing Seth talk about his work. Although when they'd first met, he'd been managing the family plumbing business, he'd always made it clear that his heart lay in renovation and restoration. Still, knowing it wasn't the same as seeing him in action. Not only was he knowledgeable, but he obviously cared about the building: sometimes he'd run his hand over one of the beams as though the house was a living thing. Certainly it was a tough one, Meg thought, having withstood the impact of a hurtling chunk of metal.

"What about finishes?" Donald asked.

"I know a guy who specializes in paint restoration. I assume you want to go with the original colors?"

"Of course. Look, I even found a sample from the dining room cupboard." Donald picked up a broken board lying against the lath of a bare wall and handed it to Seth. "See? There on the edge? That's what it would have looked like in 1750."

"Good catch, Donald." Seth handed the fragment to Meg. "These days that color would probably be called Colonial Blue, and there's a good reason for that."

"What about nails, Seth?" Donald asked anxiously. "I'm sure you know as well as I do that a lot of these beams were originally pegged together, without any metal. Like there." He pointed at some intersecting beams.

"I don't think current code will allow it," Seth said, adding, "but I'll go back as early as I can."

"Which would be what?" Meg asked.

"Hand-forged nails, mostly," Seth replied promptly. "They existed back then, but early builders used wooden pegs because nails were expensive and hard to come by. In fact, nails were considered so valuable that if a building burned down, people would scavenge whatever nails they could."

"So you can't tell the age of a building from its nails?"

"Not necessarily. These days you can still get cut nails, but they're later than this house. Sorry, Donald, but I draw the line at forging my own nails, even for you."

Donald sighed. "I understand. What about splitting your own lath?"

"That I can do." Seth smiled at him. "You want to talk about glass now?"

Feeling overwhelmed with details, Meg drifted off to study the wall construction. Clearly the beams had been cut by hand—the adze or saw marks were plain to see. It was hard for her to imagine starting with a grove of trees and arriving at a substantial building, like Donald's or her own. Yet people did it all the time back in the eighteenth century, because there were no other options. There wasn't much brick construction around here, although she'd seen elegant brick and even fieldstone buildings in parts of Pennsylvania and New Jersey when she was growing up. Not that she'd paid much attention to them. Here in this part of New England, however, it seemed that almost everything was made of wood. She wondered again about having boards cut from her own trees, to use in her house. Was it practical, or silly and sentimental? Either way, the idea of emulating her ancestors pleased her.

"Meg?" Seth's voice interrupted her.

Meg turned away from the injured wall. "You need something?"

"I've got to get to work now. You can stay and watch if you like, or you can take the van and pick me up later."

"Seth, I can drive you home if you want," Donald volunteered. "I think I can leave the place for that long."

"Meg? What do you think?"

"I love seeing what you do, but as much fun as it would be to 'help,' I think I'd just get in your way here, so I should probably go." She held out her hand. "Keys?"

Seth tossed the keys to her, and she caught them one-handed. He was already deep in conversation with Donald again, but she didn't mind: it gave her pleasure to see him so happy in his work.

What now? she wondered as she climbed into the van. Her to-do list was endless, but much of the time she didn't want to do any of the items on it. Maybe she should do something indulgent, something as frivolous as buying a new pair of shoes, or worse, some personal pampering. She thought for a moment. There weren't any spas nearby, but she could really use a haircut. She couldn't remember the last time she'd had a professional trim, rather than just chopping at the annoyingly long pieces or tucking the whole mess under a cap. But where to go? She could ask Rachel, Seth's sister. Meg hadn't talked to her in a while, since summer was Rachel's busiest season: she ran a lovely bed-and-breakfast, and her two kids were out of school. Meg smiled. Rachel probably had less free time than she did. But she might know where Meg could get a decent haircut. Before starting the van, she pulled out her cell phone and hit Rachel's number.

Miracle of miracles, Rachel answered. "Meg! How are you? Anything wrong?"

Funny how everyone seemed to expect crises from her. "No, not a thing. As a matter of fact, I have a couple of hours free, and I realized I really, really need a haircut. Can you recommend anyone?"

"Sure—I keep a list of all local services, just in case a guest asks. Hang on a sec . . . Yes, here we go: the New Hare. It's in the mall—you know, the one on Route 9 as you come toward Amherst? Ask for Laurel—I think you'll like her. She's about our age. I've known her for years and she'll do a good job for you. Listen, I've got some stuff to do, but why don't you stop by after? I'd love to see you, Meg. I can serve you iced tea on the veranda and we can pretend that we're genteel ladies."

"If you're sure you're not too busy, I'd love to."

"No problem. And I want to hear about whatever you and that brother of mine are up to. He never calls. Usually Mom has to fill me in. Everything good?"

"I think so. Let me call the hair place and I'll let you know when I'll be up your way, okay?"

"Sure." Rachel hung up, and Meg punched in the number she had given her, and found there was a slot open mid-afternoon. Perfect: she could find a bite to eat, wander through a clean, air-conditioned mall, get her hair cut, then stop by and see Rachel. That would be plenty of self-indulgence for one day.

Meg presented herself at the New Hare salon promptly at two, fortified by fast food and replacement clothing that farming had reduced to shreds. There was only one hair-stylist in sight, a slender, dark-haired woman wearing practical shoes. She greeted Meg warmly. "Hi, I'm Laurel. You said Rachel Dickinson sent you? She's good people. Come on, sit down, please." Laurel pointed to a swivel chair at her workstation. When Meg was seated, Laurel sank her fingers into Meg's hair. "You've been out in the sun a lot, haven't you?"

Meg sat and stared at her own reflection, something she avoided as much as possible. Time to get some moisturizer, apparently—something she'd never needed in her former indoor life in Boston. "Well, I've turned into a farmer in the past year, and I haven't had a professional haircut since I left Boston—no time. Mostly I just hack at the bits that fall in my eyes." She hoped this haircut wouldn't cost her a lot of money, though from the humble looks of the salon, she didn't think it would be expensive.

"I'd never guess," Laurel drawled. She stepped back and looked critically at Meg's reflection in the mirror on the wall. "I suppose you don't have a lot of time for deep conditioning and that kind of thing?"

"Nope. Strictly no-frills. Wash and wear, if you know what I mean."

"What kind of style? Length? Chop it all off?"

"I don't want to look like a twelve-year-old boy, if that's what you're asking. But I don't want anything I have to fuss with to make it look good. And I hate hair in my face."

"Color?"

Meg shook her head vigorously. "No time to keep up with it. I'm fine with what I've got."

"Got it. Clean and simple. You've got good bone structure, so you can handle it. A bit of curl, which doesn't hurt. Nice body. This should be easy. Let's get you washed, okay?"

At the shampoo station, Meg relaxed into the sensation of someone massaging her scalp with nice sudsy stuff that smelled good.

"I don't see much of Rachel in here either, what with the business and her kids. Great lady, though. How do you know her?" Laurel asked.

"I'm, uh, seeing her brother."

"Seth? He did the plumbing when we remodeled the shop here. How is he?" Laurel's voice was warm.

"He's good. He's trying to get out of plumbing and do more restoration work. Did you hear about the house in Granford that was hit by a car? That's what he's working on today."

"Sure, I heard about that. Small world, isn't it? Say hello to him for me, will you? He's such a great guy."

"I agree. And I'm always amazed at how many people know him. I'm glad Rachel recommended this place. I was surprised that you had an opening for me today."

Laurel shrugged as she draped a towel over Meg's wet hair. "Well, it's the middle of the day in the middle of the week, so it's been slow. The economy hasn't helped, and I guess a haircut is kind of a luxury these days, at least if you've got a family, so that's one of the first things people give up. But we get by, and things are looking up. What's it like, being a farmer, after life in Boston?"

"It's been a real learning experience . . ."

They chatted happily while Laurel's scissors were busy. When she was satisfied, she asked, "No goop?"

"No, it would just get messed up. Can I run my hands through it?" Meg asked.

"Hey, it's your hair! Go for it."

Meg looked at her reflection. She looked a lot tidier, and maybe even . . . younger? It felt short and might take getting used to, but it was a perfect summer cut. "Thanks, Laurel. I like it, and it feels a lot cooler. What do I owe you?"

Laurel named a price that was roughly half what Meg had been paying in Boston, and Meg added a solid twenty percent tip. "Be sure to come back when you want a trim. Should I book you for next February?" Laurel joked.

"I'll try not to wait that long. Thanks again!"

9

Rachel was sitting in one of the white rockers on the wraparound porch of her ornate Victorian home, which she also ran as a B and B, when Meg pulled up. Rachel did a double take when Meg climbed out of the car. "Wow, you look great!"

"Does that mean I looked bad before?" Meg asked, smiling, as she climbed the steps.

"Of course not, but you look better now. How've you been?"

"Busy, of course. This year we're doing a lot of watering in the orchard, since it's been so dry. We didn't need to do it last year, so this was kind of a surprise. Lots of lifting and hauling, because we have to fill our tank at the well and then drive around the whole orchard, and believe me, one tank doesn't last long." Meg dropped into a matching rocker. "No guests?"

"Not as many as in the past, and at the moment they're either all out sightseeing, or they're napping to recuperate from all their sightseeing. That's fine with me. Thank heavens Noah has a full-time job and we don't have to rely on the B and B income to survive, since it's so unpredictable! And since the kids are out of school for the summer, it's nice that they're old enough to help out a little. We're working up to washing dishes, or at least loading the dishwasher—they can handle that. I keep having to explain to them that nobody wants to see what's left from the last meal on the plate."

"I suppose if this were a hundred years ago, there'd be a batch of kids helping me out, too, collecting eggs, hanging out the laundry, picking apples."

"That's true. How's Seth?"

"He's good. Busy, while the weather's good for construction, but he really loves the renovation part. I keep wondering if I should be jealous of the old wood. He's really hands-on with it." Oops—was that too much information?

Rachel laughed. "He's always loved that kind of thing. He only went into the plumbing business because Dad was failing and we flat out needed the money, so I'm glad he gets to do what he loves now. He's earned it."

"Have you ever visited Nash's Sawmill?" Meg asked.

"Not for a long time—I think we went there on a school trip, years ago. Is Jonas Nash still running it?"

"Yes. I just met him a couple of days ago. You remember him?"

"I sure do. I had a mad crush on him, years ago. He was sort of a romantic figure, you know? The brooding woodsman, in touch with the earth."

"From what Seth tells me, now he's a businessman running a family corporation," Meg commented wryly.

"Well, life moves on for all of us. How'd you end up at the sawmill?"

"Seth needed some lumber for a new project, so I tagged along to see the place. He's working on that house that got hit by a car."

"Donald Butterfield's house? I read about that in the paper. Seth thinks he can fix it?"

"Apparently it was pretty solidly built, so the damage was restricted to one part of it. But Seth says Donald is a stickler for authenticity, so he wanted to get the right boards from the sawmill. We were at the house this morning to check on the lumber delivery, and then there was a discussion about authentic nails, and then about glass . . ."

Rachel held up a hand to stop her. "I know how that goes! So you fled?"

"Kind of. But I realized I hadn't seen you for a while, and I wanted to give myself a treat, so here I am."

"I'm glad you came." Rachel smiled at her. "Even though it's probably for the cookies rather than my charming company."

"A little of each. Bree doesn't let me off the leash very often."

"I can imagine—or maybe I can't, if you two are really watering an entire orchard more or less by hand."

"Hey, it could be worse—in the old days we'd be using a team of horses!" Both women laughed. "By the way, Seth and I were talking about getting together with you guys and your mother over the weekend—maybe a potluck cookout, so nobody would have to do too much? I live maybe two miles from Lydia, but I hardly ever see her."

"Me either. Not that she ever complains, even about not seeing the grandkids. I think it makes her happy, knowing we're living lives we enjoy. And she's still working, of course. I don't think she has to, but she's glad to have some structure to her days. Did you have a date in mind?"

"I suppose you should have first pick, since you've got a real calendar with your guests, and other people to accommodate. Me, I just mind the apples, and they don't care when I eat. Would Sunday night work for you?"

"Can I look at the bookings and get back to you? But I think it's clear."

"No rush. At least this year we seem to be able to count on nice weather. For socializing, at least. As a farmer I obviously have other concerns—it's too hot and too dry, at the wrong time. I'm so glad we have that spring up the hill."

"No wonder the orchard has survived there as long as it has. You're lucky. Is this officially a drought yet?"

"I'm the wrong person to ask. Bree would know. She tells me we need to water, and we water."

"The forests are getting pretty dry around here."

"I hadn't even thought of that, but you're right. Seth and I went over to one of Nash's properties, and he said it looked like it was well managed. You know, keeping the brush cleared out, which could reduce the risk of a fire. But I can't imagine the manpower it would take to do that over a whole lot of acres of forest. And if your neighbor doesn't, then your work is kind of wasted, isn't it?"

"Meg, there's a good reason I live in a town. I have smoke detectors throughout the house, and I make sure I change the batteries every few months. These older houses burn easily, you know," Rachel said.

"This is cheery talk. Aren't we supposed to be swapping

recipes and gossiping about our neighbors, not talking about potentially deadly forest fires?"

"Well, there is that recent death in Granford. Know of any interesting gossip there?"

"Other than that I found the body?"

Rachel stared at Meg to see if she was joking. "The paper didn't mention anything about that. Fill me in!"

"When we were at one of Nash's woodlots, I stopped to get a pebble out of my shoe, and I smelled something unpleasant, and . . . you can fill in the blanks from there."

"I'm so sorry, Meg. That it had to be you, I mean. Of course, I'm sorry the guy was dead, too. Nobody we knew?"

"Apparently someone named David Clapp, who used to work at the sawmill and then the logging company that Jonas Nash contracts some of his work out to. He was from Easthampton, not Granford, and that's about all I know."

"Doesn't sound familiar. I'm almost afraid to ask, but was there anything suspicious about his death?"

Meg shrugged. "Inconclusive, at least from what Art Preston said, and apparently Detective Marcus is not inclined to pursue it. The logger was in a place he had every right to be, so that wasn't odd. Current theory is that he fell and hit his head."

"Poor guy. You never know what's going to happen, do you?" Rachel looked away, staring across the road. "Speaking of the unexpected, there is one thing . . ."

Meg's mind immediately flew to disasters. Rachel had been diagnosed with some awful terminal disease. Or her husband Noah had. Or one of their children. Or maybe it was Lydia, who hadn't had the nerve to break it to her.

Rachel was watching her with a smile. "If you could see your face! You must be imagining the worst possible case."

"You mean I shouldn't?" Meg said, already relieved.

"No. Or at least, I don't think so. I'm pregnant. Before you do that math, Chloe is twelve, and Matthew is ten."

"Wow. Congratulations! That is, if you're happy?" Meg said.

Rachel nodded. "I am. It's just that I'm having trouble getting used to the idea. I thought all that stuff was behind us. It was, uh, kind of a surprise."

"But a good one, I hope," Meg replied, surprised at her own vehemence. After all, it was a choice these days. "From what I've seen, you're a great mother. Are there other problems? Your health? Finances? Noah can't handle the idea?"

"I'm fine. We can get by, and Noah is pleased—he comes from a big family. Mostly it's that, well, you think you have your life planned out, and then something unexpected happens and it's back to the drawing board."

"Who have you told?"

"Noah, of course. Not the kids, not yet."

"Maybe Chloe's old enough to figure it out for herself. What about Lydia?"

Rachel shook her head. "I haven't seen her lately, and I think that news like this is better said face-to-face if possible. A phone call seems so cold."

"I'm sure she'll be happy for you. Seth doesn't know?"

"Not yet—I wasn't planning to tell you either, at least not before Mom, but since you're here . . ." Rachel looked down at her hands in her lap. "Meg, I think we've talked about this before, but it's been a while and maybe things have changed. I guess I'm bringing this up now because, well . . . I know Seth always wanted kids, but I don't know where things stand with you two, and when I tell him, I'm sure he'll be happy for me, but it's kind of like rubbing his nose in what he doesn't have, if you know what I mean. But I don't want this baby to put any pressure on you—either of you—to make any fast decisions. I don't mind if you want to be the one to tell Seth, but you can do it in your own way. Are you okay with that?"

Meg felt a little blindsided. But Rachel was right: she'd been too busy being happy for her friend to think about how it might affect her own situation. And, she realized, she wasn't ready to think about that. There was too much happening with the orchard, too much she still had to learn if she hoped to make a living from it. Besides, Seth had never exactly "declared his intentions." Maybe he was happy muddling along as they had been, spending time together, going home to their own houses. She hadn't asked him. Should she?

"Rachel . . . I don't know what to say. Look, I'm really pleased that you thought you could confide in me, and I guess I understand what you're trying to tell me. Seth and I . . . well, we really haven't talked about a lot of things like that, and we're not rushing into anything. More like taking the easiest path and drifting along. It really seems absurd in this day and age to wait for the guy to make the first move, but I've always kind of felt that this is his home ground and I'm kind of an interloper. It's like he came with the package: I landed in Granford, and Seth was just there from the start. It's kind of hard to sort out what I feel."

"May I remind you that my brother can be a little dense? And he doesn't like to look for trouble. Or maybe he can't take the idea of another rejection—when Nancy left him, he took it badly. I know he cares about you—I can see it every time you two are together. You can tell me to shut up if you want, but do you feel the same way?"

"Yes, I do. I'm still sorting a lot of things out, but I guess we both have to face that we're not getting any younger. God, how old that makes me sound to say that!" Meg straightened up in her chair and looked directly at Rachel. "Look, I really appreciate what you've said. And I am happy for you, honestly. If I can do anything to help, I will."

"I'll ask, believe me. Enough said." And the talk turned to lighter topics.

It was after five when Meg tore herself away. All in all, she thought it had been a successful afternoon: she felt tidier, thanks to her haircut, and rested, although now she was weighted down by Rachel's news. It *was* happy news, but . . . she wasn't ready to be in that place, not yet. Which wasn't the same as saying never. She had always assumed that Seth would be a good father, and from what she'd seen of him with kids, or at least Rachel's, he probably wanted children. Was he waiting for some signal from her? But to put the horse in front of the cart, she did want to be married before she had a child. Sure, lots of people didn't bother with formal rituals these days, but she wasn't one of them. Did she want to marry Seth? Maybe. Probably. Not exactly a resounding "yes!" *Well, Meg, why not?*

Her mind skittered sideways, avoiding the question. No doubt they'd have to irrigate again tomorrow. The sky was cloudless, as it always seemed to be these days. The air was dry and still, oppressive even without any humidity. Was it going to rain anytime soon? She should ask Bree what forecasting services she relied on. Or Christopher. What would happen if this heat continued through the rest of the summer? Would she have any kind of apple crop at all?

She arrived home at the same time Donald was dropping

Seth off. Seth waited for her to park his van close to his office, and they met halfway between.

"Your keys," Meg said, holding them out. "If I stick them in my pocket I'll forget about them. How'd it go with Donald?"

"Good. We've mapped out a timeline that we're both comfortable with. Hey, you look good. What'd you do?"

Meg smiled. "I'm glad you noticed. I got my hair cut, for the first time since I don't know when. Seems like another lifetime anyway. And then I went to have tea with your sister and show it off, since she was the one who recommended the stylist."

"Nice. It suits you. How's Rachel?"

"Good, I think. Not so many bookings, but she's glad the kids can help with some of the chores. I told her we'd try to set up dinner with them and Lydia, and I suggested Sunday." She pulled up short of mentioning Rachel's unexpected news. *Scared, Meg?*

"Oh, right, we talked about that, didn't we? Half the time these days I feel like my brain is fried."

"I know what you mean. Did we make any plans for dinner tonight? Because I honestly can't remember. I can't even remember if there's any food in the house."

"Think Nicky could fit us in at the restaurant on short notice? We could celebrate your haircut."

"We can ask. Come on in—I'll find you something cold to drink, then give her a call."

Inside it wasn't too hot. Luckily the kitchen lay on the east side of the house, so it cooled as the sun set. Lolly lay on the kitchen floor, too lethargic to move. Meg was tempted to lay down beside her. Instead she pulled a can of cat food out of a cupboard and handed it to Seth. "You feed Lolly, and I'll make that call."

She walked toward the front of the house, cell phone to her ear. "Brian?" she said, when Nicky's husband and co-owner of Granford's newest and pretty much only restaurant Gran's picked up. "It's Meg Corey. I know it's short notice, but do you have room for Seth and me tonight?"

"Sure, things have been pretty quiet lately. I thought this was the part of the state where people came to get away, but I can't find them."

"Problems?" Meg asked.

"No, we're okay. It's just slow, but that gives Nicky time to experiment with recipes. Come on over whenever."

"Thanks, Brian. See you in a bit."

She returned to the kitchen to see that Seth had found the lemonade in the fridge. He was sitting at the kitchen table, an ice-filled glass in front of him, watching Lolly eat. "Bree left a note. She and Michael are going to see an air-conditioned movie."

"Smart woman." Meg found herself a glass and filled it with ice, then poured lemonade over it. "Brian says we can come over anytime, and Nicky is experimenting. Sound good? But first I'm going to grab a shower, in case there are other guests downwind."

10

Gran's restaurant sat on a rise above Granford's oblong town green. Meg loved to approach it in the winter months, when the golden light from inside the restaurant glowed through the dark, warm and welcoming. For summer, Nicky and Brian had hung lush baskets of blooming flowers in each bay of the wraparound porch, making it look cool and green. Small tables flanked by chairs were scattered around the porch; in the lingering heat they were currently unoccupied, but Meg knew that in pleasant weather people would bring their drinks out, to sit and admire the view of a typical New England town: the green ringed with maples, the steepled church on the right, the Victorian town hall on the left. Even though a state highway ran along one side of the green, there was little traffic. Where had everyone gone? Were they all at home, huddling around an air conditioner?

Seth escorted her from the parking lot to the front door, a sweet gesture, but even his hand on her back felt too hot. At least the interior of the restaurant was air-conditioned, and the tables' crisp white cloths, small twinkling candles, and nosegays of bright summer flowers reinforced the coolness.

Brian approached as they entered. "Hey, guys, good to see you. Where do you want to sit?"

They settled at a small table in the front overlooking the green, with Brian hovering. "Can I get you something cool to drink? Nicky's come up with a concoction using local herbs—it's very refreshing, and there's just a bit of alcohol in it."

"Sounds good to me," Seth said. "You, Meg?"

"Sure. I love almost anything that Nicky comes up with. Some people talk about someone having an eye for art. Can we say that Nicky has a tongue for food, or is that kind of weird?"

"I'm sure she'll take the compliment in the spirit intended," Brian said tactfully. "I'll tell her you're here."

When he left to fetch the drinks, Meg discreetly looked around the room. There were several other couples, some of whom Meg recognized. Not too bad for a weeknight, even if Brian had said it was slow. The restaurant had been operating less than a year, and it was making a name for itself, thanks largely to Nicky's creative cooking. It had received some good local reviews, and word of mouth was doing its job. It wasn't easy to compete in a restaurant market that included Northampton and Amherst, and Meg felt a glow of pride that she had helped to create this restaurant in Granford.

Nicky herself delivered the drinks and plopped down

into a chair to say hello. "Hey, you two—I don't see much of you these days. How're things?"

Meg caught her up on the dry state of the orchard, and Seth told her about his new project at Donald Butterfield's house. "How about you, Nicky? Is business holding up?" Meg asked.

Nicky smiled. "You'll have to ask Brian about the numbers, but I can't complain. I know it seemed ridiculous to open a new restaurant in a lousy economy, but we took a chance that we'd find a good niche here, and it looks like we were right. It's been slow but steady. Some people in Granford have cut back on their visits, even though we give a discount to our food providers, but they've been replaced by people from a little farther out in the area, and even some who've heard about us somewhere else. That plug on the news, where the restaurant appeared behind Seth's buddy Sainsbury, helped. What're his chances in the election?"

Meg waited for Seth to answer, but when he didn't, she jumped in. "We'll just have to wait for the state primary. So, what do you recommend for dinner? Nothing heavy— it's too hot."

"Not a problem. I'm doing a lot of lovely salads with an array of local lettuces, and I'm experimenting with frozen desserts. The suppliers are hurting, though, from the lack of rain. The beans are kind of stringy, and the tomatoes aren't as large as they might be. At least the lettuce is coming in well."

"Surprise us, then," Meg said with a smile.

"Coming up," Nicky said. "Oh, tell me what you think of the drink."

Meg took a small sip, and then a larger one. "It's lovely. What's in it?"

Nicky smiled. "It's modeled on an eighteenth-century New England 'shrub' recipe—no, not the plant—it's got fruit, sugar, infused vinegar, and some rum."

"Vinegar?" Meg said, raising one eyebrow.

"Yes—the tartness is refreshing, and the sugar cuts the acidity. You infuse the vinegar with fruit, or even herbs and spices, and it keeps well."

"Okay, okay." Meg laughed. "I'll just stop by regularly for a glass or three. If Bree will let me."

When Nicky bustled off to the kitchen, Meg relaxed in her chair, then straightened up again. It wouldn't do to fall asleep before dinner. "You look tired," she told Seth, fighting a stab of guilt about her afternoon off.

"It's a good tired. Are you worried about water?"

"I have to be worried. On the plus side, I have the spring. On the minus side, I don't know much about it, since I kind of inherited it. What happens if it goes dry? Will there be any warning, or could it just stop one day? Can I get municipal water, and even if I can, can I afford to use it? Or do I have to rely on the rain gods to look after me?"

Seth held up a hand. "Whoa, I didn't mean to set you off. I can look into the municipal water side of things and find out about the cost, but you'd have to tell me how much you would be using, and I have no idea how you'd calculate that. You should ask Bree or even Christopher. And the town still may have to ration it. We're already limiting things like watering lawns and washing cars, for the rest of the summer, unless things change. It may not be of much help to you."

"I know. Heck, I'm not facing anything that eight or ten generations of my ancestors didn't. I could ask Gail Seldon about historical droughts, but that might depress me more. Some years the crops fail—that's just reality."

"Well, you aren't there yet," Seth said firmly.

"You really are an optimist," Meg replied.

He smiled. "I try. Beats the alternative. Aren't you?"

"Do you know, I've never really thought about it. I'm not afraid of trying new things, or of learning something, but I do like to have a plan, not just jumping in blind. I don't assume everything will work out, even with planning, but I like to be prepared for all scenarios. So where does that put me on the scale?"

"Firmly in the middle, I'd say. You're probably more cautious than I am."

"True. But I like your enthusiasm." Seth was certainly more upbeat than Meg was, and his positive attitude drew people to him with their problems. That was a good thing, wasn't it? "On a less cheerful topic, has anybody heard anything new about that dead man?"

Seth shook his head. "I touched base with Art briefly today. He still thinks Marcus is going to write it off as an accidental death. In the absence of any real evidence, he can't prove otherwise."

Meg sighed. "I suppose it makes sense, but it feels . . . unfinished, I guess."

"There's nothing for us to do," Seth replied. "You don't really want this death to be a murder, do you?"

"No, I don't. I just don't like unexplained deaths," Meg said.

Nicky appeared with a tray full of colorful summer salads, house-made breads, cheeses, and sliced fruits, so talking stopped for a while. When the platter was bare, Meg leaned back, content. "This was exactly what I needed. Especially having someone else do all the peeling and slicing."

"I agree," Seth said. "Dessert, or are you ready to go home?"

"Home, I guess. I need to check in with Bree about the plan for tomorrow. You don't happen to have any rain gods on your buddy list, do you?"

Seth smiled. "Sorry, no. You're on your own there. Ready?" He tossed some bills on the table and stood up.

Walking outside, the heat felt like a slap in the face. It was fully dark, but the temperature hadn't dropped more than a couple of degrees. Global warming? It wasn't just highs and lows; it was extremes everywhere. Early snowstorms that ripped limbs off of trees because they were still covered with leaves. Torrential rains that dumped a foot of water in a day. There had even been a tornado that ripped through Brimfield and Monson, too close for comfort. What was next? A plague of locusts? Frogs falling from the sky? It all felt wrong.

"You're quiet," Seth commented as they made the short drive home.

"I'm thinking about apocalyptic disasters," Meg replied.

"Indigestion?"

"No, just frustration. I may be doing what my local forebears did in the orchard, but I'm pretty sure they didn't have to contend with such weird weather."

They pulled into her driveway. Lights in the kitchen indicated that Bree was home and probably still up. "You coming in?" Meg asked.

"Sorry, but I've got some sketches to make before I go back over to Donald's in the morning. Rain check?"

"Of course—but bring some rain with you, please. Are you driving the van home?"

"No, it's loaded up and ready for tomorrow. I'll walk—maybe it'll be cooler that way."

"Be safe," Meg said. She watched him walk away until he disappeared into the darkness, then turned to go in the back door.

As she had suspected, Bree was sitting at the kitchen table with various farm catalogs and computer printouts spread out in front of her. She looked up when Meg walked in. "You alone?"

"You mean, is Seth here? No, he went home. Bree, do you have a problem with him being around?"

"No, not really. At least he cleans up after himself. I'm just trying to figure out where you two are going with this."

First Rachel, and now Bree? Meg wasn't sure how to answer her. "Why can't we just go on the way we are?"

Bree shrugged. "If it works for the two of you. Look, I'm no expert. Michael and I see each other a couple of times a week, maybe, and we're good with that. I'm not going to go all gooey and say he's 'The One'"—Bree made air quotes—"but you and Seth are different. Older."

"Bree, we're not exactly ancient. I'm less than ten years older than you."

"Yeah, but you're still different. Traditional. So's Seth—he likes to do things by the book, even if the book was written in 1873. I think it's kind of sweet."

Meg wrestled with how to respond. Bree probably saw them more clearly than they saw themselves. And since she was living under Meg's roof, she had a right to be interested. But Meg had no easy answers for her. "Uh, okay. Look, if we decide to make any changes, you'll be the first to know. This is your home, and I owe you that."

"No, this is *your* home, and I happen to live here. No offense, but I never assumed this was permanent. I mean, I like living here, and it's convenient, but things can change and I'm cool with that."

"Would you move in with Michael?"

"Not where he's living now, that's for sure. But I don't think I feel the same way about him as you do about Seth."

Which was how? Meg didn't voice the question. She wasn't conducting a survey, asking other people to define her relationship with Seth. Things were good the way they were—for now. Weren't they?

She decided to change the subject. "How was the movie?"

"Cool. Thermodynamically, that is, not cinematically. That's what counted."

"What's all this?" Meg asked, waving at all the papers on the table.

"The water pump for the spring is acting up, and I'm trying to see if there's an easy fix, or if we should just give up on it and replace it if it's way past its useful life."

One more expense she didn't need. "Does that mean we have to make a decision about the whole irrigation system, if we have to replace the pump?"

"Maybe. I don't know. You should ask Christopher, or ask him to recommend somebody who can give you an opinion. And an estimate. I wish there was a better way to handle this, Meg, but we've been using the pump a lot this summer because it's been so dry, and I think it's just been too much for the poor thing. If we get more rain, we might be able to keep it going until next year."

"So if we use it too much now, it might give out. But if we don't, the crop will suffer, and even some of the trees."

"That's about it. Ain't farming grand? You fix one thing, and something else blows up."

"Sounds about right. Remind me again why we do this?"

"People gotta eat."

The landline phone rang, and Meg recognized Christopher's number. "Hi, Christopher. Were your ears burning? Bree and I were just talking about you. Why are you calling so late? Is something wrong?"

"Nothing that you need to worry yourself about, Meg, but I thought you'd like to know that the experts have found more small infestations by the Asian longhorned beetle in Granford, at Nash's sawmill and the town park, and the identification for both is confirmed. You've been vindicated, although it's not happy news for forest owners in the vicinity. I wondered if you'd like to tour our research facility here and see how we address the problem?"

"Sounds interesting—when were you thinking?"

"Tomorrow?"

Meg looked at Bree and mouthed, "Tomorrow?" Bree nodded and mouthed back, "Afternoon."

Meg spoke into the phone again. "Bree gives me permission to come over in the afternoon. What time is good for you?"

"Say, two o'clock?"

"Great. And if you have a little spare time, there's something else I'd like to talk with you about."

"I'll see if I can arrange it. See you tomorrow, Meg."

"What's up?" Bree asked.

"He says they've found more of the Asian longhorned beetles in Granford. I'm still not sure what that means, but it doesn't sound good. Christopher's going to show me the research labs at UMass. Although I'm not sure how much I really want to know about those insects—they are kind of big."

"Nice to know you were right, isn't it?"

"I guess, although I think I'd rather have been wrong. I'm going up to bed now—we'll be busy in the morning, right?"

"Right. Unless and until it rains."

11

The next day, the weather hadn't changed. Meg had never thought she'd be tired of seeing blue sky, but then, she hadn't been a farmer before. In this July's persistent heat she found herself getting up earlier and earlier in the day simply because it was cooler then, and she could enjoy a cup of hot coffee and a light breakfast. Often she wandered out to visit with the goats—and more important, refill their water trough. Even they were less frisky these days, usually resting in the shade of their shed all day long.

Meg trudged silently up the hill to where Bree waited with the water tank attached behind the tractor, parked next to the spring house. She was almost afraid to look at the trees: would she recognize water stress if she saw it? To her inexperienced eye, there were fewer apples ripening than there had been the year before, but Bree had told her that

that could happen with fruiting trees with or without drought. And setting fruit was unpredictable even under the best of circumstances. From her own reading she knew that in the early twentieth century Baldwins had been the orchard apple of choice, but they had one serious flaw: the trees bore only every other year. When the Hurricane of 1938 had severely damaged a lot of orchards, many farmers had opted to replace the Baldwins with more dependable Macintosh trees—with a sigh of relief, Meg surmised. It was, after all, a business, with no room for sentiment. You could count on Macintosh apples. Meg found them a bit boring, though, and enjoyed her few heirloom varieties, glad that they were gaining in popularity in regional farmer's markets. It would be a real shame to let them all die out.

Standing next to the springhouse, or more accurately, houses—one older, where the spring had emerged naturally who knew how long ago, and one newer, which housed the pump and connecting equipment they were using—Meg turned to survey her domain. The Great Meadow looked deceptively green. It was still damp enough to encourage plants, but Meg knew that in a normal year, there would be standing water and it would more closely resemble a swamp, with abundant cattails. Already the air was hazy in the distance, even though the sun had barely cleared the tree line to the east.

"You ready?" Bree asked.

"I guess. How long do we have to keep doing this?"

"It depends on the weather, duh. In the long run, normally I'd test at intervals. There are lots of factors in determining how much water your orchard needs, including your soil type, the kind of tree, and whether it's new or well-established. Then there's how long and how much to irrigate. It's a complex calculation, not just 'water from eight to ten every day.'"

"Have I mentioned lately how glad I am to have you on board, Bree? Because I've still got an awful lot to learn."

"You're lucky to have me, and I'm lucky to have Christopher nearby for backup. Although he's pretty busy these days, which is good for him and for the university, but he's harder to pin down. What are you two doing this afternoon?"

"Are you jealous? I told you, he said he'd show me the insect research labs at the university, as a treat in return for my first sighting of this ALB creature. I'm not sure I relish the idea of spending time in a lab surrounded by large insects, but he thought he was doing me a favor, and I didn't want to disappoint him. Besides, I can pump him for more information on irrigation."

"That is a bad pun."

"What? Oh, sorry. I will explore our irrigation options with him, okay?"

"Sure. I love free advice."

Five hours later Meg and Bree had finished watering, but Meg was surprised when Bree headed the tractor back to the springhouse. She followed obediently. Bree attached one hose to the coupling—then turned the hose on her, drenching her.

"What was that about?" Meg demanded, laughing, when Bree cut off the water.

"I haven't given you my hyperthermia lesson yet, and I want to make sure you remember."

"What are you talking about?"

"Hyperthermia. Heatstroke. Heat stress, heat fatigue, heat exhaustion. Call it whatever you want, but when you're working outside for hours in weather like this, you're at risk."

"Okay," Meg said cautiously. "How would I know?"

"You stop sweating, for one thing. You may feel faint or dizzy. You could have cramps if you lose too much salt. Oh, and of course your temperature goes up—way up."

Meg shook water out of her hair. "Thank you so much for telling me now. Why'd you wait so long?"

"Because it hasn't been this hot for this long before. Anyway, it can creep up on you, so pay attention. Keep drinking water, and splash some on yourself. Or I'll have to turn the hose on you again."

"I bet you loved that," Meg muttered. "Okay, okay, I'll be careful. Right now I'm going to go get lunch."

Meg went back to the house, while Bree returned the tractor to the barn. She found sandwich fixings—and remembered to rehydrate herself, now that she'd done it for her trees. One more thing learned. Heatstroke was not something one faced on the streets of Boston, and it never would have occurred to her. She checked her watch and finished her sandwich quickly. Despite Bree's drenching, she still wanted to grab a real shower before heading to Amherst to meet Christopher.

On the ride to Amherst she reveled in the brief time spent in her air-conditioned car, and upon arrival, she felt lucky to find a parking space fairly close to Christopher's office. Even so, she was dripping with sweat by the time she reached the building that housed his department.

When she presented herself at his door, he was quick to commiserate. "Ah, you poor child. You New Englanders are ill accustomed to this weather."

"While you look ridiculously cool," Meg retorted. "I

hear good things about this newfangled air-conditioning stuff."

"Your house is not air-conditioned?"

"It hadn't been invented in 1760, and nobody's bothered to update the place. It's on my wish list, and I'll probably get to it in maybe five years, assuming my apple trees survive this drought. I've got one cranky window unit in my bedroom, but I've got too much to do to spend time hiding out in that room just to keep cool. At least Bree's room has cross-ventilation, which mine doesn't."

"Why don't you sit and cool off for a few minutes before I take you down to the lab? You said there was something else you wanted to talk about?"

"Yes, there is. Can you tell me why, in all the years you managed the orchard for the university, you never installed an irrigation system?"

Christopher smiled. "Believe me, I thought about it. But it's a rather convoluted history. There was an experimental orchard on this campus, years ago, but those in higher positions decided that they needed that land for a new dormitory. I argued that having full-time access to an orchard was important to our agriculture program here, and that was when the lease arrangement with your family came about, as a compromise solution."

"I think you told me about that, when I first took over the place. And?"

"So we had our orchard, but since the university did not own the land, they declined to invest in any capital improvements, such as installing an irrigation system. Besides, I had plenty of free labor available from the ag students, so it did not seem as urgent as some other projects."

"What about the spring and the pump there?"

"That, my dear, was the fruit of some creative bookkeeping—I think I labeled it something like 'Supplies.' It was the best I could do at the time."

"Well, thank you for that, at least. Still, Bree and I are spending a whole lot of time and energy trying to keep the trees irrigated, and we're exhausted. But I can't afford to install a system this summer."

"I truly sympathize. What about this: perhaps I can corral some students who are around this summer and ask them to help out? And I'm more than happy to assist you in planning for a system next year."

"If my trees survive that long," Meg muttered glumly. "I'm sorry, I don't mean to sound ungrateful. You've been a terrific help. I'm just hot and tired and frustrated. Be honest with me: is this drought going to go on? Is this the new normal?"

"I wish I could tell you, Meg, but I'd have to be God. This is indeed an unusual weather pattern for this region. There are those who argue that this is one manifestation of global warming; others who claim that it is a normal if unfortunate variation from the norm, but all will be well—sometime. It makes little difference to you farmers, on a day-to-day basis." He looked at her critically. "Are you ready to take the tour, or would you rather sit here a bit longer?"

"Door Number Two, please. Can you explain what's going on with this beetle menace, before I go meet them up close?"

"Of course. How much do you know, so I won't repeat myself?"

"I did some online research, so I know the basics, and Bree has filled me in. But the closest infestation has been in Worcester. I didn't think this thing flew very far or fast, so what's it doing here?"

"Worcester is perhaps fifty miles from here, as the crow flies, but I would agree that it didn't fly here. As I may have already told you, usually the first insects are carried in, in packing crates or other wood products."

"Bree said something like that."

"I'm glad she's been paying attention. Unfortunately, most infestations that have been found were well-established before they were noticed. The Worcester site was discovered after the pest had spread some ten miles in all directions, which meant it had begun years earlier. It originated in a packaging center, where many wooden crates passed through. I mention that only to say that the beetle could have arrived in Granford some time ago, but no one was looking for it, so it went undetected. We may never determine the source."

"There aren't people out there monitoring forests for pests like this?"

Christopher sighed. "Would that it were so. Unfortunately, there is the problem of chronic underfunding and understaffing in cases like this. Most of the insects, including the ones in Worcester, have been found by ordinary homeowners who happened to notice an unusual creature and made an effort to report it—which in itself requires some persistence. It is an imperfect system."

Meg was beginning to feel more human now that she had cooled off. "This new sighting or whatever you call it, you said it's confirmed?"

"It is, unfortunately. As soon as the first one was found, I sent it off to the appropriate government agency, and I followed suit with the second sample."

"So what happens next?"

"There is a standardized procedure in place to address the issue of any discovery of an invasive species. When the insect is found, its identification must be confirmed by an approved authority, and that has been done. Then APHIS— the federal government's Animal and Plant Health Inspection Service—will send out a team of inspectors, who will begin at ground zero, where the original insect was found, and examine trees at increasing distances from that spot. Not just looking at the trees from the ground, as you and I did, even with binoculars. They will have to actually climb the trees, or try to maneuver a cherry-picker truck in, to get a closer view. The inspectors will continue until they have established an area of at least a half a mile around the site in which no insects have been found. And then they will go in and cut down the infested trees, as well as all potential host trees within the perimeter they have established."

"Ouch!" Meg said. "Is the landowner compensated for losing his trees?"

"Unfortunately not. They are deemed a public hazard. Moreover, the wood may not be used: the only proven method to eliminate the insect is to reduce the affected trees to chips and leave them where they were found. They cannot leave their point of origin."

"I seem to remember reading that in Worcester, nearly thirty thousand trees had to be cut down and destroyed? This thing doesn't attack apple trees, does it?"

Christopher smiled. "No, it is primarily a forest pest, although it attacks trees that might at one time have been found in a forest but that are now used as ornamental trees. In some suburban neighborhoods the effect has been devastating, at least in aesthetic terms."

"Isn't there any other way to attack them?"

"Not that we scientists have discovered—yet. That is why labs such as ours exist."

"So tell me, what do you do in your lab?"

"We rear insects for research purposes. We make them available to other researchers across the country."

"Can they escape?"

"We certainly hope not! You will see the precautions in place when you take the tour."

"Are you the only lab doing this?"

"No, there are others, but all are carefully monitored."

"I hope so," Meg said fervently. "As Bree keeps telling me, we have more than enough pests to deal with already—and molds and blights and I don't know what."

"Ah, my dear, I never promised you that maintaining an orchard would be easy, did I?"

"No, I can't say that you did. Blast Johnny Appleseed! He brainwashed us all into thinking it was simple: plant a tree and wait for it to grow up and produce apples."

"Mr. Chapman did not have to concern himself with aesthetically pleasing apples, since his intention was always to turn them into cider and allow them to ferment."

"How hard is it to get a distillery license in Massachusetts?" When Christopher immediately looked concerned, Meg held up a hand. "Just kidding. I really don't feel like learning a whole new set of skills right now. Well, shall we go tour your lab? I'm ready to meet creepy-crawlies."

"Of course. Are you squeamish about insects? I've met many women who are, so it's no disgrace."

Meg thought briefly of her instant response to move away from the one beetle she had seen, and that one had been dead; now she was going to meet a lot of them,

face-to-face. "I'm working on it. The big ones still freak me
out a bit, but I can handle it. I don't get much choice, do I?
I'm a farmer, and insects come with the territory. So
lead on."

12

Christopher led the way through polished and nearly empty corridors.

"Not many people around in summer, are there?" Meg commented.

"Not students," Christopher agreed, "but there are many employees, those who keep the experiments going. Science, I fear, does not recognize holidays."

"Neither does farming, unless you count winter. We're crazy busy nine months out of the year, and then we have three months to recharge. I still haven't figured out how to get outside projects like painting or roofing done, since I never have time during good weather, and I can't do it when I do have time in the winter."

"The eternal dilemma," Christopher said. "Ah, here we are." He courteously opened a door and let Meg enter first, but she was forced to stop because there were yet more doors in front of her.

"What's all this?" she asked.

"This is the entrance to our quarantine facility. The area you are about to enter must be kept sterile, so that the experiments are not contaminated by outside agents—other insects, bacteria, and so on. We also must ensure that you do not carry invasive species out of this area, as they may pose a threat to the environment. This is where we have to suit up. There are three chambers we have to pass through. You'll notice that there are lights on the wall opposite the doors—we hope any insects that do try to make a break for it will be attracted to those first, and we'll notice before we open the next door. See the light panel by the door? You can't open the second door until the first door is securely closed and the light turns green. Here you go." He held up some bedraggled Tyvek jumpsuits, complete with feet, that looked for all the world like giant baby's pajamas. "If you pick up anything while you're in there, we will see it and remove it before you leave."

"I never thought of that," Meg said, as she struggled to get her feet into the limp garment. "What about your ventilation systems? Can't things pass in and out through there?"

"A smart question, but we have long since addressed it. That's why it's expensive to build laboratories such as this, both in terms of the physical infrastructure and rather esoteric specialized equipment. Let me show you."

They passed together through the chamber. On the other side, Meg followed Christopher through a maze of small offices and labs.

"Hey, slow down!" she said, after passing through another set of doors into a hallway that looked like every other hallway they'd passed through. "Will you leave a trail of bread crumbs, so I can follow you if we get separated? Because I have no idea where we are now. Why is everything so jumbled?"

Christopher stopped and smiled at her. "Ah, I forget how accustomed I am to this labyrinth. What you see is the fruit of bureaucratic wrangling over an extended period of time. Project funding is somewhat unpredictable. Often research begins with high hopes, accompanied by significant outlays of monies for setting up a laboratory, hiring staff, acquiring special equipment, and so on. Space is allocated according to the importance and scope of the study. But often such studies lose, shall we say, their sex appeal? And funds are diverted to another new project, leaving the older one to run dry, unless the researchers can locate additional funds elsewhere. But, as you might guess, it costs money to reconfigure the space each time this happens, so people usually make do, simply changing the title on the door and adding or removing partitions."

"How many projects do you usually have going at any one time?"

"I'd say between five and ten, but don't hold me to that—often there's some crossover. For example, an employee may be funded partially through two different projects, spending equal time on each. Equipment may be transferred from one project to another as well."

"The bookkeeping must be a nightmare!" Meg laughed.

"It is," Christopher said, "but happily that is not my concern, except in the broadest managerial sense. I merely wave my magic wand and say, 'Make it so!' and somebody does. One of the perks of my senior position. Ah, here we are." He opened another door and stepped back to allow Meg to pass him. "The ALB center."

To Meg it looked like everything else she'd seen in the laboratory part of the building. There was a large room ringed with various pieces of equipment. Some were clearly for refrigeration, but beyond that Meg could only speculate. She could see doors opening onto what appeared to be staff offices or storage. Workstations occupied the center of the main room, and there were several people working there.

Christopher's cell phone rang, and he apologized to Meg before turning away to take the call. He was back within a minute. "I'm so sorry, my dear, but I fear there's yet another crisis at the new building, and apparently I'm the only person who could possibly resolve it. Would you mind terribly if I turned you over to one of the research assistants?"

"Of course not, Christopher. I appreciate your taking as much time as you already have. I'll be fine."

"Excellent. Gabe?" Christopher called out.

A twentysomething young man in a more or less white lab coat looked up from what he was doing. "Yes, Professor?"

"Could you join us for a moment?"

Gabe stood up, revealing himself to be slightly taller than Meg but definitely broader. He was dark haired and bearded. When he smiled, his teeth looked startlingly white. "What do you need, Professor?" he asked.

"Gabe, this is Meg Corey—she took over the former experimental orchard in Granford. Meg, this is Gabriel Aubuchon."

"Hi, Meg," Gabe said. He held out his hand, and when Meg shook it she was surprised by the strength of his grip. "Great orchard you've got—some nice old varieties. You having a tough summer with this drought?"

"I am. I spend a lot of time watering."

"Gabe," Christopher said, "we're here because Meg

found a dead ALB a few days ago, on a wooded lot in the north end of Granford. We've done a quick survey of that site but found no sign of infestation, although as you well know that's not conclusive. But now with the more recent discovery, it looks as though we have a real problem on our hands, and I've notified the appropriate authorities—I'll let you know when they arrive. Since Meg was the first to discover this invader in Granford, I thought she might like to acquaint herself with what we're doing here, and with the creatures themselves. She seems to have a good eye, and she can watch out for further appearances. Do you mind giving her a tour?"

"Sure, no problem."

"Thank you, Gabe. Meg, I leave you in good hands. We'll talk soon." Christopher made his departure. Obviously he knew where he was going. Meg wondered if she could possibly find her way out or if she'd be reduced to looking for a window to climb out. There were none in sight from where she stood.

She smiled at her new escort. "So, where do we start, Gabe? Why don't you tell me what you do here?"

"Sure. I was hired about five years ago, right after college, as a technician for the ALB project, when it was first set up. How much do you know about funded research projects?"

"Um . . . assume I don't know anything."

"Okay. The Asian longhorned beetle has been declared a harmful species, so the U.S. Department of Agriculture has allocated funding for it, among many, many other similar projects. They do have their own research facilities, but they're directed more toward attacking and eliminating the insect, rather than understanding what makes it tick.

Not that there isn't overlap, but they usually leave the more
theoretical stuff to us. We have some joint agreements with
them, so we share data and we collaborate on various aspects of the research. We've been working on some biocon-
trol measures, like bacteria or natural enemies. Want
to see?"

"Sure," Meg said gamely.

"This way." Gabe led her through yet another door, and
she found herself in another enclosed room.

Looking around at it, Meg found it curiously informal.
If she had anticipated an austere space filled with gleaming
trays and cabinets, she was disappointed. What she saw
were large cages made of wire screening and metal; there
were tiers of racks holding trays. Some areas were filled
with plastic petri dishes, others with plastic or glass jars.
Some of the cages held segments of logs, while others had
only clusters of fresh leaves. The whole room measured no
more than twenty feet square, and in addition to what Meg
assumed was the paraphernalia for the experiments, the
space was crowded with desks and tables, holding both
equipment and piles of papers and journals.

Gabe stood by, letting her take it all in, then said proudly,
"This is our rearing facility. Over there"—he pointed to a
cluster of cages—"we've got the adult females, laying eggs
under the bark on those logs, and then we'll harvest the
eggs and rear them out, over there." He pointed to one of
the tiers of trays. "That's where they hatch. Then as the
larvae grow, we put them into jars with a special diet. Oh,
and they've got to be glass jars—we've found the critters
can chew their way right through plastic. We've even seen
a couple gnaw through metal."

Now that was unsettling, Meg thought. "How many do you produce?"

"We can rear up to three thousand in one batch."

Meg tried to imagine three thousand adult beetles like the one she had seen, armed with jaws that could cut metal, and suppressed a shudder. "And what on earth do you do with that many?"

"We use them for our own research, but we also distribute them—under the watchful eye of the USDA—to other research facilities. We seem to have better luck with rearing than other places. Here, let me show you the temperature-controlled room." He opened the door to what looked like an industrial-strength refrigerator, but the air that rushed out was warm, and noticeably humid. "We can control temperature, photoperiod, humidity, depending on what we're rearing at any given point."

"What happens if there's a power failure? Do you lose all of these?" Meg asked.

"Oh no, we've got a backup generator, and somebody's always on call to make sure it's working—usually me. Hey, want to meet a live ALB, up close and personal?"

Not really, Meg thought, but it seemed rude to say no.

Gabe reached into one of the containers and almost tenderly extracted a wiggling insect. "Hold out your hand."

Meg swallowed and held out one hand, and Gabe deposited the beetle on her palm. "She'll try to bite you, but it's unlikely she can penetrate your skin—looks like you've been working in the orchard a lot. Lots of calluses."

"I have," Meg said, keeping an eye on the beetle. Objectively it—or she—could be called handsome, and the long and constantly moving antennae were certainly unusual.

When Meg moved her hand slightly, the insect reacted by trying to clamp its—what, jaws? Pincers?—into her skin, but as Gabe had predicted, it had little luck. Gabe hovered anxiously, protecting his beetle like a mother hen—which, since he had reared it and nurtured it since its birth, was probably logical.

After a couple of minutes, Gabe said, "Seen enough?" When Meg nodded yes, he took the beetle from her and placed it carefully back in the container, then led Meg out of the room, closing the door behind him. "Let me show you how we mix up the diet. We've been working on a new system. This way." Gabe led her out one door, down a maze of corridors lined with six-foot metal cases, more tray racks, and other things that Meg couldn't begin to identify, until they arrived at another room, dominated by a ten-foot-tall contraption with a funnel-shaped stainless steel tank in the middle. "This is our new diet mixer—it can make a few hundred pounds at a time. It really makes things go a lot faster."

"What goes into the diet?" Meg asked.

"Things like wheat germ, molasses—you can smell that, can't you? Some other bugs are really finicky, and sometimes it's hard to come up with a mix that makes them happy. There's a lot of trial and error, but we've been pretty lucky here. Of course, what most insects really like is an endless supply of whatever their host plant is, but that's not always easy—either they're not available around here, or hard to get, or just too bulky, like if they prefer whole tree branches. Same problem with getting them to lay eggs— some don't care and will do it anywhere, others insist on having the right kind of tree branch, right bark, right size, before they'll even think about it."

This was more than Meg wanted or needed to know, but

she didn't have the heart to interrupt enthusiastic Gabe. "There must be a lot of human work involved," she said.

"Oh yes. Some things you just can't automate. You've got to harvest your eggs at the right time. You've got to transfer the larvae at the right time, onto clean medium. You've got to make sure the food doesn't rot and mold doesn't grow. And you've got to grow the bugs to the adult stage, and keep them alive. It's harder than you might think."

"Do you do this by yourself?"

Gabe seemed to preen a bit. He was plainly basking in the attention, especially from an outsider. "I'm in charge of the rearing lab, so I need to be up to speed on all of the insects we're raising, so I can direct the staff. We get a lot of student help, during the term, but that drops off in the summer, which is exactly when you need it most, so I keep pretty busy. And the researchers at other places always want a steady supply, like yesterday. I swear, some of them think you can just open a catalog and order a couple of thousand insects, like that."

"Is the ALB harder or easier than average to raise?"

Gabe shrugged. "About average. But as I said, mostly it's figuring out what works best, and then after that it's just keeping the rearing facilities clean and uncontaminated."

"Where do you get the breeding stock for your insect lines? Aren't some of these prohibited in this country?"

Gabe nodded vigorously. "Meg, you ask really good questions. Yes, we have to be very careful about importing any insects. Most of the insects we study these days come from the Far East—China, Korea—because trade with those countries has expanded so much and so fast, and since not all the safeguards were in place when the growth began, some pests sneaked in, like in packing crates, or even something as seemingly harmless as pinecones imported for Christmas decorations. Once they're here, and identified as a problem, we research guys get into the act. When we want to start a colony for research purposes, we usually import the initial stock from the source, whatever country they are native to. The risky ones—the ones on the government watch lists—come directly to our quarantine facility here, either hand carried by an employee or shipped by an authorized agency, so we can track them all the way. You've seen the precautions we take: once they're in here, there's no way they can get out."

Meg had the feeling that Gabe would be happy to continue talking about insects for hours, but it had already been a long day, and Meg was tired. "Gabe, thank you so much for such an informative tour. I've learned a lot, but I should be going now. I'm a working farmer, and that keeps me busy."

"I hear you! Hey, I'm glad you came by—I don't get to show off too often. Listen, if you have any more questions, just give me a call." He handed her a business card. "I'm here almost every day. Heck, I see a whole lot more of bugs than I do of humans!"

Meg smiled. "Will you lead me out?"

"Oh, right." They went back out to the main room, then exited by a door opposite the one they had come in through. Three minutes of winding corridors later, Meg recognized the air-lock thingy. "Let me make sure you aren't carrying any passengers." When Meg looked blank, Gabe said, "I mean that none of our insects have latched onto you." He did a careful visual search and pronounced her insect free. "You'll have to take off your white suit after you go through the air lock—just hang it on one of the hooks there." He pointed.

"Thanks again, Gabe. I really enjoyed the tour."

"My pleasure," he said.

She could feel him watching as she left, carefully following his instructions. But better to be safe than sorry: she didn't want to be responsible for spreading the unwanted insects.

13

 "Dinner?" Bree said hopefully, slouching in the doorway to the dining room, watching Meg feed Lolly after her return from the UMass lab.

"You volunteering?"

Bree made a rude noise. "Any cold cuts?"

"I doubt it. Lots of veggies, though." Thank goodness the farmer's market was close by and they all liked vegetables. Still, she kept running out of other staples, like cat food. The bag of kibble she kept on hand for Seth's dog Max was running pretty low, too. He was spending nearly as much time here as his master.

"Meg?" Bree broke in. "Food?"

"Salad," Meg said firmly. "If you want protein, add cheese. Or ice cream. Not to the salad, but after."

"Hey, maybe ice cream salad could catch on! It could save on dishwashing."

Meg threw together some ingredients, did a bare minimum of chopping and dicing, tossed in some herbs, and set the large bowl of salad in the middle of the kitchen table.

"So, how was the bug lab?" Bree asked, filling a bowl for herself and searching out a box of crackers.

"I wouldn't want to get lost in there, because I'd never find my way out. Did you have anything to do with the lab research end of things, when you were in school?"

"I think I saw the labs maybe once, but it wasn't like they wanted herds of undergrads trampling through polluting the place—you must have noticed that."

"You mean, all the precautions? I suppose they have to be careful. The guy directing it is not much older than you—Gabe something?"

"He got a beard? I think I remember him. He really seemed to like his work, but not many members of my class were all that interested."

"Yes, he really seemed into what he was doing. Oh, and I did ask Christopher about why there was no irrigation system on my land here, and he told me that the university balked at spending money on land they didn't own. I guess that makes sense, so I'll have to blame my mother, the absentee landlady. Not that she expected me to get stuck with the problem."

"Have you heard from your folks lately?"

"Nope, but that's not unusual. That's just the way we operate. It's not like we're feuding or anything, we're just . . . formal, I guess. How often do you see your family?"

"Not much." Bree didn't volunteer anything more. She seldom mentioned her family. Meg knew she had an aunt somewhere nearby but wasn't sure where Bree's parents were at the moment. Back in Jamaica, or harvesting something somewhere?

Meg wondered briefly why the two of them each kept most of their relationships at arm's length—she with Seth, Bree with Michael, both with their families. Of course, they were busy, but that was a lousy excuse for avoiding human contact. "Hey, Seth and I have been kicking around the idea of having a big get-together—you know, with Lydia, and Rachel and her family. Potluck. Do you and Michael want to come?"

"Maybe. When?"

"That's the part we haven't figured out. Sunday, maybe? Maybe we could look up a rain dance, and we could all perform it together. Strength in numbers, or something like that."

Bree grinned reluctantly. "You'd better bone up on your local tribes, so you don't offend their gods."

"I'll look into it. I think part of King Philip's War took place around here, but I doubt that would be a very happy memory."

"King who?" Bree asked.

"King Philip, also known as Metacomet, was a Wampanoag Indian who fought the British sometime in the seventeenth century because the settlers were kind of shoving the Indians out of the way, including around here. And that's about all I know."

"Got it."

Meg laughed. "Good. So to get back to Sunday, at least we can all get together and eat—outside."

They finished their leafy dinner companionably, and after taking care of the few dishes, Meg went out to see how her goats were doing, hoping that it would be a bit cooler outside than in the kitchen. It wasn't. The goats looked up at her from their shady corner and nodded but didn't even bother to stand up. She couldn't blame them. She leaned on their fence and contemplated the Great Meadow, which at the moment looked like a kind of Small Meadow.

She heard Max before she heard Seth approaching. The goats gave Max a wary eye but still didn't move. "Hey, there," Meg said. "I hope you aren't looking for food, because Bree and I already ate. Or maybe a better term is *grazed*, since it was mostly green stuff. The kind of stuff that Isabel and Dorcas would have been happy to share with us."

"Hey to you, and don't worry, I've already eaten. How was your day?"

"Hot and dry, no surprise. I went over to Amherst in the afternoon to see the university's insect research labs. Christopher offered it as some sort of reward for my finding the ALB here, and I didn't want to disappoint him. What do I know about insects?"

"Enough, apparently," Seth said. Max dropped to a grassy spot at his feet and settled down, panting.

"What've you been up to?"

"A couple of small jobs, then working at Donald's. The framing's done, and even the lath, but we're waiting on a real plasterer, and he doesn't want to work in this heat—says it affects how the plaster sets up. Donald, needless to say, is not happy, but I can't rush the expert, so he'll just have to wait."

"No air-conditioning at his place, either, unless you count natural air. Ah, well, our ancestors survived, so I suppose we will. Have you talked to your mom about getting together on Sunday?"

"Not yet. I'll call her tomorrow."

"How's Max holding up? He's got a lot of coat on him."

"I've finished up that dog run behind my house—there's plenty of shade, and I make sure he's got water."

"So," Meg said, unsure of what she wanted to say.

"So," Seth agreed amiably.

"Are you staying?" she asked.

"Do you want me to?" Seth countered.

Meg smiled. "This is a ridiculous conversation. Of course I do. By the way, Bree thinks you spend more time here than at your place."

"Is that a problem?"

"No. Not for Bree. Or for me. She says that at least you clean up after yourself, which for her is a major compliment. I gather Michael is more, uh, casual about such things."

"I'm impressed that she noticed. Shall we go in, before the mosquitoes show up?"

"Sure, although it's no cooler inside. Well, maybe in the bedroom."

"I could get you a better air conditioner at cost, you know."

Meg sighed. "I know, but if I got used to it, I'd probably find too many excuses to stay inside wherever it was, instead of doing what I need to do. I'd get soft. Check back with me at the end of summer, will you? Maybe I'll have exhausted my pioneer spirit by then, and besides, they should be on sale, right?"

"If there are any left. You want Max in or out?"

"Wherever he's most comfortable. Lolly probably won't even notice—she's very good at finding the places where the air moves best, and Max can't reach most of those."

Once inside, Meg rummaged through the refrigerator, savoring the cool air. "There's still some iced tea, if you want."

"Sounds good."

Seth sounded tired, and when Meg turned with the pitcher

of iced tea and poured him a glass, she thought he looked tired, too. It was hard, doing physical work in this heat—she should know, because she was doing it, too. They made a fine pair, half-catatonic after a long day. *I wonder when the most babies were born in New England?* She idly counted on her fingers. If everyone was too exhausted in summer and during harvest to even think about making babies, then the lowest birth months should be . . . April through June. She wondered if there was any way to prove her thesis.

"You look amused," Seth said. "What are you thinking about?"

Her mouth twitched. "Making babies, historically. Or more specifically, *not* making babies, because it's too hot even to think about it this time of year and farm couples were exhausted." When Seth looked confused, Meg waved away the subject. "So whose schedule is more complicated? Your mother's or Rachel's?"

"I'd bet Rachel's." He eyed her curiously. "Has she told you—"

"That she's pregnant? Yes, she told me yesterday. Does your mother know yet?"

"Yes, Mom told me. Rachel talked to you before Mom?"

Why was he asking? Was he hurt that she'd known before he had?

"Yes, but only because I happened to be there, after I got my hair cut. I don't think she planned it—I kind of dropped by, and that's when she brought it up. She said she wanted to tell Lydia in person, but I was right there in front of her. I guess she was wondering what my plans were, in that area." *Why did I even bring up babies?* Meg wondered.

"For babies, you mean?" Seth's expression was unreadable.

She shrugged, avoiding his eyes. "I've barely got a handle on the orchard, and that's my livelihood. I can't just walk away for a chunk of time, and right now I can't afford to hire someone to fill in for me."

When she finally looked back at Seth, he had turned away and was staring out the kitchen window at the growing darkness. "That's a very practical assessment," he said carefully.

But it leaves out the whole question of loving someone and wanting to build a life with that person, one that included a child or children. And I'm really screwing up this conversation, which is probably what Rachel didn't want to happen. Meg took a deep breath. "Seth, this is something we should talk about, but not right now, okay? We're both exhausted."

He looked at her a moment, his eyes oddly blank. "You tell me when you think you're ready to have this conversation, all right?" He stood up abruptly. "I think I'll head home after all." He gathered up Max and went out the back door, leaving Meg sitting at the table, stunned.

What had just happened? Had she misread something he'd said, or had she failed to interpret what he hadn't said? Bree was right: they'd been drifting toward couplehood for a while now, but they hadn't really discussed the how and the why. And now it seemed she'd hurt him, without meaning to. But she could fix it, couldn't she? Just as soon as she figured out what she wanted. She had to do what was best for her, and at the moment that meant pouring all her energy into the orchard. If she was so important to him, and having children was, too, why hadn't he said anything to her about it? Once burned, twice shy? And if she was honest, she wasn't exactly pushing for a commitment either.

Sure, they'd known each other for more than a year, but there was so much on her plate that their tentative relationship and where it was going had not been a first priority for her. Maybe that was wrong. They had to talk about it, but not right now, not yet.

14

Seth called early the next morning, as Meg was finishing her coffee. He sounded strangely formal. "Meg, I talked to Mom and Rachel last night. Sunday's good for everyone for this dinner thing."

"Did you tell them it's potluck?"

"I did. Are Bree and Michael planning to come?"

"I think so. Bree said she'd ask Michael."

"So that's nine, if you count Rachel's kids. Just wanted to know how much of everything we'll need. Where do you want to set up?"

"Is here all right? I can put tables on the orchard side of the house, where it's out of the direct sun."

"Fine. Anything you want me to bring?"

"Ice? Do you want to handle the grill?"

"All right."

This conversation was getting weirder and weirder, like

they were trading scripted lines, and it made her uncomfortable. "Seth, I'm sorry about what happened last night. I didn't mean to open up a whole can of worms. And I didn't mean to cut you off. We need to talk."

There was a pause, and then he said, "We will. I'll see you tomorrow, maybe around six so I can start the coals. Bye, Meg."

What had she done wrong? All she had said was that she didn't have time to think about having a baby right now. She hadn't even said whether she wanted to or not, just that this wasn't the right time. And who was Seth Chapin to leapfrog right over things like "I love you, I want to spend my life with you, I want you to bear my children"? There were definitely some gaps in that discussion, and he had to know that. Or was having children the deal-breaker, an issue that Seth wanted to clear up before things went any further between them?

Meg wasn't sure how she felt about the whole boiling mess. She was sorry she had joked about it so casually, but she hadn't realized it was such a touchy subject for him. Clearly they weren't communicating very well. Rachel had tried to warn her, but she'd dismissed it.

"Yo, Meg, you ready?" Bree said, dragging Meg back to the moment.

"I guess. More irrigating?"

"Until we don't have to anymore. I hate to say it, but I'm beginning to worry. The soil's drying out, and there's no rain in the forecast. So I think we have to go to daily watering."

"You're the expert. It's got to rain sometime, doesn't it?"

"I sure hope so," Bree said.

Well, Meg thought, if she was sabotaging her future

happiness, not to mention her potential progeny, she'd better make sure the orchard flourished. "Let's go."

Four hours later they were back in the kitchen, all but inhaling another pitcher of iced tea. The orchard was watered, but Meg and Bree were drenched with sweat, liberally sprinkled with dusty soil, and exhausted. The thermometer on the shady side of the house read ninety-seven degrees.

"Maybe I should check my e-mails," Meg said. "Maybe I've won a lottery in some exotic location and all I have to do is send all my financial information and the check will be in the mail." In fact, she couldn't remember the last time she'd read her e-mail, not that anybody was sending her anything of importance. She'd lost track of most of her Boston friends, and her Granford friends she either saw regularly or they were too busy to e-mail, as she was.

Bree snorted. "Yeah, right. Then we can buy an irrigation system for the whole property, and a bunch of guys to manage it, when they aren't serving us cold drinks by the pool. Oh, no pool? We'll have them build one in their spare time."

Meg looked at her and started laughing. "You know, we are definitely getting punchy. I need to take a shower, then I'll go find food supplies for tomorrow's dinner. Are you going to talk to Michael about it?"

Bree looked blankly at her for a moment. "About what? Oh yeah, the cookout. Yeah, I'll call him."

"Okay, well, I'm going to clean up, and then I'm going to get into my air-conditioned car and drive to the nice air-conditioned store and just stand there for a few hours, staring blankly at food products while keeping cool."

"Sounds about right to me," Bree said.

Meg started for the stairs in the front of the house, but passing the dining room table, where she had set up her laptop, reminded her about the e-mails. Fatigue was really doing a number on her concentration. She sat down and booted up and waited for her e-mail to appear. When it did, most of the messages she could delete without reading. But Christopher had sent something—a formal report directed to somebody at the Animal and Plant Health Inspection Service, which he had forwarded to her with the added comment:

> Meg—I thought you might be curious about the juggernaut of a process the ALB discovery in Granford has set into motion. This document signals that the next official phase has begun. I have notified the appropriate governmental authority, the identity of the creature has been confirmed by their designated experts, and one or another agency will now send a preliminary group of experts to assess the extent of the problem. You need not concern yourself any further if you're not interested. I hope I will see you soon.

Was she interested? Meg felt strangely responsible for the whole string of events. If she hadn't remembered, or hadn't said anything, what would have happened? She hit reply and typed in a quick *Thanks—keep me informed, please,* and as an afterthought added, *I'm having a potluck cookout here tomorrow at six. We'd love to see you—as a guest, not a consultant!—if you can break away.* Then she shut down the computer, went upstairs for her much-needed shower, and drove to the supermarket.

As she had predicted, entering the cool supermarket was close to stupefying: she stopped dead just past the entrance and breathed deeply of delightfully refrigerated air. How long could she spin out her shopping? What was the greatest amount of food she could get that required the least amount of cooking? Something the kids would eat, for a start, lots of liquids, charcoal for the grill . . . An hour later Meg stood in the checkout line and for once wished that the young checker would run through her cans of cat food more slowly. No such luck, so Meg took a last lingering breath of the chilled air before plunging back outside into the parking lot, where the acres of asphalt intensified the heat. She all but threw her food into the trunk, then shut herself into the car, turning the AC up full blast. She waited until the temperature had dropped at least ten degrees before setting off for the liquor store and finally the farmer's market.

Meg arrived home as hot and tired as when she had left, despite her brief intervals in the cooler air. When she struggled into the kitchen, clutching all her bags, Lolly, draped across the shadiest corner of the floor, opened one eye to look at her, then closed it again. Meg had just finished putting the groceries away when she heard rapping at her screen door. It was Lydia Chapin, Seth and Rachel's mother. "May I come in?"

"Of course," Meg said quickly as Lydia opened the screen door. "Can I get you something to drink?"

Lydia waved a vague hand. "Whatever you've got is fine."

Meg filled two glasses with iced tea, added ice, and sat down again. "So what brings you here, and why aren't you at work?"

"My boss closed down the office a couple of hours early.

Nobody was getting any work done, and he figured he'd save on air-conditioning. As for why I'm here . . . I understand Rachel told you about the baby?"

"She did. I think it's great! Why—is there some problem?"

"No, not at all. She's thrilled, Noah's pleased, the kids are excited, and I love being a granny." Lydia stopped.

Meg looked her in the eye. She had an idea about what Lydia wasn't saying. "How does Seth feel about it?" she asked carefully.

"He's happy for her, of course. He loves her kids. Forgive me if I'm overstepping, but has this created some friction between you?"

Meg didn't rush to answer. "I guess I'd have to say yes. Somehow I made an offhand remark that I couldn't imagine having children anytime soon because I'm so busy with the orchard, and Seth just shut down. What have I done wrong?"

"Nothing, Meg," Lydia said gently. "But you should know that it was one of the central problems when Seth was married to Nancy. He wanted kids then, and she was looking for a bigger, better life first, and maybe kids later. So I'd guess your remark, no matter how innocent, brought that all back again. If he didn't tell you, you couldn't have known. And he probably wouldn't be happy if he knew I'd told you, but I wanted you to know."

She still ought to have guessed, Meg thought. "I never meant to hurt him. I just thought it was something we would discuss—later. When the time was right."

Lydia leaned back and gave her a long look. "Meg, *do* you want children?"

Meg fought back a moment of panic at the direct

question. "I think so. It's just that I've never been in a position to seriously think about it. Seth kind of caught me by surprise when we were talking. But I hope he didn't hear what I said as a 'no.'"

Lydia nodded once, apparently satisfied. "Give him some time. When he thinks about it, he'll know you didn't mean anything final. Believe me, I understand your position. Full-time farming takes a lot out of you. Our female ancestors here managed, but they had more help—and frankly, many of them died too young as well, simply worn out from struggling with both work and childbearing." Lydia took a long drink of her tea. "All right, that's all I had to say about that. What do you want me to bring to dinner tomorrow?"

"Whatever you feel like. Don't overdo. Oh, by the way, I asked Christopher Ramsdell if he'd like to come." Meg watched Lydia and thought she detected a hint of a blush. "And Bree's Michael, too, so it won't be just family."

"I think that sounds lovely, dear," Lydia said, with a small smile. She stood up. "Don't worry about this misunderstanding with Seth. We're all hot and stressed out, and not always thinking clearly. This, too, shall pass!"

"I hope so," Meg said, holding the door open for Lydia.

The next morning dawned fair and fine, as usual. *Why can't we stockpile these days for when we really need them, like in February?* Meg grumbled to herself as she brushed her teeth. Downstairs, the thermometer outside the kitchen window read eighty-two degrees, and it was only seven o'clock. Meg started slicing fruit for a fruit salad for dinner. At least it would be cool and juicy. She'd stocked up on

plenty of ice cream and had crammed her refrigerator with
as many bottles of juice and iced tea as it could hold. She
was debating whether it would make sense to set up
the tables and take out the chairs and benches now, before
the day got too hot, when Bree came downstairs. "Morning," she muttered.

"Yes, it is."

Bree turned from the refrigerator and looked curiously
at her. "Is what?" She gathered up English muffins and butter and set about making herself some breakfast.

"It is morning. To be followed by afternoon and evening.
We are entertaining this evening, if you recall."

"Meg, you're getting strange. I talked to Michael—wave
free food at him and he's interested. But he's not much into
meat. There'll be plenty of salad stuff, right?"

"Sure, no problem. Can you help me haul some tables
and folding chairs out back in a few minutes, while it's still
cool out?"

"Okay. You figure maybe a dozen people?"

"More or less. And a dog."

"Max doesn't need a chair."

"No, he does not," Meg said, making a face at Bree, then
continuing, "I invited Christopher by e-mail, and I hope he
comes—it seems like I only talk to him when I have a problem, which isn't much fun for him. He's a sweetie, and I'd
love to hear more about his life. So that makes us an even
ten, with you two, me and Seth, Rachel and her family,
Lydia, and Christopher."

"You're not playing matchmaker, are you?"

"What, you mean with Lydia and Christopher? Well,
they did seem to be getting along nicely the last time I saw
them together, but I'm not pushing anything. If it happens,

it happens. Lydia's not an old woman, though, and it would be nice if she had somebody in her life, that's all."

"Uh-huh," Bree said dubiously. "She's old enough to make up her own mind. What if she likes living alone? It's not like she's isolated—she knows plenty of people around here, and she still goes to work. And I don't notice *you* joining things around town. So far you've got me and a cat. And sometimes Seth. Which one of us is going to last the longest?"

"The cat," Meg said, refusing to be drawn into the argument. "Lolly loves me. You just want a paycheck."

"Sure do—I earn it. And Seth? Where's he fit?"

"The jury's still out on that one. I'll let you know as soon as I do."

15

Seth arrived at six as promised, bringing Lydia and Max with him, and started to set up the fire on the grill. He seemed his usual cheerful self, although Meg sensed that there was a certain ease missing between them. Still, in the midst of preparing to feed a hungry crowd, there was no way they could talk about anything personal.

There was a shady nook on the uphill side of the house, where there was a rickety lean-to, and some previous occupant of the house had made a halfhearted effort to lay down a patio large enough to hold two tables and a bunch of folding chairs. Meg brought out several coolers to keep the salads and drinks chilled until it was time to serve, and Seth positioned the barbecue grill a few feet onto the grass, a safe distance away. The air was so still and almost physically dense with heat that when he lit the fire, the smoke rose nearly straight upward. Meg looked beyond, where rows of her apple trees marched over the crest of the hill. Did they look a touch yellow, or was she just feeling anxious?

Rachel and Noah, their two kids in tow, arrived shortly after six. Seemingly impervious to the heat, the children threw a Frisbee for Max to catch. Meg was rinsing some lettuce at the kitchen sink when Christopher arrived, carrying what had to be a couple of bottles of wine. She dried her hands and went out to greet him.

"Christopher, I'm so glad you could make it! I was telling Bree that the only time I seem to see you is when I have some kind of problem. Should we swear not to talk shop tonight? At least, not too much?"

"It is difficult, though, isn't it? I was delighted by your kind invitation, and please accept my humble offering." He held out the wine bottles, beaded with condensation.

"Wonderful, thanks," Meg said. She sent him around back to the others while she finished up in the kitchen, then went out to join the group herself. Bree and Michael rounded the corner just as Meg settled in a chair next to Rachel, who was watching everyone with a smile on her face.

"Well, the gang's all here," Meg said. "I'm so glad I don't have to cook. If this heat keeps up, Bree and I are going to find ourselves gnawing on raw vegetables. You have AC, don't you, Rachel?"

"We do. The B and B wouldn't stay open long if we didn't, drat those demanding tourists."

"Window units?" Meg asked.

"No, there's something else between a window unit and a full installation. I saw it on a This Old House episode a few years ago, and Seth approved of it, so he installed a partial system. I think we were his guinea pigs, but it's worked really well. You should think about it, at least for some part of your house."

"Oh, I *think* about it a lot—I just don't do anything about it. No time or money yet. I thought putting in the new septic system was a bit more critical than cool air. I'm still waiting for my bank account to recover."

"I agree with your priorities."

Meg watched Seth retrieve an errant Frisbee and send it sailing across the lawn to Max, the kids chasing after, giggling. She felt a pang again—he was having so much fun with his niece and nephew. "So, does everybody know about . . . ?" Meg nodded toward Rachel's midsection.

"Yup. I'm calling him—or her—Pumpkin, which sounds better than Turkey, which is closer to when the newest Dickinson will make an appearance. Probably December."

Meg turned to survey her guests: Lydia and Christopher were deep in discussion about something or other; Seth came back to the grill to flip a variety of meats and even a few large slices of vegetables like eggplant and zucchini, with Michael nearby; Bree and Noah were chatting about something; and the children and Max had all finally collapsed on the grass, panting. A nice, happy scene.

The relaxed mood carried through dinner. As they ate, the sun set slowly behind the orchard hill, casting their little patio corner into deeper shade, and Meg lit a number of citronella candles and offered insect repellant all around. Barn swallows swooped through the air, catching any insects foolish enough to be out this late; the swallows would turn over their shift to the bats as soon as it was dark.

"Much as I hate to break up such a nice party," Rachel announced, shortly after eight, "I've got to get these two home to bed." She nodded toward the kids, subdued now, as her husband yawned widely. "Or maybe I mean three! Thanks so much for having us, Meg—this was really nice. Don't get up. We can find our own way out."

Rachel gathered up her family and herded them around the house. Meg followed orders and stayed where she was. She could hear their SUV start up in the driveway, and a moment later she waved as they passed on the road in front of the house, heading toward Amherst.

Christopher, still seated next to Lydia, looked around as though startled that night had crept up on them all. "I, too, should make my exit. Thank you so much, Meg, for including me in your get-together. It has been a pleasure not to have to deal with building codes or university politics for at least a few hours, and in such delightful company. I'll keep you informed on that other matter."

Did he mean the ALB problem? She was glad he hadn't brought it up over dinner, and that they'd all avoided talking about David Clapp's death, so they'd managed to have an untroubled, pleasant meal.

"That would be fine, Christopher. Let me walk you to your car. If I sit here any longer I'll fall asleep," Meg said. Christopher made his good-byes to the others, and he and Meg walked around to his car on the other side of the house. Meg sniffed and smelled smoke. "Seems like the rest of the neighborhood had the same idea we did about cooking outside."

"It was indeed an excellent idea. We'll talk later." He got into his car and followed the same road that Rachel's family had taken. As Christopher pulled away, Meg admired the view over the Great Meadow, looking so peaceful in the growing dusk . . . except for the wisp of smoke that came curling out of the woodlot on the far side. Meg stiffened and focused her attention. Yes, there was another wisp—and then she saw a tiny golden flicker of flame, somewhere within the stand of trees. The smoke she'd noticed wasn't from a grill, it was from a real fire.

What should she do? Ask Seth, of course. Meg turned and ran back around the house, to where the remaining people were gathering up trash and stuffing it in a bag. "Seth?" she panted.

He looked up from his task. "What?"

"I think there's a fire in the woods down the street."

His demeanor changed instantly, as he shifted from relaxed social to official mode. "Show me," he said brusquely.

Meg led him around the house and pointed. Now there was no mistaking it—more flames were visible, extending from the edge of the road to a point about twenty feet into the trees; they'd moved fast in the minute she'd been away. Seth took a brief look and said, "You're right." He pulled out his cell phone and punched some speed-dial button. When someone answered he said tersely, "There's a fire in the woods on the Ludlow road, about a quarter mile past Route 202, on the north side. Send a couple of the trucks, just in case, and let's see if we can catch it now before it spreads too far." He ended the call quickly, and his eyes went back to the fire.

"Do I have anything to worry about?" Meg asked quietly.

He turned to her as though he had forgotten she was there. "Here? No. It's not likely to cross the Meadow, and the ground around the house is clear of brush. I can't say as much for the properties on the other side." Seth was shifting from foot to foot in his eagerness to take some sort of action.

"Does Granford have its own fire department?"

"Yes. Paid, not volunteer. Three engines, plus a tanker and some other smaller vehicles. Plus an ambulance. There are over two hundred fire calls each year, and I'd bet this year will go higher. They should be here fast."

Meg thought wryly, *If it was a volunteer department, Seth would be part of it, no doubt.* "Where is the station?"

"It's on the far side of town, in the same building as the police department, so you must have seen it." Seth showed no signs of leaving his post, where he could oversee the fire activity. The trucks did indeed arrive soon; there were two, and Meg wondered if the second one had been dispatched because of the risk that the fire would spread quickly, with so much dry underbrush. As the first truck approached, Seth signaled the driver and waved him farther down the road. The second truck followed behind. While the sun was mostly gone, the flashing lights illuminated the night, flashing erratically off the trees.

After a few minutes, Art Preston pulled up and stopped at Meg's driveway. When he climbed out of the car, Seth called out to the police chief, "Couldn't stay away, eh?"

"Yeah, guys and fires, right? Looks like they've got it under control. It's not the first one this week."

"Firebug?" Seth asked.

Art shook his head. "Nah, probably some idiot tossing a cigarette. Can you believe people still do that?"

"And all our public service announcements can't stop them," Seth said. "Anything else we should do?"

"Nah, but the summer's not over yet. Let's make sure all the fire equipment is in good working order." Art took one last look at the scene and watched as one of the trucks pulled away. "I guess I'll head home now."

As he left, Lydia came out of the back door.

"Did you miss all the excitement?" Meg asked.

"No, I was watching from the kitchen window. The fire department seems to have handled it quickly."

"Yeah, they're good guys," Seth said. "I'm just worried that they're going to be busy until this damn drought breaks."

"We can expect more fires?" Meg asked.

"It's all too likely. And unfortunately the town hasn't been keeping up with clearing brush—including in that park we were talking about—which raises the danger. That's another casualty of budget cuts—we can't afford to hire the crew to do it."

"That's too bad. But you said my property is okay?"

"I'd say so. Which reminds me—I should put out a mass e-mail to the rest of our good citizens and remind them to clear flammable items away from their homes and outbuildings." He stood up. "You ready to go, Mom?"

Lydia glanced between Meg and Seth before saying, "I guess this heat has taken a lot out of me. Thank you, Meg— this was a good idea, and it was nice to see Christopher again."

"I'll go get Max. Be right back." Seth disappeared around the other side of the house.

Lydia smiled tentatively at Meg. "Trouble in paradise?"

"I really don't know. We haven't had time to talk, and I feel like this weather has everybody on edge and exhausted at the same time. I'm sure it will be okay. I hope. It was good to see you, anyway. You and Christopher seemed to be getting along well."

"Are you fishing?" Lydia said, with a gleam in her eye. "He's an intelligent and interesting man, and I enjoy his company. And that's all there is to it—for the moment. I'll let you know if that changes."

Max came bounding around the house, followed more slowly by Seth. He did look tired, Meg thought. "See you tomorrow?" she asked.

"Probably," Seth replied. He kissed her cheek briefly, leaving Meg unsure whether it was just out of habit. Things were definitely not quite right between them. She waited until they had pulled out of the driveway, took one last look at the remaining fire truck down the road, whose lights were no longer flashing, then went inside.

16

 Meg's breakfast the next morning was interrupted by a phone call from Christopher. "Ah, Meg— sorry to bother you so early," he apologized.

"No problem, Christopher—this is the coolest part of the day, and I usually get up early to enjoy it. What can I do for you?"

"First, I wanted to thank you for a delightful evening, but I also wanted to tell you that the government agency has moved extraordinarily quickly: they are sending a preliminary inspection team to check out the ALB sites today."

"Wow, that is fast. Didn't you just tell them about the sighting a couple of days ago?"

"Yes, and this is indeed unusually quick turnaround. But the process is facilitated because they already had a team in place nearby, at Worcester. Let me note that this is just the first inspection. They'll send a few people to look at the site from the ground, and if they decide it's warranted, they'll send a larger official crew out to determine the parameters of the infestation. There are protocols in place for events like these."

"Where are you sending them?"

"You mean, which physical locations? The Nash lot, for a start, although I assume they'll want to expand their search from there, and there's a lot of other forested land in that direction, although no one could check all of it. I thought I might direct them to the Granford town forest as well."

Meg wasn't even sure where that was. "Why? Has anybody noticed anything there?"

"Not to my knowledge, but it wouldn't hurt to check, and it's public land, so there are no issues about gaining access there."

"I hadn't realized access was a problem. Are you saying that an owner has to grant permission for a government agency to inspect their property?"

"Essentially, yes. Legally it's a rather murky issue. In the Worcester situation, most of the pests were found on suburban properties, so it hasn't been too controversial. As you might guess, however, a forest, whatever its size, presents a different challenge, both practically and legally."

"I never thought of that. Have you told Jonas Nash yet?"

"No, but it falls to the inspection team to get in touch with the owners, rather than me."

So Jonas didn't know yet. "Christopher, what would have happened if I hadn't noticed that one insect, or hadn't reported it?"

"Someone would have noticed signs of the infestation

eventually. But it's good to have an early start in dealing with it."

"Will you let me know if they find anything significant?"

"Of course, my dear."

While she had learned a lot about agricultural pests in the past year, forest pests had not been on her radar, although she had the impression that the Asian longhorned beetle had been in the news intermittently but consistently. The government agencies were taking the threat seriously, it appeared.

"Christopher, how serious is this? I know the Worcester infestation had gotten a lot of press in the state, but sometimes I wonder if that's because it's such a large, showy bug. I swear I've seen the same footage of one of them climbing up a boy's arm, every time the news stations give us an update. It certainly has shock value."

"There is a certain visual appeal to the insect that serves well to alarm the public. It's more difficult to generate concern about a pest that is hard to see. It's as though people have trouble connecting a tiny insect with the destruction of a tree, or worse, a forest, for all that it's a true threat."

Political theater, Meg thought to herself. "Will you be involved?"

"I'm not directly responsible, but I have friends and colleagues who will no doubt fill me in, since this is occurring in my backyard, so to speak. In case you're wondering, the research that we do on campus and the government eradication program such as that at Worcester are not connected. I'll let you know what they find or don't find. Well, I should leave you to your tasks."

"Thanks for keeping me in the loop, Christopher." They hung up simultaneously.

Meg gazed into space, sipping her lukewarm coffee. She could pat herself on the back for doing the socially responsible thing in reporting the one she had found, but that would be the end of her involvement. She hoped.

When Meg returned to the kitchen table, Bree was there, munching on cold cereal. "What was that about?" she asked.

"Christopher's latest insect update. The Feds are coming."

"That's fast, for them."

"Looks like it. Thank goodness these things don't eat apples, right?" Meg buttered some local whole-grain bread. It was too hot outside to toast it.

"Right. Lots of other trees, though, like maples, elms, even willows. But slowly. They're kind of sneaky—they burrow under the bark and tunnel up and down, out of sight, so by the time you notice that the tree looks sick, the damage has been done. Not that it kills the tree, or not right away. It just weakens it. In populated areas people worry about the weak trees or at least their branches falling on houses or cars—or people. Left alone, it might take decades to kill trees, but that would screw up the forest ecosystem, which has bigger effects. Back a century or two, most of the land around here was open fields, so what we've got now is secondary forest. Which has more maples, which the beetles really like to eat, so they can do more damage more quickly in a maple forest. And if the ALB goes after all those maples that turn pretty colors in the fall, the leaf-peeper tourists are going to be unhappy. And they bring dollars to places around here. So it all ties together."

Meg sighed. "So the USDA is indirectly helping Massachusetts hold on to tourist dollars? Who would have thought? But this is not something I have to worry about for the orchard, right?"

"Yeah, if you're thinking just about your own needs rather than the greater good."

"I am, believe me. Keep the orchard alive and producing—that's all I want for now. What're we doing today?"

"I'll give you three guesses." Bree grinned.

"Watering," Meg said.

"Got it in one."

Through the kitchen window Meg saw Seth's van pull into the driveway. She stood up quickly. "I'm going to talk to Seth before we head up the hill. You want to go ahead?"

"Yeah. I'll take the tractor up. Don't talk too long."

"Don't worry," Meg said. Seth hadn't seemed in a talkative mood over the last few days anyway, but she wanted to fill him in on what Christopher had told her. It might affect the town, right? So he should know. That was her story and she was sticking to it.

She and Bree left by the back door, Bree heading up the hill and Meg going toward Seth's office. She found him sorting through piles of papers on his desk. He looked up when she knocked and said, "Hi," but his tone was neutral.

"Hi, yourself," Meg said. "You look busy already."

"I'm trying to find the cost estimates for the structural parts of Donald's house. He wants everything done yesterday, but I want to be sure the billing is right before we close in the walls."

"How's it going?"

"As well as can be expected. The nice part is, everyone around here knows the house, and a lot of people in the restoration community have volunteered materials or skills. They respect that he wants to do things right."

"That's good to know. Did he lose much in the way of personal heirlooms?"

"Some. Those are irreplaceable."

"Have you talked to Jonas lately?"

"Only in passing. Why?"

"Christopher called this morning, and he says the federal agency's confirmed the beetle identification, and they're sending a team out to do a preliminary survey—today. They'll look at the Nash land, but he mentioned they might also want to look at some town-owned land. Isn't there a public park on the other side of town, just past the center?"

"Yes, where our ball fields are, and picnic areas and hiking trails, not that it's all that big. It's just over two hundred acres of former farmland. The town bought it with the help of matching funds from the Federal Land and Water Commission. It's got something for everyone: a pond for fishing and skating; picnic areas; three baseball fields; hiking trails; a two-ring horse arena; a dog park; and a relatively new playground. No swimming, though."

"Nice," Meg said. "How much is forested?"

"Most of it. Since it used to be farmland, a lot of it is secondary growth, mostly maples. We've got a recreation commission who manages it—during the school year we hold a lot of baseball and soccer events there. So they want to see if there are beetles there?"

"That's what Christopher says. I assume you—I mean the town selectmen—haven't heard from the agency yet?

Because they seem to have jumped on this pretty fast. Christopher said they'd be contacting Jonas, too."

Seth shook his head. "Not that I know of, but it's public space, so they have every right to roam around and look. I'd be more concerned about what happens if they do find something."

"What happens then?"

"Well, in the Worcester case, a lot of trees got cut down. Certainly the town would want to cooperate, if it's a real ecological threat, but I don't know what that would mean for the wooded parts of the park. I'd bet there are some folk around here who might be upset if they cut down a lot of the trees."

"Can they stop it?"

"I really don't know, Meg. This is new territory for me, and for the town."

Seth was not making this conversation easy. Meg tried changing the subject. "You know, it's been a week since David Clapp died. Has anybody said anything more about that? Has Art mentioned anything?"

Seth shrugged. "Marcus doesn't always keep Art up to date, you know. I'd guess he hasn't said anything because there's nothing new to tell. The forensics might not prove how the rock came into contact with his head, and absent any physical evidence, Marcus doesn't have many choices, so I'd guess he'll either leave it as open and move on to other cases, or he'll declare it an accident."

"It doesn't seem right, though, that he should be forgotten so easily. Especially if Jonas knew him."

"I wouldn't be too hard on Jonas—he's got enough troubles of his own."

"What do you mean? Or is it none of my business?"

"I know you won't spread it around," Seth said. "Jonas told me that he may have to close the sawmill—it's just not financially viable anymore. He's had some indications of interest from developers about selling the place. The sawmill site has parking, easy access, and it's a sound building that could be modified for another purpose."

"It would be a shame if he had to sell it—hasn't it been in his family for generations? What about the timberland he holds? Isn't that worth something?"

"Not the timber itself, if he's going to lose the trees to this beetle. And most of the lots are scattered around, away from main roads. Not as attractive as the sawmill site. He and his family are going to have to make some kind of decision soon."

If Jonas Nash was trying to sell his property, Meg thought, and David Clapp found ALB on Jonas's timberland, that gave Jonas a motive to silence him—to prevent him from undermining any deal with a developer. Meg filed that away to think about later. "It's too bad."

"Was there anything else you wanted, Meg?"

Meg debated holding her tongue, but she was getting tired of his cold shoulder treatment. "Yes, there is. Why are you mad at me?"

He looked at her, then slumped into his battered office chair. "You really want to get into this now?"

"Yes, I do. We had an awkward conversation the other day, that I never intended to mean anything, and ever since then you've been shutting me out. If you have a problem with something I said, I want to know what it is, and why."

He shook his head, more to himself than at her. "You

know, there are a lot of things we haven't talked about, but what you said, about being too busy to think about having a baby—well, it brought back some unhappy memories."

"I was making a joke, and apparently it failed—I didn't mean to upset you, or to treat it lightly. We've both had relationships before that ended badly. So we're cautious, I guess."

"Some people might say emotionally paralyzed."

"Okay, fine. But can we find a time to talk?"

"Put it on the calendar, you mean?"

She was trying to fix things, and he was being sarcastic. She tried to swallow her annoyance. "Seth, you're not making this any easier. I'm sorry it I hit a nerve. I didn't mean to. So let's talk about it."

He scrubbed his hands over his face. "I'm sorry. I'm being a jerk. It's hot and I'm tired and Donald keeps nagging me, and there's always some new problem with the town— like this beetle thing, and now there's this developer sniffing around looking at town properties, so I have to deal with that—and I feel like I'm chasing my tail all the time and getting nowhere. I shouldn't take it out on you. I agree—let's find a time when we can sit down like calm, rational adults and talk about things that really matter, not bugs and Colonial paint colors. Okay?"

Meg smiled at him. "Okay. That's all I want." She turned to leave, then stopped and turned back. "Wait—did you say a developer is looking at town land, too? Haven't we been through all that? When the strip mall went in?"

"This is something new. Some commercial builders think the economic tide has turned, and some of the properties along Route 202 look more attractive now. This is all very preliminary, but I have to take it seriously on behalf of the town. I'm meeting with one of them this morning, early. Just one more thing to add to the to-do list." He stood up. "I really need to get going."

"So do I. Are we okay?"

He finally smiled. "Yes, we are."

17

Meg and Bree were wrapping up the watering for the day, well past the lunch hour, when Meg's cell phone rang.

It was Christopher, and he sounded excited. "Meg, the inspectors will be here shortly, and there's something you might like to see."

All she wanted at the moment was a very long drink of something with a lot of ice in it, not a jaunt into the woods to hunt for bugs. "What is it?"

"The APHIS people brought their insect-tracking dogs! They're going to give them a run in the town park, if you'd like to watch."

"I had no idea there was such a thing," Meg said, stalling. She was hot, sweaty, and tired. How much did she care about watching dogs hunt for bugs?

"It's a fairly new effort, but the team has demonstrated

some success in other areas. People will still do the standard visual inspection, but they want to see how well the
dogs' finding correlate." He must have sensed her reluc-
tance, because he added, "Please don't feel you must
come—it's just that I'm tickled by this new-old technology.
I can fill you in later on the results."

Meg smiled to herself. Christopher's enthusiasm was
infectious, and she hated to let him down when he was so
eager to share it. "Hang on a sec." She covered the phone
with her hand. "Bree, are we about done here?"

"I guess. What, you want to go play again?"

"Not exactly. Christopher wants me to watch dogs hunt
beetles in the town park here."

"Oh well, if it's for science . . ." Bree grinned at her.
"Go. I can finish up. You can tell me all about it over dinner. Your turn to cook."

Meg told Christopher she'd meet him at the town park,
then went slowly down to the house, feeling as though she
was wading through the thick air. The sky was almost yellow; the grasses in the Great Meadow below looked yellow,
too. In the kitchen she drank down a glass of ice water
quickly, then a second one more slowly, and splashed water
on her face and arms. No point in cleaning herself up: it
didn't matter how she looked to the scientists or inspectors
or whatever they were. She was just an interested observer.
She filled a water bottle with more cold water and set off
for the town park, which lay beyond the town center, on the
west side of the main road. It was easy to find.

Meg pulled into the parking lot, reluctant to leave the
air-conditioned cocoon of the car, but Seth was there, and
he'd already seen her and motioned her over. When she got
out and came close, she said, "Do you know, I've never

been here before? Of course, I don't have a lot of time for recreation. How'd your meeting go this morning?"

"With the developer, you mean? That was just exploratory. We went over what properties the town controls, and he told me what his company is looking for. He asked about the park here, and I told him that it's heavily used, plus there are restrictions on its transfer that would make it complicated to purchase."

"What does he want to build?"

"Primarily homes, with maybe a few offices along the highway. We didn't get into details, but he said he'd talk to me again, or the board if we wanted a formal presentation. I didn't commit to anything." Seth looked over at the gathering of scientists. "I think they want us."

As they started to stroll toward the waiting group, Meg asked, "What did Christopher tell you?"

"He said he wanted a good test site for the dogs that the state is bringing in. This is Granford's largest public park, plus a lot of it is wooded, so it seemed like a good place to start."

"What happens if they find something?" Meg asked.

Seth shook his head. "I haven't had time to find out. One step at a time, okay?" He watched as Christopher's car pulled up near Meg's, followed by a van with government license plates. The driver of the van and the passenger climbed out and came around to open the side door, and two dogs jumped down and started running in circles with their noses to the ground. As their handlers were gathering them up, yet another van appeared, disgorging several more people. The whole gathering looked incongruous in the middle of the near-empty park.

Christopher was the last to get out, and he spoke with

the others before approaching Meg and Seth. "Seth, these
are the members of the State Plant Health Inspection team,
and they're here to perform a Level 1 survey of your town
park." He named them all, and then he introduced Seth.
"This is Seth Chapin, a Granford selectman—he's repre-
senting the town. Seth, we've already gone over Jonas
Nash's woodlot. Since he already allows access to the public, it wasn't a problem."

"What did you find?" Seth asked.

"We found evidence of a small infestation there," one of
the inspectors said directly to Seth. "That was the site
where the first example was found, right?"

"Yes," Meg answered him. "I'm the one who found it
there. I'm Meg Corey—I run an apple orchard a couple of
miles from here."

"Good to meet you, Meg. Thank you for reporting it so
promptly," the lead inspector replied. "A lot of people
wouldn't have."

"I'm a farmer, so I have to pay attention to insects. When
I found it, I . . . was a little distracted, but when I remembered the beetle again, I told Professor Ramsdell here, and
we went back and retrieved it."

"We're lucky you noticed it. We did find more insects
there."

Poor Jonas, Meg thought. He couldn't seem to catch a
break.

"What do you need to do here?" Seth asked.

"Check out the trees, both in the wooded parts and those
that are freestanding. Since it's too early to tell where the
initial infestation site is, we need to look at a broad area."

"The Nash property is a couple of miles away. Can the
insects fly that far?"

"They are capable of flight, but usually they're brought in by way of firewood, or they hitch a ride on vehicles. Do you allow cooking fires in the park here?"

"We do," Seth said. "We hold various events here, which sometimes involve barbecues, and there are a limited number of camping sites."

"All possibilities for introduction of the insect," the inspector said cheerfully. "Shall we get started? Let me introduce the dogs—we use shelter rescues and give them special training . . ."

Meg dropped back to let Christopher and Seth listen to the scientist. After their first flurry of activity, the dogs had settled down to business, each managed by a handler. Seth led the group away from the highway, toward the wooded area at the back of the park. As Meg watched the people in front of her, she thought how odd it was that this group of federal and state officials, not to mention dogs, had gathered to hunt . . . insects. Or, as her reading had informed her, "foreign invaders," bent on munching their way through tasty native trees. She looked around her: the trees looked reasonably healthy, under the circumstances, but she wouldn't recognize an insect-damaged tree even if she fell over it. She did notice that the underbrush looked dry, but when the town was clamoring for so many other municipal services from a limited staff, brush-clearing probably landed at the bottom of the list. Did the fire department keep an eye on campers' and partiers' fires here? At least the fire department was close by, maybe a quarter mile down the highway.

Meg continued to hang back, watching the dogs in action. Two of the humans aimed binoculars at the tops of trees, while a third recorded their comments and clicked what appeared to be a GPS unit—marking the location of each tree? The dog handlers, in contrast, were focused on the ground, and when one or the other dog nosed a patch of something, they made a note of that, then pointed out the tree to the binoculars people. They all spent more than an hour in the forested part, where at least there was some shade, then headed back toward the camping area, where the dogs appeared to find little that interested them. By the end of the second hour the group seemed ready to fold up their tents and leave. They conferred with Christopher, thanked Seth, made general "we'll be in touch" noises, loaded up their vans, and pulled away.

When Christopher, Seth, and Meg were alone again in the dusty parking lot, Seth asked Christopher, "What did they tell you?"

Christopher looked concerned. "There is clear evidence of infestation here, which means that there are now at least three identified sites in Granford, and possibly more. They wouldn't commit to the age or the extent because they wanted to go over their data first, but said they'll get back to me. Since they have confirmed these sites, they will need to extend the perimeter of their search—they are required to examine all potential host trees within at least a half-mile radius of the initial find, and when they find more, a half-mile beyond the outermost find. There are more details, but that's the short version."

"So we're in the middle of it, right?" Seth said. "And this may spill over into other towns?"

"That may already have happened. Beetles are not known for respecting human boundaries."

"That's going to make Granford real popular," Seth said, sounding depressed. "They have any clue how this started?"

Christopher smiled ruefully. "They're government employees. They aren't about to guess until they have a lot more data. But it's safe to say that the creature is here and it must be dealt with. I'm sorry if that increases your municipal burdens, Seth."

Seth shook his head. "Not your fault. That's the way our luck's been running for a while now. We just can't seem to get ahead. You'll let me know when they report back to you, Christopher?"

"Of course. No doubt they'll send you a copy of their report as well. Meg, I hope you enjoyed this little excursion?"

"Uh, sure. I still wonder if things would have been better if I'd just kept my mouth shut."

"Ah, but you're an essentially moral person, Meg, and you did the right thing. I need to get back to campus and see what I've missed. Nice to see you both, although I might wish the circumstances were more pleasant."

After Christopher had pulled away, raising yet more dust, Meg asked Seth, "What does this mean for Granford?"

Seth shrugged. "I have no idea. I guess I've got some homework to do. You going home now?"

"I guess. Bree tells me it's my turn to cook. Want to join us?"

"If it's no trouble," he answered.

"At the moment, my plan is to light a fire and throw a chicken at it. I might tear up some lettuce. All I can see in my mind is a large pile of ice cubes. But we've got to eat."

"That we do. I'll meet you there. Mind if I bring Max over?"

"No problem. Think he'd make a good candidate for a bug-sniffer? Maybe you can rent him out."

"Max?" Seth raised one incredulous eyebrow.

Meg laughed. "Sorry—what was I thinking? See you in a bit."

She went home and immediately jumped in the shower. Fifteen minutes later, half of it spent standing under the cool running water, Meg was back in the kitchen, wearing the lightest-weight cotton dress she owned and standing in front of the open refrigerator. Chicken—check. She should flatten it and marinate it a little before sending it out to the grill. At least six kinds of lettuce from the local farmer's market, mainly because they were pretty, along with some small but colorful peppers. A half-full container of crumbled feta cheese. That was salad—done. And there was plenty of ice cream for dessert.

Why was the heat so exhausting? She and Bree weren't doing anything more difficult than they had been doing earlier in the summer, but it seemed to be taking more out of them. Should she give in and indulge in another window unit air conditioner for the first floor? Where would she put it? As she had told Seth, she'd probably find an excuse to spend all her time in whatever room it landed in, leaving her apple trees—including the baby ones they'd planted with such high hopes only a couple of months earlier—to die a lingering and untimely death. She couldn't let that happen. She'd just have to toughen up and keep hydrated, just like her trees.

Seth rapped on the screen door shortly after six. "Hey," he said, letting Max into the kitchen before him. Max promptly flopped onto the wooden floor, plastering as much of his belly against it as he could. "You look nice."

"Thank you. You look exhausted." Meg smiled. "Come on in and get something cold to drink. I've started the grill, so the chicken'll take maybe half an hour."

Seth rummaged in the refrigerator until he found a cold beer, then dropped into a chair. "Thanks. I'd probably be having cold cereal at home, except I'm out of milk."

Bree came into the room and knelt to greet Max, who grinned and slobbered at her but didn't stand up. "Hey, Seth," Bree said. "How'd your afternoon go? I haven't heard the story from Meg yet."

"Granford has bugs—that's the headline. Apparently the state inspectors have now found three local infestations of Asian longhorned beetle, and there may be more."

"So what's that mean?" Bree said, grabbing a cold soda from the refrigerator.

"I don't know yet. More inspections, I'm pretty sure. I'd bet that somebody is going to want to cut down some trees, although I couldn't tell you how many. Which means somebody else will protest. That's the way it goes."

"And you're supposed to keep it all in order, right?" Bree grinned at him. "You don't even get paid for the job."

"I know. I'm just trying to do my civic duty, but there are days . . . Did Meg tell you about the bug-sniffing dogs?"

"No! Where do they come in?"

Meg left Seth to explain about the dogs while she dropped the marinated chicken on the grill and covered it, then stepped away as quickly as possible. The grill was hot. The air was hot. This had to end sometime, didn't it?

After dinner, Bree cleaned up the few dishes and disappeared to her room, which at least had a slight breeze. Seth seemed distracted, but Meg didn't take it personally—she was having trouble focusing, too. "Want to go out and see if there's some moving air out back?"

They meandered outside and settled themselves on the Adirondack chairs overlooking the meadow. Meg reached out for Seth's hand, and he took it; it seemed to be as much as they could do. They sat silently as darkness gathered.

Meg heard the distant ring of her cell phone back inside but couldn't summon up the energy to go answer it. She was surprised when Bree came out with it in her hand.

"It's Christopher—he says he needs to talk to Seth." Bree thrust the phone at him.

"Thanks." Seth took the proffered phone. "Hey, Christopher, what's up?"

Meg watched as he listened, frowning and nodding. "Can it wait until morning? And is it okay if Meg sits in?" Another pause. "See you then." Seth hung up.

"What was that all about?" Meg asked.

"I'm not sure," Seth said slowly. "He said the inspectors found something odd and I need to know about it. He's going to stop by here early. You can hear whatever he has to say, too."

"How early is early? Before we start watering?"

"He said around eight. Does that work for you?"

"I guess so. I wonder what on earth would be odd about an insect infestation. But I guess we'll find out tomorrow. I'm going in—I'm wiped out."

"I'm right behind you."

18

Christopher came rapping at the kitchen door a few minutes past eight the next morning. "Coffee?" Meg asked.

"Please."

As Meg filled a mug for him, she said, "Seth's out in his office, sorting out what he needs to do today, but I'm sure he heard your car arrive. He said you sounded very cryptic last night."

"It's an odd situation. Good morning, Briona," he said as Bree came down the back stairs.

"Hi, Christopher. What're you doing here? Did I miss something?" she said.

"That phone call last night?" Meg prompted, handing Christopher a mug of coffee.

"Oh yeah, right. I need coffee."

Meg could hear Seth whistling as he approached, plus

the scratch of Max's claws on the back steps. Seth's mood had lifted a bit. Last night had been . . . nice. Easy.

"Hey, Christopher," Seth said as he walked into the kitchen. "What's all the mystery about?"

"I'm sure you're wondering why the results arrived so quickly, and the inspectors were careful to say that this may be merely a coincidence, but what they found was that all the infestations are virtually identical."

"What does that mean?" Meg asked.

"As you know, they looked at three sites in Granford—and they will be looking at more in the vicinity, as I explained yesterday—and it appears that all began at approximately the same time."

"How do they know that?" Seth said.

"They located a central tree with the highest number of holes and other indicators—and the dogs agreed—and worked outward from there. They were able to establish a perimeter fairly quickly, at least on the first pass. It would appear that these infestations began no more than two years ago."

"Is that odd?" Meg asked.

"Not the age of them. If they had first arrived in the summer two years ago, they wouldn't have spread very far in the first year, but now they've moved demonstrably outward from the origin. What *is* unexpected is that all three sites conform to the same pattern. They're not contiguous, so there is no reason they should align so closely." Christopher looked at his audience as if waiting for a response.

Meg's brain seemed to be working slowly. "Why is that important? What are you saying?"

"I'm still not sure. If these creatures all appeared at the same time, why in those separate locations? I can imagine that wood products move onto the sawmill site with some regularity, so that is a potential source there. Seth, you mentioned that people bring firewood onto the park site. However, the logging site is more isolated, and if anyone wished to build a fire there, there would be plenty of material available on the ground—why carry it in? It seems highly unlikely that infestations at all three sites would have sprung up at the same point in time. The first and perhaps most logical conclusion is that these sites were created artificially. That is to say, someone planted the original insects, then sat back and waited for them to spread, which they did."

"Why would anyone do that?" Seth demanded.

"I don't know," Christopher said simply. "I can think of no reason. What I do know is that the inspectors, who will be returning to the area today, are inclined to suspect a human perpetrator who is manufacturing this situation."

"Are you saying someone just picked up a bunch of the insects and dropped them in the woods around here?" Meg asked. "But why? Who the heck benefits?"

"It's not clear," Christopher replied. "To tell the truth, I've never heard of any such incident, nor have my colleagues. It's not even clear that there is any criminal act associated with this. I *can* tell you that there are hefty fines associated with transporting insects out of a quarantined area, if someone removed them from another location, such as the Worcester area, to bring them here. Look, Meg, Seth, I've told you what little I know. There will be more information coming in over the next few days. There is no action that you need to take right now. And even if this does prove to be a deliberate act of mischief or vandalism or whatever you choose to call it, the outcome will be the same: your town and Jonas Nash will still lose some trees. The protocols must be followed, once the problem has been publicly recognized."

"Of course," Seth said absently, working through the ramifications. "Thanks for letting me know, Christopher."

Christopher stood up. "Having delivered my doom-and-gloom pronouncement, I must get to my office. I'll forward any information that comes to me. I hope this doesn't ruin your day. Give my regards to your lovely mother, Seth. I'll see myself out."

When he was gone, Seth, Bree, and Meg remained seated at the table. "Is this weird or what?" Bree asked.

"Definitely weird," Seth agreed. "Is somebody just messing with us? It sounds pretty easy to do: take one forest, add beetles, and wait. Maybe it's some new kind of domestic terrorism."

"Please, let's not jump to a conclusion like that!" Meg protested. "Nobody's brought that up with Worcester."

"That's because in Worcester they've got a pretty good idea how it started," Bree said. "Imported wooden packing materials. Seth, has the town bought any park benches or picnic tables from foreign sources?"

Seth shook his head. "We haven't replaced anything in the park in the last two years, as far as I can remember, and even when we do, I usually farm out the work to local guys, and they use local wood. And that wouldn't explain the infestation on Nash's sawmill property, anyway."

In her mind Meg went back to the location where she'd first seen the insect. A dead adult insect. Near a dead adult logger. An awful thought started brewing. "Seth, what if David Clapp died because of this? Maybe he stumbled over someone trying to leave bugs behind, and that's why I saw the one I did. Or maybe he was the one who was planting them and somebody caught him in the act." Someone like Jonas Nash? She hesitated to bring up Jonas directly since she knew he was Seth's friend.

Seth didn't answer immediately. "I suppose it's a possibility, but why would anybody kill over this? Why the heck would it be so important?"

"We already have an idea of why," Meg said. "Jonas loses a lot of timber that's valuable to him. The town park is stripped of its trees, which makes it less attractive, so that affects the town. There's got to be a motive in there somewhere, against Jonas or the town or both. Should we talk to Art? Or Marcus?"

"Meg!" Bree was quick to protest. "Trees and water, remember?"

"Yes, I know," Meg said impatiently. "Seth, can you see if Art knows anything new about the death? I mean, it makes a big difference whether David Clapp fell or was hit."

"Sure. I agree that Art needs to know, but let's tell him before we go running to the state police. Anyway, Art's probably surprised that we haven't been hounding him."

"Don't make fun of it—I'm the one who found the body, remember?"

"I'm sorry, you're right." He thought briefly. "Look, even if we assume that Clapp saw something he wasn't supposed to, we have no idea why somebody thought he had to die. Most people wouldn't know what the insect was."

"Maybe that part *was* just an accident," Meg suggested. "Maybe he startled someone in the act, and that person pushed him and he tripped. But there's still a crime, right? Or maybe he was doing it himself, got spooked by something or someone, then fell and hit his head when he tried to hide. Or he was doing it and somebody surprised him and a fight happened. No matter how it went, nobody's come forward to report seeing him or anyone else on the Nash property."

"What are you suggesting, Meg?" Seth asked. "That he was involved in planting the bugs? Which side was he on?"

"I . . . don't know. Look, we just found out about this, and we need to think it through."

Seth looked at his watch. "I'm supposed to meet Donald in half an hour, and that's what's paying the bills. Let me see if I can get together with Jonas Nash. Maybe we can share some information."

"Will he talk to you?" Meg wondered if Jonas had had something to do with any of this, although he stood to lose the most from the infestation. Was there such a thing as insurance against insect invasions?

"Probably. Besides, we're not accusing him of anything. He should know what Christopher told us, if he doesn't already know from the government people. And I'll call Art, too. Let him decide whether it's worth passing on to Detective Marcus."

"And somebody had better explain what laws apply here," Meg muttered. "You go ahead, Seth. I want to think about all this—while we water, Bree."

Up the hill, Bree handled the calculations for how much water was needed to simulate the best natural rainfall, a phenomenon Meg could barely remember. She'd read one suggested guideline for amateur orchardists with a tree or two in their yard: a five-gallon bucket of water once a week for young trees. She tried to imagine hauling five gallons of water to each tree and quailed. Of course, the system she and Bree were using dated back more than a century, only now a gasoline engine, rather than a team of horses, provided the power to move the water tank. But that tank had to be refilled regularly back at the well, so it was a time-consuming process.

That left at least part of her brain free to think about the beetle problem. To state it simply, the insect was where it shouldn't be. Well, it could be there, but not as it had been found. Ergo, somebody had put it there, or possibly in two or three separate "there"s, and maybe more. Why? That was the big question.

From what she had read, it looked like the bug was a threat, all right, but its timetable was years, not weeks. It wasn't like a plague of locusts, which could strip a tree bare in minutes. Now, she didn't want to downplay its importance in the grand ecological scheme of things, but it certainly wasn't something that would catch someone's eye and cause panic. If she hadn't happened to see one dead adult, it could have gone unnoticed for who knew how long. So if someone had planted it there, he or she didn't have a timetable and was content to wait, even for years? It didn't make sense. She would have expected whoever was doing this to want faster and more obvious results.

Time to refill the water tank again. She and Bree traded off driving and managing the water distribution hoses. The wellhead that provided the water was smack in the middle of the older part of the orchard, which often meant they had a long trek back to it, but thank goodness it was there at all, because Meg didn't know what would have happened to her trees and her crop without it. So far they had managed to keep up with the trees' water needs, and the spring was holding up fine. But if they had to cut back on watering, not only this year's crop but next year's as well could be affected. And the poorer the crops, the less likely Meg would be able to afford the drip irrigation system that would deliver water consistently and improve the crops. It was frustrating.

What did the beetle infestation mean? The government apparently had a lot of rules in place about destroying trees that were infested, and also destroying trees that *might* become infested if they were located nearby. The end result was a lot of trees lost. Gone. Bree had told her that the felled trees couldn't be used for something else like lumber. They couldn't leave the quarantine area. That might have an impact on motive. Would someone in Granford want the trees? Unless they were right here, they were in for disappointment. Or did they want to get rid of the trees? Was the underlying land the issue, with or without the trees?

And where were the creatures coming from? From what she'd seen of Christopher's lab, they were well contained there. How many would it take to establish a single infestation? Surely more than a handful. Dozens? Hundreds? And then multiply that times three, at least. Could just anyone order up a batch from a research lab like the one at the university, or were there screening procedures in place?

Too many questions. She needed more information.

She and Bree had gotten a late start because of Christopher's visit, so they finished late. They had just returned to the house when Meg's phone rang.

It was Seth. "Meg, I finally tracked down Jonas Nash, and I think we've got stuff to talk about. You want to come over to his office at the sawmill? It's air-conditioned . . ." Seth dangled the incentive in front her.

"Sure. Now?"

"There's one small catch: can you pick up some sandwiches and something to drink on the way over?" he asked.

"I think I can handle that. Give me an hour. I want to shower first."

"You going out?" Bree asked when Meg had hung up.

"Yeah, I'm going over to talk with Jonas Nash with Seth." When Bree looked blank, Meg explained, "You know, the guy with the sawmill and the woodlot where I found the first beetle?"

"Oh, right, him. I think Michael and I are going to go see another nice, cool movie. I only hope I can stay awake." Bree hesitated a moment before asking, "Hey, are you and Seth okay? He's been kind of funny lately."

Meg debated about filling Bree in on their issues and decided against it. "He's got some things to work out. Nothing you need to worry about. You and Michael go have fun. I claim the first shower."

Clean once again, Meg headed out to the local market to pick up sandwiches and assorted juices and sodas, then found her way to Nash's sawmill with only a couple of wrong turns. Jonas and Seth were waiting outside, talking; Seth waved when he spotted her. Neither one looked upset, if she was reading their body language right. Seth came over to take some of the bags with the food and drinks, and Meg seized the moment to ask, "Have you asked him anything yet?"

"No, I just got here myself. We've been discussing Donald's requests for matching moldings, but that's as far as we've gotten."

"Okay." Meg raised her voice. "Hi, Jonas. Ready for a late lunch? Or is it an early dinner?"

"Either one works for me. Come on in," Jonas said amiably. "I hear you're air-conditioning deprived."

"You've got that right."

Distributing food and drinks occupied several minutes, and Seth kept the conversation light until they had nearly finished their sandwiches. Jonas kept eyeing them, but he didn't ask any questions until he'd balled up the wrappings from the meal and thrown them away. Then he sat back in his chair and said, "Okay, what's this really about?"

Seth avoided answering him directly. "Jonas, have you received anything from the USDA this week?"

"Like what? A letter? An announcement? I haven't had a chance to go through my mail for a couple of days. Let me check." Jonas stood up and went to his paper-covered desk and rifled through a couple of piles until he pulled out an express envelope. He ripped it open and read the single page he pulled from inside. Then he came back and sat down, looking bewildered.

"What does this mean?"

Seth answered. "I got one like it, at the town office. The government is officially informing you that they have found an invasive species of insect on your property or properties."

Jonas looked stunned. "Asian longhorned beetle? Here? Damn, that's bad news."

"Yes, it is," Seth said gravely.

19

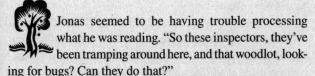Jonas seemed to be having trouble processing what he was reading. "So these inspectors, they've been tramping around here, and that woodlot, looking for bugs? Can they do that?"

"I don't know all the legal details, but since both places are nominally open to the public—you give tours here, and there are picnic facilities at the other site—they believe they have the right. You haven't seen anyone out looking?"

"Not that I've noticed, but we're talking a lot of acres. And I haven't been around my office much." Jonas glanced at Seth's face. "There's more," he said flatly.

"I'm afraid so," Seth replied. "They've found infestations on both of your properties." Meg waited for Seth to explain about the curious timing and was surprised when he didn't. Instead he said, "You know about this pest? Have you seen any around here? Say, on one of your woodlots?"

"I know about it in general terms, after what's happened in Worcester and Shrewsbury, but I haven't spent a lot of time walking through the woods the past couple of years. You know I've contracted that side of things out."

Jonas appeared sincerely surprised, but Meg wasn't going to go on her first impression. She didn't know the man—she'd have to wait for Seth's take. Meg said, "They've confirmed its presence on that lot and in a Granford park. Do you know what that means?"

Jonas scrubbed his hands over his face. "Of course. They're going to want to cut down a lot of my trees. Damn. That'll probably be the last straw. Same thing with the town park, Seth?"

"Yes," Seth said, "and that doesn't make me very happy either—that park is used a lot. But I think there are some bigger issues here."

Seth looked at Meg, who explained, "Jonas, I found a dead beetle near David Clapp's body last week and brought it to the attention of Christopher Ramsdell at the university, who reported it to the authorities." She took a breath and continued. "Do you have any reason to believe that David Clapp's death is connected with the beetle that was found next to him?"

"I'm not sure what you're saying," Jonas said. "You think he found it?"

"Or he put it there."

"What? Why would he do that?"

"Jonas, you tell us," said Seth. "You know what it means if your property is found to be infested: you lose a lot of trees. Your business is shaky anyway, so that could shut you down. You just said so."

"Are you saying you think I killed David Clapp to shut

him up? C'mon, Seth, you should know me better than that. He worked for me for years. My kids hang out with his— they compete in Little League. Besides, I thought it was a stupid accident—he tripped and fell. There haven't been any cops coming around and questioning me, after that first time."

"It may well have been an accident, Jonas. Did you and David part on good terms?"

"Sure. He knew my financial situation, and I recommended him to the company he was working for. Everybody won—he knew my trees, and I trusted him to make good choices for cutting. Hell, I went to his funeral. You can't think I'd do anything to David?"

"I don't. But if not you, then who would want to keep him quiet about the insect? Look, didn't you tell me something about talking with a developer about selling the land?"

"I have been, for this site, in a very preliminary way. What's the connection?"

"How would losing a lot of your trees affect its value to a developer?"

Jonas leaned precariously back in his chair and shut his eyes. "We've been talking about a high-end residential development—you know, big houses on big lots. If a lot of the trees were gone, they might think they could get it at a lower price. But to kill someone to knock off a few thousand bucks? I can't believe that." He leaned forward again and looked directly at Seth. "I can't believe any of this. I've been careful with my properties. You know that, Seth. I've worked with the state to meet their standards. I've made it available for public use. I'm a friend to every bunny and birdie out there. How could something like this pest have slipped in without my noticing?"

Seth glanced briefly at Meg, and she assumed he was trying to warn her off from saying anything about what Christopher had told them. Then he responded to Jonas. "We all have a lot of questions, Jonas. We're learning about it as we go along. Since the town park is infested, too, it's not just your problem. It's not clear where David's death fits. Maybe there's a connection, maybe not. The police are not pushing the investigation very hard, and I can't say I blame them—there's not much physical evidence, and as you say, they haven't come back to you about it. Maybe it would help all of us if you could tell us what you know about David Clapp."

"I've told everything I know to the state police," Jonas protested. "More than once. I knew him, I worked with him, I liked him. I never had any reason to distrust him. How much do you know about commercial logging, Seth? Meg?"

"Not much," Seth said.

"Almost nothing," echoed Meg.

Jonas paused a moment to gather his thoughts. "All right. The Nashes have owned land around here since before the town of Granford existed. If you know anything about Massachusetts history, you know that the forests that the first settlers found were pretty much cut down, and then after some decades of farming, the forests came back, and right now are going strong."

"Yes, Seth explained that to me," Meg said. "Go on."

"The sawmill's been operating for more than a century, and the family still owns plenty of forest around here to supply it. But after four generations, there are a lot of members of the extended family who are holding bits and pieces of that land, and the operation doesn't generate enough income to support everyone, so they've gotten regular jobs. Besides, not a lot of people want to go into logging these days. Some time ago, all the Nash owners got together and decided to hire a forest management organization to take care of it for us—for a fee, of course, but we still make money."

"How does that work?" Meg asked.

"The organization has both foresters and managers on staff. They follow sustainable forest management practices and look after all aspects, including when and what to cut. Only a small portion comes to our sawmill, which as I mentioned is pretty much for demonstration these days— although Seth's bought a lot of specialty products from us over the past few years. But the rest of the lumber, the forest management company sells to the highest bidder, which can change over time. Everybody wins: we know that our forests are being managed responsibly, and they make money from it and so do we. They can afford to look at the big picture because they manage so many properties—they aren't dependent on any one lot or even region."

"But you still hold title to the land," Seth asked.

"Yes, although we have a long-term contract with the company. We could have sold it to them outright, but then we could have lost control of it. There are companies around who will buy a forest, clear-cut it, sell the lumber, and walk away, and that's not good for the community. Maine and Vermont have enacted legislation to prevent that, in the last decade."

"And if you sell?" Seth said.

"A developer would want this lot. As for the woodlots, most likely it would be directly to the management company, because they've done a good job with them and I think they'd be fair on the price. It's not like I'm putting it on the open market."

Seth nodded, once. "This is great information, Jonas," he said, "but we're kind of getting away from our original question. Who gets hurt, or, conversely, who'd benefit if there's an infestation of beetles and the government steps in and cuts down a lot of trees?"

"Not me, that's for sure."

"Has anybody—either your management company or someone from outside—come looking to buy any of your forest property recently?"

"No. At least, nobody's approached me about those, just the sawmill lot. Nobody else in the family has mentioned any approach, although I can't speak to how they would feel about selling."

"Let me get this straight," Meg interrupted. "It's the management company, not you, who hires the loggers who actually choose and cut down the trees?"

"That's right. I know the company tries to use local staff, so they were happy to have David. Those guys usually come and go on their own schedules. Sometimes, if they were going to be working near the sawmill, they'd give us a heads-up, but it was more a courtesy than a requirement. I've had nothing to complain about since we've been working with them. Is any of this helpful? Like I told the police, I have no idea why David was found dead. He hadn't told me he'd be around, but he wasn't obligated to tell me. He had every right to be on the property, but I can't say if there was a planned cutting anytime soon, and that would be the only reason for him to be there. Look, I told the police all this, so I assume they talked to the logging company. They haven't come back to me with any more questions."

"The autopsy was inconclusive," Seth said.

"And why do you know that, or care?" Jonas demanded.

Seth met Jonas's look squarely. "Because it happened in my town. Because Meg was the one who found him, and we've had some experience with murders around here lately." He glanced briefly at her. "I would have been content to let the staties handle it, until this beetle thing came up. Now I'm wondering if there's something more going on." Before Jonas could protest, Seth held up a hand. "I know, there's no obvious connection. But I'm bothered by the way this is playing out. Look, as I understand it, generally these insects can be traced to some initial point of origin, most often shipping containers. In the case of our town park, someone could have brought them in with firewood. That might be the case for picnics at your woodlot, but not here at the sawmill, right?"

"No, or at least not in theory. I don't allow fires here, but that doesn't mean that people don't sneak in and build them anyway. But why would they need to bring in wood? There's plenty of dead stuff lying around there."

Meg had been watching the volley silently. Seth was doing his best to be impartial. But he hadn't yet mentioned that maybe the beetles had been deliberately introduced, which would tip the discussion a different direction. What would be gained by infesting Jonas's land? Particularly if Jonas wanted to sell it and he seemed to have a willing buyer in the wings? She could already see more than one possibility. One, Jonas didn't really want to sell and was contaminating the land to give himself an out. Two, somebody else held a grudge against Jonas and was trying to hurt his business, or if they already knew he was in financial straits, make sure it closed. Three, some buyer had his eye on the land and was trying to drive down the price. The last would work if the buyer wasn't a logging company but someone else entirely—like that developer Jonas had mentioned. Was that the same developer that had approached Seth recently about land in the center of Granford?

"Jonas, who else knows you're thinking of selling?" Meg said suddenly.

He looked at her as though he had forgotten she was there. "I've mentioned it to a few family members, but I haven't done anything official yet. As I said, the sawmill has been in the family for four generations, and the land longer than that. It's something of a local institution. I don't want to sell, but I'm not sure there's any alternative."

"How much would the value drop if you lost all the maples, and maybe some other trees, too?"

"I don't know, specifically. Maybe twenty percent? From what I've heard, no one can use the trees that are cut down for anything other than wood chips. What a waste."

They all sat silently for a few moments. Meg could think of nothing more to say, and she didn't want to give anything away by asking the wrong question. Since Seth hadn't chosen to share the deliberate infestation information, she wasn't about to either. Besides, she was still trying to think through what it might mean.

Jonas stood up abruptly. "Hey, guys, I appreciate your coming by and telling me about this, even if I don't want to hear it. Can you keep the fact that I'm thinking about selling quiet for now? What you've said may mean I have to rethink some things."

Seth stood up as well. "Of course. Look, Jonas, I'll be really sorry to lose the sawmill. Maybe that's selfish of me, but you've always done good work, and people recognize that. I wish there were more of them who were willing to pay what that's worth. Let me know if there's anything I can do—personally or on behalf of the town."

"I will, and I appreciate the compliments. Meg, someday I'd like to meet you without something awful hanging over us."

"I know what you mean, Jonas. I'd like that, too."

They made their farewells, and Meg and Seth trekked back to the parking lot. He was still curiously silent.

"Problem?" Meg said.

"What? Oh, nothing new, I guess. I hate to see the saw-mill close. That's another piece of Granford history lost. And another business. Maybe I picked the wrong time to get into the restoration business, but I figured people would stay where they were and try to preserve their homes. Which is true, until they see the price tag. Donald may be a pain to work with, but he's really committed to saving what he's got, and I value that. That, and the fact that he's willing to foot the bill."

Meg wondered if she should play Pollyanna and tell him that everything would turn out fine. Maybe it would— someday. Just not in the foreseeable future. She was putting off replacing her roof, much as it needed it, but when the time came, would she go with the option that most resembled the original, or would she be forced to opt for the cheapest? So far she'd managed to avoid decisions like this by not deciding at all, which was the coward's way out.

Before getting into her car Meg asked, "Do you think Jonas is telling us all he knows?"

"I think so. He's always been a straight shooter with me. I want to think that he wouldn't lie to me. I've been wrong before, but I'd rather trust people than not. I can tell that

Jonas loves his work, and his prices are fair. I'll bet it really hurts him to have to shut down the sawmill. He doesn't deserve the problems, like David Clapp's death or this beetle thing on top of that."

"Seth, so far nobody can explain why Clapp is dead. Jonas doesn't think he was involved with the beetle problem, but he claims they were friends, so maybe he doesn't want to believe it. Maybe the logging company David was working for was using him to pressure Jonas to sell. Or the developer was. Or it could still have been an unfortunate coincidence. Speaking of coincidences, what's the name of the developer who's approached the town?"

"I forget. Nobody local, because I'd remember that. You're wondering if it's the same developer that Jonas has been talking to?"

"Yes, I am. That might make a difference," Meg shot back promptly. "And another thing. We've always assumed David Clapp was working on his own. What if there was somebody else there with him, friend or foe? Whoever else was there could have taken away evidence."

"If there was any evidence," Seth said dubiously. "But what?"

"A weapon. Traps. Poison. A stash of illicit drugs that he was hiding?"

"You are kidding, right? I have trouble seeing drug dealers wandering around the woods. I won't say we don't have any drugs in Granford, but most of the hard-core stuff takes place somewhere else."

"Exactly my point. Who would be looking here? And it would be easy enough to put a GPS tracker on the drugs, to make it easy for anyone to find," Meg pushed, glad to see she managed to at least wangle a smile out of him.

"You know, Meg, this is getting absurd. I can't see Jonas as a criminal, or even as turning a blind eye to any criminal activity. And I can't see anyone trying to do him harm either. Which leaves us no further ahead than we were."

"Based on what little I've seen of Jonas, I agree with you. So what now?"

"I'll swing by my place and pick up Max—he's been cooped up all day. Then I'll bring him over to your place. Bed. Sleep. Start all over in the morning."

Meg smiled. "Works for me. See you there."

20

Meg was jerked from sleep the next morning by the muted buzzing of Seth's cell phone. Even without opening her eyes she could tell it was already growing light, so there was no hope for going back to sleep. She listened with half an ear to Seth talking quietly.

"Yes, I know . . . Don't worry about it . . . I'll be over at eight . . . All right, seven thirty . . . yes." He shut off the phone with an exasperated sigh.

"Donald?" Meg asked.

"Who else would call at dawn worrying about the profile of his shelf moldings?"

"No one I know, thank goodness," Meg said, sitting up.

"You don't have to get up."

"I do. I need to get out there before it gets too hot. Has anybody forecast any rain? Ever?"

"It might snow first," Seth said, pulling on his jeans.

"Why is Donald worried about moldings?"

"Actually, it's kind of interesting. The car crash took out one of the interior closets, and I had to re-create a couple of shelves. Some survived, but they'd been in place since the house was built, and they'd been painted a couple of dozen times. It was only after I stripped off all that old paint that we realized there was a decorative edge to them. Now Donald wants to make new ones that match exactly."

"Is there some point where this passes from authenticity into obsession?"

"I think Donald's hovering on the brink. I'm going to go take Max out and start the coffee."

"Bless you. I'll be down in a couple of minutes." After Seth left, Meg lay back down for a while, relishing what little cool air there was so early in the day. She hated listening to the mechanical drone of the elderly air conditioner at night, and it cost a lot to run it, so she'd turned it off and opened some windows. Meg had never labored so hard, so steadily, in her life, nor had she ever expected to. Her former city banking job hadn't involved any tough manual labor. She felt strong now, but she was perpetually exhausted. And as if the work wasn't enough, there was the death of the logger David Clapp and now this peculiar insect infestation to worry about. She wanted rain, with an almost physical longing, but at the same time, rain would only complicate Seth's construction projects.

It was truly curious that Christopher had said that the bugs might have been planted in the plots they knew of, and there could even be more affected sites. Still, the "why" was missing. Terrorism by insect? She'd never heard of such a thing. Then it struck her: hadn't Christopher or Gabe told her that the insects were hard to rear? You didn't just go to a supermarket, or even online, and order up a batch, because they were on something like a watch list with the government. Therefore they could come only from approved and regulated vendors—such as government agencies or government-sponsored labs. So if they weren't there naturally, where had Granford's beetles come from? And if they were so carefully regulated, would there be any way to find out who had bought or requested them? Could someone have stolen them from the UMass lab? How long would they last, outside of their carefully managed environment? How many would they need to seed the forests? Would David Clapp have had the expertise or the contacts to get hold of them? She'd have to ask Christopher. Energized at last, Meg swung out of bed and pulled on her work clothes.

Downstairs, Bree and Seth were sharing the table, eating breakfast. Meg poured herself a cup of coffee and sat down. "Same again today, Bree?"

"Yup. I'll test the soil for water content, but I don't expect any changes. We're going to be watering every day until it rains."

"That's about what I figured. Seth, I had some thoughts about the bug infestation, but let me follow up on them before I tell you about it, okay?"

"Fine, as long as I don't have to do anything about it— I'm jammed today. There's a whole stack of paperwork at town hall that I haven't even had a chance to look at."

"You guys find out anything useful yesterday?" Bree asked.

"I don't know," Meg said. "Not much fits together at the moment, but it's early days yet. Seth, is there anything more to be learned from the Granford town park? Like, why would someone want to damage it? And would that be the same motive for trashing Jonas's land?"

"Let me think about it." He drained his cup. "I'm out of here, before Donald calls me again and wants me to learn how to hand-forge nails."

"Can't he learn how to do some of this stuff himself?" Bree asked.

"He'd probably lose a finger or two along the way. But on the bright side, he pays on time. See you later, Meg?"

"Dinner?"

"Sounds good. Bye, Bree." Seth was whistling as he went out the back door.

"My, he's certainly in a better mood," Bree said, avoiding Meg's glance.

"Yes, he is. Stop prying or I'll ask you embarrassing questions about Michael." She stopped suddenly, then said, "Speaking of Michael . . ."

"No, don't go there," Bree said firmly.

"This is business, not personal. He's still connected to the local Green community, right?"

"Something like that. Mostly the organic people. Why?"

"Say someone was actively seeking to harm local forests, or the people who owned and managed them— would Michael be likely to know about it? Even if it's just rumors?"

Bree turned her full attention on Meg. "Why are you asking?"

"Christopher said it was possible that the beetles were deliberately planted. Yesterday we were trying to figure out why anyone would do that, and we came up with a list of possibilities, but it's hard to fit the dead man in. Let's say someone objected to the Nashes' use of the land—which they contract out to a company that isn't local—and wanted to punish them by damaging their trees. I'm not saying that's likely, but would Michael hear about that kind of hostility?"

"And the logger was just collateral damage? Or are you thinking that logger guy had something to do with this?" Bree asked.

"Either. I'm just filling out my list of possibilities. I don't like coincidences. David Clapp was found within a few yards of the dead insect, so I'm not willing to rule out a connection."

"Okay," Bree said cautiously. "You went and talked to Jonas Nash. You think he's involved in this?"

"I don't know him, but Seth trusts him. I'm not sure I can see any motive for him to do this, especially on his own land, but I don't think I'll rule him out just yet. Maybe there's a motive I haven't figured out yet. Maybe I'm looking for problems where there aren't any. The poor logger tripped and fell, and the beetles showed up all by themselves, end of story." Did she believe that?

"So what do you want from Michael?"

"If there's a remote possibility that this is a misguided protest against something, I'd like to know if Michael knows anything. I don't want him to betray any confidences among his friends, but this is a federal crime, I think." And somebody died, but she wasn't going to mention that.

Bree thought for a moment. "Okay, I guess I see where you're going with this. How about I ask him over for dinner, or whatever pitiful meal it is we eat in the evening, and you can ask?"

"Perfect. I'm just trying to check things off my list."

"Then let's go check a couple of thousand apple trees off that list of yours."

The day dragged on like all the prior days, as far back as Meg could remember. Logically she knew that this was not a drought of biblical proportions, although she'd heard it was coming close to rivaling the great Dust Bowl of the 1930s, but up close and personal, it was hard to tell the difference. Each day they watered; each day the water disappeared into the dusty earth, and patches of dry grass between the apple trees crackled beneath their feet. Nobody was even willing to guess when it would end. After the day's round of hauling hoses, she and Bree trudged down the hill, took showers, and retreated for a nap.

Meg was back in the kitchen trying to figure out what to offer Michael, who seemed to have vegetarian leanings, for dinner when Seth's van pulled in, followed closely by Art Preston's car—his personal car, not a police cruiser. When she went to the door, Seth greeted her. "Look who I found. His wife has left him high and dry, so I invited him to dinner."

"Hi, Meg," Art said. "Hope I'm not intruding. My wife's still at her sister's place on Cape Cod. She said I could call her when the temperature went below eighty and she'd think about coming back. We brought supplies!" He held up a plastic bag. "Burgers and hot dogs, and some monster zucchini that people keep dropping off at the station, trying to get rid of them."

"Oh, and we brought cold beer. Lots."

"Welcome, weary travelers," Meg said, laughing. "Come on in."

"I'm going to set up the grill, okay?" Seth said, suiting his actions to his words.

Art came in and deposited the food on the kitchen table. He pulled out a beer and offered it to Meg, who took it and opened it, then he opened one of his own. "Thanks for having me."

"Good grief, Art, this is about as low-key as hospitality gets. We haven't seen much of you for a few days. Here, give me the zucchini and I'll slice them up."

Art complied. "That's usually a good thing, isn't it, when you're talking to the chief of police?"

"Yes. Although if you're really itching for something to do, there's this little problem Seth and I have been gnawing on."

Art sighed. "I knew it was too good to last. He was hinting around it when we ran into each other. I don't have to do anything official, do I? Because then I can't finish this beer."

"Don't worry! We're just kicking around ideas."

Art grinned at her. "I've heard that before," he said, then drained his bottle.

Michael's car appeared, and moments later he rapped on the back door. Bree let him in. He seemed nonplussed at seeing the Granford chief of police sitting in the kitchen, but it was hard to be sure, since Michael never said much under any circumstances. "Hi, Michael," Meg said cheerfully. "You know Art, right? Can I get you a beer?"

"Uh, yeah, sure," Michael said, shuffling his feet.

"Hey," Bree said, nudging his arm, "this is just a friendly dinner—nobody's gonna get arrested."

Meg handed Michael a beer, which he took gratefully, looking glad to have something to do with his hands. "Did Bree tell you that I wanted to talk to you?"

"Uh, yeah?"

"It's not urgent. Art, are you going to go play caveman and help Seth burn meat?"

"Sure, why not?"

Meg handed Art a platter laid out with burgers, hot dogs, and sliced zucchini brushed with olive oil and herbs. She added utensils. "There. Go!"

Since all the cooking was happening outside, Meg sat down and motioned for Michael and Bree to join her. "Michael, I wanted to talk to you because I've got a question about something related to local ecology. Or something like that—I'm not sure what the right terminology is. Did Bree fill you in on this beetle problem that's been discovered this week?"

"Kinda." Michael focused on peeling the label from his beer bottle with his thumbnail.

"Well, Christopher Ramsdell says that the inspectors thought the distribution of the insects was suspicious, and they're very quietly wondering if they could have been introduced artificially. Don't spread that around, okay? Anyway, none of us has come up with a convincing reason why anybody would do something like that. I mean, no matter what your ecological philosophy, invasive pests like this will ultimately do harm to forests, right?"

Michael nodded. "Yeah, sounds about right. What am I supposed to tell you?" At least now he was beginning to look interested.

"Look, we're just spitballing here. Suppose somebody wanted to make a political statement, and they used Asian longhorned beetles as their weapon. The insects were originally imported, mainly from Asia, so no natural enemies, and now they destroy forests. What's the message?"

"Huh," Michael said, looking at a spot above Meg's head, presumably thinking.

"Come on, you can do better than that." Bree nudged him with her elbow.

"Okay. Bree told me one of the sites was a tree lot, and the trees are used for lumber?"

Meg nodded. "Yes. The lot belongs to a local lumber company run by a family that's owned and managed it for generations. But they contract out for the logging, and a hired logger was found dead there. One of the other properties is a town-owned park."

"Oh yeah, I think Bree told me about the logger guy. Nobody logs the park?" When Meg shook her head, Michael said, "Then I don't see how the two fit together. Okay, say somebody decided that commercial logging was bad, or the way they were doing it was too destructive, so they scatter the site with the bugs to destroy its value for logging. It wouldn't make sense, because a lot of the forest would still get destroyed either way, so nobody comes out ahead. The park makes even less sense, because it's a public asset that serves all sorts of people. Why try to destroy it?" He took another swallow of beer. "Is this helping?"

Meg nodded. "Yes, by eliminating possibilities. So in your opinion, there's no protest group that might be doing this?"

"I don't know everything that goes on around here, but I haven't heard of anything like this. It's not like we all coordinate, but this doesn't sound like anyone I know. Nobody wants to destroy the good stuff."

"Thank you," Meg said. "That's about what I was thinking, but I wanted to check."

Bree had been silent, but now she said, "Who pays for

all this—I mean, clearing out the trees? The government? State or federal?"

"Uh, I don't know," Meg said. "Why?"

"Because it could be somebody who wanted to attack either the Nash family or the town, or both, depending on who's responsible for the costs. It's probably public knowledge that the town is strapped. I don't know about the Nashes."

"I do—they're hurting, too," Meg said. "I don't know who has the cash for this kind of thing, but it's not like they have a choice, if the government says they have to remove the trees. Let's hope it doesn't come out of the owners' pockets—there may be some remediation funds."

Bree pressed on. "Another question for Christopher."

"You're right," Meg replied. "Thanks again, Michael—you've been a help. Keep your ears open, will you?"

"Sure."

21

 Bree and Michael took off shortly after dinner, leaving Meg, Art, and Seth sitting around the kitchen table, feeling sluggish.

"Anybody do anything interesting today?" Meg asked hopefully. "Because all I've been doing is irrigating. Seth, anything new at Donald's?"

Seth smiled. "Now he's decided he wants to bring in a consultant on paint colors. He may even decide to mix his own paint."

"What did they use for paint in seventeen whatever?"

"Milk paint, for one," Seth said.

"As in, cow's milk?"

"Yup. Milk plus lime and pigments—about as simple as you can get. Donald wants to be sure he gets his colors right. He's sent off some samples from the damaged parts to someone who knows about these things, who's going to analyze the paint layers."

"I am so glad I have a newer house," Art said, leaning back in his chair, his hands laced behind his head, legs outstretched.

"Lucky you," Meg said. "Ice cream, anyone?"

After Meg had dished up ice cream and they'd eaten it quickly before it melted, Art said, "Okay, guys, I appreciate the meal and all, but I know you want to pick my brain, assuming you can find it. You'd better get down to it before I fall asleep in my chair."

Meg and Seth exchanged a glance, and Seth nodded at Meg to go first. She quickly outlined the Asian longhorned beetle problem and what Christopher had told her about the government report, and the possible deliberate use of the insects. Art followed her narrative with a slightly bemused expression.

"Are you saying there's a crime in here somewhere? Am I supposed to do something?"

"That's the problem, Art," Meg told him. "We have no idea. It could be anything from malicious mischief or vandalism to domestic terrorism. Christopher's not aware of any other examples of deliberate misuse of insects like this. And where does the death of David Clapp fit?"

Art nodded. "You think they're connected? You aren't buying the accident theory? Because as far as I know, Marcus is. I haven't heard from him in a week."

"I figured as much. I'll admit that may be what happened, but I don't think we can rule out other possibilities. Say, for example, that this Clapp person was planting the insects, although what he stood to gain puzzles me. Maybe he was doing it for personal reasons, although Jonas Nash swears they were on good terms. Or maybe he was working for someone else. Either way, it's possible that somebody found him and tried to stop him physically, and then when things went wrong he got scared and ran. Maybe killing him wasn't intentional, but the poor guy's just as dead."

Art looked at her and then at Seth, his expression skeptical. "Are you really saying that these critters are worth killing anyone for? I mean, so a few trees die or get cut down—does that really justify murder? Sometimes I wonder why I talk to you two at all—you create more problems for this town, not to mention me, than anyone I've ever known." Art's smile softened his statement. "What is it you want me to do?"

Seth finally spoke up. "Nothing, at least for now. Yes, the impact of an insect infestation is serious business, but you don't have to worry about the details. You'll be hearing more about it because the town park is affected. To get back to the unexplained death, maybe we're seeing demons where there are none. But we keep coming back to the basic fact that a man is dead, and it's possible that somebody else knew about it and didn't tell anyone. Whether or not that's connected to this insect thing isn't clear. Do we know enough about him?"

Art was silent for a few moments before speaking again. "I'm sure the state police have checked the guy's background. On the other thing, assume somebody is in fact planting this pest in various places around here. What's the motive? Who stands to gain?"

"That's where we're stuck, Art," Meg said. "Or rather, we have a number of possible motives but no way of figuring out which one is the right one. And they all sound kind of absurd."

"Give me the short version," Art said.

Meg ran through her list: doing harm to Jonas Nash, either personally or through his business; trying to influence property values; or simply making trouble, although there should be easier ways of doing that than sneaking around scattering exotic insects. "Does that cover it, Seth?" she said when she had finished.

"Sounds about right," he said.

"Oh, I forgot—while you guys were out cooking I asked Michael whether there were any environmental groups that might have reason to do this, and he said he didn't know of any. That doesn't mean they aren't out there, but he's pretty plugged into the local scene, so he would likely have heard. It seems a stretch anyway—if someone wants to save a forest, you wouldn't send in a pest that could destroy it, right?"

"Wouldn't make sense to me," Art said. He stood up and stretched. "I'm going to call it a night, folks, and think about what you've told me—not that Marcus would welcome me poking my nose into his investigation, if there even is one, and I'm not sure there is. But I agree that it feels like another one of those pesky coincidences that just doesn't sit right. And I do take it personally when somebody dies in my backyard. Thanks for the dinner. Don't get up—I know the way out."

When he was gone, Meg continued to sit at the table, too tired to move. "Well, I guess we've done the right thing. What's next on your agenda?"

"I've got a backlog of town business to deal with. One of the letters I opened today was a follow-up from a commercial developer I've been talking to."

"I thought Granford was done with all that, now that the shopping complex is up and running?"

"I'd hoped we were. I don't want to see Granford turn into every other town with a string of strip malls with the same stores. But developers are getting hungry again. I mean, look at how much that stretch of Route 9, this side of Amherst, has been built up recently, even since you've arrived. Stores, hotels, restaurants."

"You're right—I noticed that, when I went to get my hair cut. And it does look like any other generic strip in the country, once you get past Hadley. But what would anyone want with Granford?"

"You forget that Route 202 is a main highway. There's still land available along there. Like the park."

She stared at him for a moment. "And the developer has his eye on that site in particular?"

Seth nodded. "Along with a few others. The developer wants to meet with the Board of Selectmen and discuss possibilities for working with the town."

"Are you going to meet with them?"

"I'll tell the board members about it, and we can decide if we want to take it to the next step. I'm guessing we wouldn't—I'm sure you remember what a mess it was last time, for a variety of reasons—but I have an obligation to hear the guy out, if his intentions are legitimate."

"It's not your decision?"

"Not a personal decision, no, and not solely mine."

"But it's still on our list of motives," Meg said, almost to herself.

"I guess so."

"If the government or whoever has to come in and cut all those down, what kind of impact will that have on the park? Or any other wooded site around here, for that matter. People go there to enjoy the woods and nature and all that, and if you take away the forest, or the majority of it, then what? Does it serve its purpose anymore?"

"I guess I see your point. But it's not that simple. The park is part of a town-wide recreational use plan, and it would be difficult to change that. We'd have to look into ownership issues, which are complicated by the fact that some government monies were used to acquire it. And all of this would take time—maybe years."

"Maybe there are developers who take the long view. After all, there's only so much land."

"True. Oh, and I ran into another odd problem, when I stopped by the town offices, that I'm supposed to do something about. Looks like somebody's been siphoning off electricity from the town."

"And you know this how?"

"In case you haven't noticed, we have a municipal power provider here—Granford Power and Light. The town doesn't manage it directly, but we do have oversight. The town administrator usually reviews the bills and authorizes payment, pro forma, but over the past year or two she noticed an unusual spike in usage, more than can be accounted for by new users like the shopping center. It's not a lot, which is why it took her so long to identify it—it wasn't a high priority. It was a good catch on her part."

"Are you supposed to do something? You think it's more than just some hard up homeowner tapping into a line to save some money?"

"Looks like it. At that level, it would take us a while to catch on. After all, it's town money that's paying for whatever this is."

"Could it be something illicit, like, say, a meth lab, or a chop shop?"

Seth laughed. "Meg, you've been watching too many crime shows. I guess it's possible, but it's not likely."

"How do you track it down? What do you look for?"

"Mostly follow the power lines around and see if anybody's patched something in that shouldn't be there."

"Shouldn't the power company be doing that?"

"Yes, and they are. I'd just be another set of eyes. There's still a lot of unoccupied land around here, and I drive around a lot on the back roads. For that matter, if whoever it is has done a good job, it would be hard to find. Just one more niggling little problem."

"Of which there are many, I gather. I don't know how you do it all."

"Some days I don't either." Seth smiled. "Hey, want to come along while I take Max for a walk? It should have cooled down a bit by now."

Meg stood up, feeling her muscles protest. "Sure. Some fresh air might be good. Don't forget bug spray. Betcha this is the leading edge of an insect uprising."

"With a coalition between mosquitoes and Asian long-horned beetles? I find that a little hard to visualize."

"Never say never," Meg said, reaching for the spray she kept by the door.

Max had to be coaxed to leave his comfortable space on the floor, but once outside he perked up. He went over to greet the goats, who were also taking advantage of the cooler evening air to stroll around within the confines of their pen, then he took off toward the back of Meg's property. At least his golden coat made him easy to follow in the growing dark. Meg and Seth linked arms and strolled after him at a more leisurely pace.

"Do you think we'll ever know what really happened to that poor logger?"

"You know, he probably knew that park. Didn't Jonas say their kids both played in Little League there?"

Meg stopped dead and looked at Seth. "Seth, do you realize what that means? He would have known both the park *and* the Nash land. If I weren't so tired I'd be excited— that's actually a clue, sort of. At least it links the victim to two properties."

"It does. I'll tell Art in the morning. He can take it to Marcus, if he wants—maybe he can score some points with the detective." Seth laughed. "My, what a romantic conversation we're having."

"I'm too tired to be romantic. Let's collect Max and go in before the mosquitoes find us."

22

When Meg came downstairs the next morning, Bree was seated at the kitchen table with various pads and notes spread out in front of her. Seth had left earlier, headed toward his office, and he'd taken Max with him. Meg helped herself to coffee and sat down across from her.

"That looks serious," she said.

"Maybe," Bree responded. "I hate to say it, but I'm beginning to worry about our water supply. The water level's been dropping."

Not the way Meg wanted to start the day. "What does that mean, in practical terms?" she asked.

"I can't tell you. We don't have a lot of history on the well supply—maybe it's just a blip. But this year's been so dry . . . I'm worried."

"What happens if we can't irrigate?"

"With no rain? Uh, it depends."

"Come on, you can do better than that!" Meg said.

"Okay, if you really want to hear it. Fruit growth happens in two phases. The first is from bloom to about fifty days after bloom. We came through that just fine. The second phase runs from fifty days to harvest—that's when your apples grow. And that's what depends on available water, during the hottest, driest time of the year. That's where we are right now, and we've got a drought on top of the normal summer heat. We've been able to compensate with the well water so far, but if we can't use that, the apples will stop growing. The older trees with deep roots will do better than the new ones."

"Which means we should concentrate our watering on the newly planted trees, even though they're not producing apples yet, rather than the ones that are?"

"If you're thinking long term, yes. Those new trees need to get well-established now. They're producing wood for the future. But even in the older trees, drought stress can reduce fruit set for the next year."

"Are my trees stressed?" Meg asked.

"You tell me. The signs are wilting, yellowing leaves, falling leaves, and fruit drop."

Meg thought about what she'd seen in the orchard. Things weren't exactly looking lush, but were they that bad yet? "Uh, maybe?"

Bree shook her head. "We're okay for now—just. But another week or two like the past few and we won't be."

"Can I go back to bed now and pull the covers over my head?"

Bree smiled reluctantly. "Nope. As long as we have water, we're going to irrigate. But maybe some prayer might help."

"I'll consider it." Meg stood up and refilled her coffee mug—her own form of irrigation. "Anything else you want me to worry about, that I'm helpless to control?"

"No, that should do it for now," Bree said cheerfully. "I'll be ready in five."

Meg finished her breakfast and went out to greet the goats while she waited for Bree. "Hey, ladies," she greeted them. "Hot enough for you?"

Dorcas and Isabel stared at her with their unnerving eyes. Their rectangular pupils always surprised her.

"You have enough water? Shade?"

The pair walked away and resumed grazing.

"Thanks for the moral support, you two," Meg said as she turned to go up the hill. She was surprised to see a university van pull into her driveway, and a young man she recognized by his dark beard climb out. What was the UMass researcher doing here? she wondered. "It's Gabe, right?" she said, as he came into earshot.

"Sure is. Gabe Aubuchon. Nice to see you again, Meg."

"What brings you out here?"

"Christopher Ramsdell sent me out—not because *you* have any problem, personally," he hurried to reassure Meg. "He thought I should take a look at the ALB in the wild— thought it might give me some new insights into the rearing process. I spend most of my time in the lab, but yesterday I tagged along with the state inspectors, to learn how they spot them. So now I'm just checking out random patches of forest, to see if I can spot any more ALBs."

"Well, I don't have a lot of wooded land. Mainly what you can see on the other side of the meadow there, and more toward the back of the property. You haven't seen it in a forest?"

"Not an active infestation, before now. There aren't many, thank goodness. I mean, I've seen chunks of log that show the damage the ALB has caused—they make some big holes and tunnels! But it's not the same as seeing them on their home ground."

"Have the inspectors found any more infested sites?"

"They have, although not big ones. The chainsaw gangs should show up by next week. You mind if I look at your wooded land?" Gabe asked.

"Go right ahead," Meg said, although she had to admit to herself she wasn't sure she wanted to hear bad news if Gabe found anything.

"What about up the hill?" Gabe asked, gazing at Meg's orchard.

"That stand of trees at the top belongs to the Chapins. Like I said, I haven't seen any inspectors. You think the insects are here?"

"You might see the state crew come by. They'll start from the spots they've already identified and work their way outward from there, until they get a clear half-mile perimeter. So far the finds have been a couple of miles north of here, closer to Amherst. Can I take a look at the trees up the hill?"

"Sure. I was headed that way anyway. Do you suspect there's anything there?"

"Nope. I'm just checking things out. You never know, and if I find something, maybe I can score some points with the inspectors."

But not the landowners, Meg thought sourly.

As they trudged up the hill, Gabe asked, "How many trees you got here?"

"In the orchard? Maybe two thousand, or more. If you

look over there to the right, those are new ones we just planted this spring—that's a thousand right there. But they're planted more closely than the older trees were."

"And it's just you doing all the work?"

"Me and my orchard manager, Briona Stewart. We hire pickers in the fall, and for a couple of days in the spring to clean up the place and prune. But, yes, mostly it's just Bree and me. It's manageable, if we're willing to work really hard."

"What're you doing now? It's too early to pick, right?" Gabe seemed eager to learn. Meg wondered how often Christopher let him out of the lab.

"We spend a lot of time irrigating the orchard. I'm lucky to have a well in the middle of the older part, so I've got water, but Bree and I are the official delivery system, which means filling tanks and hauling hoses. We really need some rain."

"Bet you do!"

Meg checked her watch, and then saw Bree climbing the hill. "Well, Gabe, I'll leave you to it—I've got to get to work. Happy hunting!"

"What was that all about?" Bree demanded when she came closer to Meg.

"That's Gabe, the guy who works in the ALB lab at UMass. I met him the other day. Apparently Christopher let him out of the lab long enough to see the beetles he's rearing in their wild state, and he's checking all over."

"You know, I think I remember meeting him when I visited that lab a couple of years ago—you don't run into many beards like his these days. So he's been there awhile."

"I think he told me five years," Meg said. "You haven't

seen any of the official inspectors around our land, have you?"

"Nope. Aren't they supposed to notify you when they want to take a look?"

"I have no idea. They wouldn't need to look at the orchard, because apples are not one of the host trees, but they might want to look at the wooded areas around my property. I'm not going to object, if they happen to ask."

"I don't care what they do, as long as they don't get in our way. Let's get going."

Meg saw Gabe headed back down the hill, giving her a wave and a thumbs-up after he'd looked over the Chapin trees. Meg assumed that meant he hadn't found anything there. There were a couple of old maples in front of her house—should she worry about those? They shaded the house, and she'd hate to lose them, but at the same time they *were* old and their dead limbs were just waiting to take a shot at her already battered roof . . .

Meg and Bree finished the morning's watering and were poking at lunch in the kitchen when Seth stopped by later that afternoon.

"You don't look happy," Meg said. "You want something to eat? Drink?"

"I'll take that drink, but what I really want is a clone of myself."

"Why?"

He filled a glass with ice, then water, and dropped heavily in a chair. "The good news is, the State Plant Health Director and the State Plant Regulatory Official have the pest invasion situation well in hand, and it's a pretty impressive operation, I have to say. The problem, however, is that one of the requirements is public outreach, which means press releases, interviews, public meetings, mass mailings, interacting with community interest groups, and so on—all of which falls to me."

"You can't ask one of the other members of the board to take it on? Or your staff?"

"You've seen our staff—the town clerk, one administrator, and two other select board members. I'm the best qualified, which isn't saying much. But I'm the only one who knows anything about all this."

"You have heard of the word 'no,' haven't you?" Meg smiled to soften the comment.

"I've heard rumors. It's okay—Granford isn't very big, and we've got the mailing lists and e-mail contacts on file anyway. But still, it's just one more time sink, and I'm already running behind on everything else. It's kind of hard to earn a living when I keep getting distracted by things like this. Funny, the bills keep coming, whether or not we're under attack from giant killer beetles."

"I don't suppose working with Donald makes things any easier," Meg said.

Seth shook his head. "He's a great guy—he knows his stuff, and he really cares about it—but he does require a lot of hand-holding, which I don't have time for at the moment."

"Anything new from Art? Do you know if he passed that info about Clapp on to Detective Marcus?"

"I haven't heard. Again, it's kind of a can of worms—I'm sure we could identify hundreds of local parents who've had kids who played on the park fields *and* who have taken the history tour at the sawmill, who would know the place as well as he did."

"But how many of them ended up dead in the woods?

How many of them have any kind of expertise with forests and their pests?" Meg demanded.

"Meg," Seth snapped, "if you think it's so important, *you* tell Art about it." He drained his glass and stood up abruptly. "I've got to go."

"Hey, peace. I'm just asking. So the answer is no, you haven't discussed this with Art?"

"Yes, the answer is no," Seth said, his tone only slightly less annoyed.

"Will I see you later?" Meg called out at his retreating back.

"I'm having dinner with Mom," he tossed back over his shoulder, and he headed toward his van.

Meg sighed. With Seth these days, it seemed to be two steps forward, one step back. Right now, the ongoing heat was making everyone snappish, and that included even-tempered Seth. She turned to Bree. "So it's just you and me?"

"Sorry, Michael and I are going to find someplace with air-conditioning. You're on your own."

A few hours later, after Bree had gone, Meg wandered slowly through the house. It was nice having a little alone time. Of course, that gave her time to give the house a hard look and remember how many things needed to be done. Or *could* be done—it was still standing, even with a few leaks. If the big maple by the front corner turned out to be infested and had to be taken down, she'd suffer the consequences for a long time—as long as it took to grow a thirty-foot maple. How many other homeowners were facing the same problem, if this insect threat turned out to be widespread?

Actually, from the inside the house didn't look too bad.

The parlors flanking the front hall were in pretty good shape, probably because no one had ever used them much. She'd done a lot with the kitchen when she'd moved in, out of necessity, so she could check that off her list. Of course, there were pitifully few electric outlets, at least by modern standards, but she was managing. Storm windows would be nice, but that was down the road somewhere. And a second bathroom—now that was a dream. She refused to contemplate how colonial residents had managed things like basic hygiene. She hadn't found any archaeological trace of an outhouse, but then, she hadn't looked very hard. She shouldn't complain, but she did harbor dreams of a roomy, well-ventilated bathroom, maybe one with a Jacuzzi tub— just the thing to stretch out and wallow in after a hard day in the orchard. But that was going to have to remain a dream for a while longer.

In the end she settled for a cool bath, with Lolly perched on the bathroom counter for company, followed by a mystery novel she'd been saving to read, except that she fell asleep before she finished the first chapter.

23

The next morning Meg could tell it was hot again before she opened her eyes. Even the birds seemed to have given up the effort to sing. This weather had to end sometime, didn't it? She was willing to accept the reality of global warming, but she had never thought it would hit so hard and so fast. And why did it have to happen to her? Her orchard had been getting along fine for a couple of centuries, but now that she had taken it over, it was going to be devastated by the weather? Surely there wasn't some cosmic message there, directed at her?

Get over yourself, Meg! she told herself as she stumbled toward the bathroom, passing Bree on her way out. "Nice night?" she asked.

"At least it was cool," Bree said, without elaborating. Sometimes Meg wondered just what Bree and Michael's relationship consisted of, but it wasn't really any of her business.

"Same old, same old today?"

"You got it. See you downstairs."

In the kitchen Meg fed Lolly, then contemplated her coffeepot, wondering if she really wanted to boil water. Caffeine was dehydrating, she had read, so maybe it wasn't a good idea, but without it she would be a zombie. The need for caffeine won, and she went through the motions, then stood numbly watching the coffee steep in the French press.

"Tell me there's something good in the weather forecast?" Meg said when Bree arrived, her hair wet.

"Ha!" was Bree's only answer, as she buttered an English muffin. "There's a front somewhere doing something, but the forecasters don't agree on much of anything. Except that it's hot."

Meg's breakfast was interrupted when her landline rang, with a caller ID she didn't recognize. "Hello?"

"Is this Meg Corey?" a vaguely familiar voice asked.

"Yes, it is. What can I do for you?"

"I'm sorry to bother you. This is Donald Butterfield. I'm looking for Seth Chapin. We were supposed to meet this morning, and he hasn't arrived. He's usually quite dependable about such things."

Why was Donald calling her? "I haven't seen him this morning, Donald. Have you tried his office number? Or his cell?"

"Yes, of course," Donald said impatiently. "There's no answer at his home number, but I recalled that his office is behind your house, and I wondered if you might check to see if he's there?"

Holding the phone, Meg went to the back door and looked out at the drive: there was no sign of Seth's van or his car, but he had been known to walk over to his office from his home, except he wasn't home. Unless, of course, he was avoiding answering Donald's phone calls. But Seth would be unlikely to walk if he had a business appointment. "I don't see either of his vehicles. When did you expect him?"

"At seven thirty. I'm an early bird, and he said he wanted to beat the heat, so that's the time we set."

Meg checked the clock, which read eight. Half an hour was definitely late for Seth, and anyone could travel from one end of Granford to the other twice in that amount of time. "Maybe he's had car trouble. I'll keep trying him at his home, but other than that I don't know what to tell you. Maybe you could try the town offices, when they open. I'm sure he'll show up."

"Thank you, Meg. I'll stay here and wait, in case he was delayed."

Meg hung up thoughtfully. "What's the problem?" Bree asked.

"Seth didn't show up for an early meeting with Donald. That's not like him. He said he was having dinner with his mother last night—I'll see if I can catch her before she leaves for work, in case he told her something about his plans."

Meg hit a speed dial number and waited for three rings before a breathless Lydia Chapin answered. "Hi, Meg—you just caught me as I was headed out the door. What's up, so early?"

"Did Seth have dinner with you last night?"

"Yes, but he left fairly early. Why?"

"He had an appointment this morning and he didn't show up. Did he say anything about what he was doing this morning?"

"Not that I recall. Wait—it's that Donald person, isn't it?"

"That's the one. He said he tried Seth's other numbers, and then he called me."

"Seth says he's a bit of a fussbudget, but he did mention that he was planning to meet with Donald this morning. That's all I know. Maybe the van broke down or something. Sorry I can't help, but I've got to leave for work."

"That's okay, Lydia. I'm sure he'll turn up. Talk to you soon."

Meg put the phone back in its cradle. Now what? Was she supposed to worry? His own mother didn't seem too concerned. Seth was an adult with a lot of responsibilities. Maybe there had been some crisis at town hall. Or maybe he was just dragging his heels because he didn't feel like dealing with Donald right away.

But Seth was seldom late, and if he said he was going to do something, he did it.

"You ready?" Bree asked. "Those trees aren't going to water themselves."

"Yes, I'm ready." Meg made sure her cell phone was in her pocket as they closed up the house and walked up the hill.

They'd been watering long enough by now that Meg could do it on autopilot. Fill tank from well; drive to a section of the orchard; dispense water until the tank ran dry. Repeat. And repeat again, until her eighteen acres were watered. It could have been worse, Meg reminded herself once again. And they had the option of irrigating, so they didn't have to sit by helplessly and watch the trees wither and the immature apples drop. Maybe they were lucky.

So why didn't she feel lucky? Because she was hot, sticky, dusty, tired, and frustrated. And now she had to add worried: Seth's van had not appeared while they were watering the orchard, nor had he called, at least on her cell phone. Not that he owed it to her to keep her informed of his every move, but she was a little surprised. He had seemed kind of ticked off the day before, when he had left. Or maybe he'd been tired, like she was, not to mention overcommitted. Maybe the state agencies had grabbed him and locked him in a room to turn out cheerful press releases about the beetle. Or maybe he was just playing hooky.

No, not Seth. He didn't do things like that.

They finished the watering by noon and went down the hill to stow the equipment in the barn. Inside the house, Meg checked her phone messages: four from Donald, the most recent only half an hour earlier. She didn't feel like listening to them, but she could guess the substance: no Seth. What now? She drank down a couple of glasses of water and threw together a sandwich of sorts, then told Bree, "Seth's still AWOL. I'm going over to his house to see if there's any sign of him."

"Jeez, maybe he's just busy."

"Maybe, but it's not like him just to vanish, especially when he knows someone is waiting for him. Is there something here you need me to be doing instead?"

"Nope, you're clear. Go track down Seth and tell him you can't live without him for more than six hours at a time."

Meg swallowed a snappish comment. Bree was right, in a way, but Meg was still worried. She debated walking over for about twelve seconds, then rejected the idea in favor of a nice, cool drive in her air-conditioned car. "I'll take the car. Do we need anything else while I'm out? Food? Drink?"

"The fridge is as bare as I've ever seen it, so you'd better stock up on something."

"Got it." Meg went to her car and started it up, then sat

in it for a few minutes while the interior cooled, as she made a mental shopping list. She felt sluggish and uninspired. Would this heat never end?

She drove the mile or so to Seth's house—farther by road than on foot—and pulled into his driveway. His car was there, but not his van. Maybe that was a good sign? He'd left the house on his way to Donald's house and then . . . what? No signs of life in the house. Just in case, she climbed reluctantly out of her cool car and knocked at the back door, with no response. But she was startled to hear barking from behind the house. She went around back to find Max in the enclosure that Seth said he had built recently. Why would Seth have left Max out there? Yes, there was shade, and the dog's water dish was still half-filled. He must have planned to come back and collect Max after his early date with Donald. But Max seemed pathetically happy to see Meg; how long had Seth been gone?

"Hey, Max, want to come with me?" Max jumped up and put his paws on the fence, panting. She took that as a yes. "Okay, let me find a leash for you and we'll go over to my house."

She found a long leash hanging on a nail on a wall near the pen, then let Max out and attached the leash to his collar. "Let's go, boy."

Max willingly followed her to the car and jumped into the backseat. Meg wondered just what was going on. She pulled out her phone and tried all Seth's numbers: no answer at any of them. What now? Water for Max, first. Could she leave him in her house? She still had errands to do, but she couldn't take Max along and leave him in the car.

She headed home, then opened the back door for Max to jump out, and led him in the back door. Seth's van was not

parked in her driveway, eliminating one hope. Bree was
still in the kitchen, and she looked surprised to see Max.

"What's up?"

"No sign of Seth, but Max was outside in his pen, and I
don't think Seth would have left him out all day, in this heat."

Finally Bree registered some concern. "That's not like
Seth. I can see him blowing off Donald, but not Max."

"You haven't heard anything?"

"Nope. You still going to do those errands?"

"I thought I would, and I might swing by town hall to
see if they know if Seth was working on something for the
town. Can you keep an eye on Max? I shouldn't take more
than an hour."

"Sure, no problem. He's good company."

Meg set off again, this time toward town. Might as well
stop at town hall before buying food, which would wilt in
minutes if it sat in her car in the sun. She pulled into the
small parking lot at the side and went in the front door. "Hi,
Sandy," she greeted the woman at the desk inside.

"Hey, Meg. What brings you here?"

"I'm looking for Seth. Have you seen him today?"

"Nope, but he's not here every day. You probably know
his schedule better than I do. Did you need something in
particular?"

Meg debated about how to answer that without sounding
like a nervous idiot. "He missed an appointment this morning, and that person called me looking for him—I didn't
know what to tell him." Then she recalled that Seth had
mentioned something about checking for bootleg power
lines. "Wait—were you the person who was looking at
those electric bills? Something about someone siphoning
off electricity? Would he be working on that?"

"He told you about that?" Sandy looked surprised. "Normally it wouldn't be noticeable, but with everybody pulling power for their air-conditioning at the moment, we're pretty much up to maximum usage, and every bit counts."

"I hadn't even realized we had a municipal system until Seth told me."

"Sure—always have, since about 1900. None of the bigger companies has offered the town a better deal. Most of the time we don't pay much attention to it—if it ain't broke, don't fix it, right?—but this little jump showed up, and I started looking back and found it had been going on for a while, so I told Seth. He said he'd look into it, but he didn't seem to think it was urgent."

"Sounds about right." If it wasn't urgent, there was no reason for Seth to have ditched his appointment with Donald, who was paying him, to run around the back roads looking for unauthorized power lines. "Any other fallout from this drought, for the town?"

"Fire company's been keeping busy. Doesn't take much to start a fire these days, and then it moves fast because everything's so dry."

"I know—there was a small one near my place a couple of days ago. It was the first time I'd seen the fire department in action. I thought they did a great job—showed up fast."

"I think they're still grateful for the new municipal building the town put up a couple of years ago, so they're on their best behavior. Anything else I can do for you, Meg?"

"No, I don't think so. If you see Seth, tell him Donald was looking for him. Of course, maybe they've already connected by now. I'll let you get back to work, Sandy."

"Good to see you, Meg." The phone rang and Sandy

turned to answer it, so Meg left. She braced herself to step from the relatively cool interior of the town hall building to the sweltering heat outside, and she stopped on the top step for a moment to adjust. The town hall building, once a gracious Victorian summer home, sat on a rise, and below her lay the town green, ringed with sugar maples. Meg felt a pang of alarm: how far away was the town forest and park? If there were insects there, would the trees around the green fall within the mandatory clearance area? Would the state come in and take down the maples? That would be a true loss to the town, stripping it of one of the more appealing aspects.

She returned to her car and made her rounds, picking up food and other necessary supplies. It was after four when she returned. Bree came out as Meg was unloading the car.

"Let me grab those," Bree said, reaching for some bags.

"Thanks. No word?" Meg didn't elaborate; she didn't need to.

"Nope. Not at town hall?"

"No." They shuttled their burdens into the house and distributed them, mainly in the refrigerator. When they were done, Meg said, "I'm going to call Art."

"Isn't that kind of extreme? I mean, seriously—it hasn't even been twenty-four hours."

"Maybe, but Art's our friend, and he knows Seth. I'll just ask if he's seen him. Maybe something came up about David Clapp and he talked to Seth."

Bree shrugged. "Go ahead, then."

Meg went to the cooler front of the house and speed-dialed Art's personal number.

"What?" he barked. "Oh, sorry, Meg, I didn't see it was you. Problem?"

"I can't find Seth." It sounded stupid to her ears even as she said it.

"What do you mean, you can't find him?" Art sounded exasperated, and Meg couldn't blame him.

"He missed an early appointment at Donald's, and nobody's seen him today. And he left Max outside his place in the heat."

"Huh. Doesn't sound like Seth." Art's tone changed to one of concern.

"You haven't seen him or heard from him?" Meg asked, trying not to sound pathetic.

"Nope, not today, but that's not unusual. He took the van?"

"He did—his car's at his place, but I haven't seen the van anywhere."

"I'll keep my eye out for it, then, but apart from that there's not much I can do. We've got plenty of other problems—mostly small fires popping up." He covered the phone with his hand and yelled something at someone else, then returned. "Sorry, Meg, gotta go. I'm sure Seth'll turn up." He hung up, leaving Meg listening to dead air.

What was she supposed to do now? Other than worry?

24

All right, admit it, Meg—you're scared. Seth wouldn't just walk away from his responsibilities, even if he wanted to, so for him to be out of touch this long meant he had to be in some sort of trouble. But what on earth could she do? She'd called everyone she could think of; she'd looked for him at his house, and she could see his workplace from where she sat, so she knew he wasn't at either. Unless he was deliberately hiding in his own basement and avoiding people, there weren't a lot of other places to look for him. Besides, he wouldn't have abandoned Max. Something had to be wrong.

She jumped when the phone she was still holding rang in her hand. She recognized the number. "Art?"

"Yeah. I found Seth's van—it's parked a few yards off the road that runs north of town, heading toward the Butterfield house. No sign of Seth, but I don't have time to

check it out—there's a fire west of there that's blowing
smoke over the highway, and I've got to go direct traffic."
He hung up abruptly, leaving Meg with a lot of questions.

She took a deep breath. All right, the location made sense.
Seth would probably have taken that road on his way to Donald's house for his early appointment. But why would he have
stopped, and where could he have gone? Art hadn't given her
much to work with. He'd made it clear that the van hadn't been
in an accident, and even if it had, Seth would have let someone
know. Had he left his phone in the van? That might explain
why he hadn't answered all day. But if whatever it was had
happened early in the day, on his way to meet Donald, why
hadn't he surfaced by now? Had he gone for a walk in the
woods and gotten lost? Unlikely: Seth had grown up roaming
these woods, and he knew his way around. And why would he
have stopped if he was on his way to an appointment?

Meg checked her watch again. It was past four, so there
would be at best four hours of daylight left. She could go
find the van, since Art had said it was just off the road, but
what was she supposed to do when she found it?

Max. Meg almost hit herself in the forehead. She had
Seth's dog, who would no doubt be eager to help find his
master. He wasn't a trained tracker, but he could find Seth,
couldn't he?

"Bree?" she called out.

"Yo?" Bree replied from upstairs, then came tumbling
down the back stairs. "What's up?"

"Art spotted Seth's van on the north side of town, empty.
He's busy trying to manage the traffic around some fires up
that way, so he couldn't check it out. I'm going over to
where the van is now, and I'm taking Max—maybe he can
find something."

"You want me to come?" Bree offered.

Meg was torn. Two sets of eyes could be useful, but Bree probably wasn't any better at tracking someone in a forest than she was. "Why don't you stay here and hold down the fort? If you hear from Seth, or anybody else, you can call me." Meg patted her pocket to reassure herself that her phone was there. "I don't know how long I'll be—if Max doesn't pick up a trail, then I don't have any other ideas." Meg took a hard look at Bree. "You think I'm overreacting."

"I . . . don't know," Bree said reluctantly. "Maybe. But better safe than sorry, so you go ahead. I'll be here."

"Fine." Meg was itching to head out the door, but she reluctantly acknowledged she didn't know the roads of Granford all that well, and she should take a look at a map before setting off. She pulled out the most detailed local map book she had and opened it on the kitchen table. Her house lay at the southernmost end of Granford, and Seth's was maybe a mile north of that. If he had left from his house, how would he have driven to Donald's? Donald's house was about as far as you could get from hers, in the northeast corner, and only one local road led in that direction—the road that some idiot driver had been taking far too fast when he swerved and hit Donald's house.

The map showed a lot of forest in that direction. Once past the town center, the whole north end of Granford was forested, running up the mountain and on into Amherst. Some of the green areas on the map were marked as state park, or actually, multiple parks. Wasn't Jonas Nash's sawmill up that direction? Would Seth have stopped to talk to him and . . . gotten diverted?

Wait, Meg –are you thinking Jonas might have done something to Seth? She had trouble believing that, but could

she say she was a hundred percent sure that Jonas wasn't
involved in David Clapp's death? He'd known David. If David had come to him after finding a beetle, Jonas could have
lashed out at him. But wouldn't he have done a better job of
hiding the body? He had plenty of places to choose from.
Meg shook her head to clear it: she had no tangible reason
to suspect Jonas Nash of anything, but if she was going that
direction, she could swing by the sawmill and see if Seth
had been there. Besides, she was running out of ideas: from
her brief look at the map, she couldn't see anything else that
would distract Seth on his way to Donald's house.

At least she should be able to find the van easily enough,
and that was a start. "Come on, Max." Max looked up at her
eagerly from where he had flopped on the kitchen floor.
"Let's go find Seth, okay?"

The mention of Seth's name brought Max to his feet.
Meg grabbed the leash from the doorknob where she'd
hung it and led Max out to her car. He seemed to sense that
something was happening, and jumped into the backseat
willingly.

Meg started the car and pulled out of the driveway,
heading for Route 202 north. She could tell that there were
fires somewhere nearby: the heat haze that had become
normal was now intensified by a smoky smell, even through
the air-conditioning, and the air seemed hazy. She wondered where the actual fire was. Or was there more than
one? Art had said that it was close enough to the highway
for the smoke to affect driving. He had sounded harried,
and he wasn't even a firefighter, but he did have to manage
the situation and make sure that the fire trucks had clear
access by road. What if the fires were far off the road? Meg

had no idea how anyone would handle those. Contain them and let them burn themselves out?

The air grew thicker, with a peculiar yellow cast. Max whined in the backseat—picking up on her anxiety, or troubled by the unfamiliar smells? In the center of town, rather than follow the highway Meg turned on a smaller local road that she knew led north and would intersect with the road leading to Donald's house. She could only hope that it wouldn't lead her into the fire's path.

There were few other cars on the road. She easily spotted Seth's van after she'd made the turn onto the second road and passed beyond the small cluster of houses and a cemetery near the intersection. Art had misspoken: the van was not pulled onto the verge, but rather, it was turned into what looked like the beginning of an overgrown, unpaved lane, perpendicular to the road. She pulled up behind it and got out of the car. There was smoke in the air, but not too thick. Nothing but silent woods in sight. She made her way over to the van and peered inside. Nobody there—no surprise. The doors weren't locked; the keys weren't in the ignition. The parking brake was engaged. She would have laughed at herself if she hadn't been so worried. What had she expected? Signs of a struggle? Bloodstains? She had to shut her eyes for a moment at that thought. *Meg, you're getting too far ahead of yourself.* Obviously Seth had parked here and then gone . . . somewhere.

Meg stepped back from the van and looked around her. There was nothing resembling a path, except for the rutted lane, which didn't look as though it had seen much use anytime recently. Still, it was a sign of civilization, and it led away from the road, deeper into the woods. Whose land

was this? Meg wondered. Where was the nearest house?
She had no idea.

Still in the car, Max began barking, probably annoyed at
being ignored. She went back to the car to let him out, making sure his leash was securely attached to his collar—all
she needed was to lose the dog in the woods now. She
wasn't sure Max would come to her if she called. She knelt
down in front of him and looked him in the eye, glad there
was no one to see her acting so foolish. "Max, find Seth.
Got it?"

Max barked again, once, and set off along the lane, pulling hard on the leash, and Meg had to rush to keep up. She
should have changed back into her work clothes, including
her work boots, before setting off. Her sneakers were ade-
quate, but she kept tripping over roots and fallen saplings,
which in turn slowed Max down as he strained forward.
After a few minutes she forced him to stop, which he did
reluctantly, and listened for a moment. Nothing, save a
crackle in the underbrush off to one side that could be any
of a number of small woodsy creatures. There was no wind
here in the trees. No sound of cars or planes—or sirens.
Max barked again, startling a large black crow that took off
with a squawk, flapping noisily.

What do you think you're doing, Meg? she asked herself.
*You're a city girl, lately an apple farmer, but right now
you're bumbling around without a clue.* She might be the
least qualified person in Granford to find someone in the
woods.

Still, she had to do something, and this was the only
thing she could think of. Max was still pulling on his leash,
so she let him have his head again. He was intent on following the rough lane, which was good—if they set off

cross-country through the trees, she'd be hopelessly lost in minutes. After a while she noticed what she assumed were electric wires, strung on poles parallel to the lane. She hadn't noticed them before. Did that mean that someone actually lived in this direction? Seth had guessed that someone might be bootlegging electricity from the town— maybe that was what he had been pursuing when he had walked into the woods and disappeared. *If* he had walked into the woods. What if this was just some huge scam, designed to make it look as if he had disappeared, when in reality he had been skimming funds from the town for years and was at this moment on a plane for some island paradise with no extradition, with a healthy bank account waiting for him?

Meg, you're getting hysterical! Something like that was completely beyond Seth Chapin. Honest, decent, hardworking, caring, efficient, responsible Seth Chapin. He had to be here somewhere. Max certainly thought so, as he kept pulling her forward, deeper into the woods. The lane followed a more or less straight path, shifting now and then around a tree that had probably been there for a century or more. Meg tried to visualize the map, but all she could remember was a lot of green space at this end of town. Maybe she could pull out her smartphone and call up a map app and zero in on any structures nearby with aerial photographs. Maybe she should have thought of that before she set off on this insane hike. As it was, the phone screen was too small to be of much help, and if the aerial images were current, all she would see would be the tree canopy. Lots of trees, in full leaf, which would block the view of anything on the ground.

How long had she been following this blasted lane, and

how far had she gone? A half-mile? A mile? She had no
idea. Max had not lost enthusiasm, and finally she noticed
what looked like a thinning of the trees ahead. Another
minute and she realized it was a clearing. When she emerged
into the open space, she saw that in the center was a ram-
shackle wooden building that hadn't seen paint in a long time,
if ever. It was more than a shack but something less than a
house. It looked as though it had been thrown together from
whatever scrap materials had been handy, and it was weath-
ered so that it blended into the background.

The power line she'd noticed ran straight to the building.

Did someone actually live here? Was she trespassing?
Did she really believe that some hairy hillbilly would
emerge with a shotgun and run her off? Max was barking
furiously now. If Meg had hoped to approach quietly, that
wasn't going to happen—but why would she have needed
to? In any case, Max's noise hadn't produced any response
from inside the building or from the surrounding woods.
She knelt down next to him again and said, "Find him,
Max," and unhooked the leash.

Max ran straight for the building, but not for the sorry
excuse for a front door. Instead, he went around to the side,
where a sort of lean-to with a slanted roof clung to the
side of the main building. Max had parked himself in front
of the lean-to's door and was scratching and whining. Meg
came closer and called out, "Seth?" No answer, but Max
didn't stop. On inspection, Meg found there was a surpris-
ingly new and unrusted hasp and padlock on the door.

Now what? She pounded on the door: no response. Max
continued to paw at the doorsill. All right, she'd get the
door open, somehow. It fit closely enough that prying it
open with a branch wouldn't work—she'd have to break the

lock. She looked around until she found a rock. *Welcome to the wonderful world of breaking and entering, Meg*, she thought as she raised the rock and brought it down on the lock. It didn't budge: somebody had done the job right and bolted it through the door rather than just screwing it into the surface. She tried again, and again, until finally the hasp snapped, sending the padlock tumbling to the ground. At the first sign of a gap, Max pushed himself into the small structure; Meg followed more slowly, hesitating a moment to let her eyes adjust to the dim light in the windowless space.

The space was crammed with a hodgepodge of old wooden boxes and a few newer cardboard ones stacked on top. The floor was occupied by a body: Seth's.

And he wasn't moving.

25

Meg dropped to her knees beside him, even as she took in details. The space was tiny, so he was jammed into a small space with no way to move. He was breathing, so she knew he was alive, and wrapped clumsily but thoroughly with duct tape. Nothing over his mouth, but she guessed that even if he yelled, there was no one around to hear him. Max, of course, had not hung back, and was bouncing around ecstatically licking Seth's face. Meg reached out a hand and touched Seth's face: it was hot. Too hot. It was then that she realized how incredibly hot the airless enclosed space was. It had to be over a hundred degrees in the lean-to, with the sun hitting it full on.

Her face was already dripping sweat. Seth's wasn't.

The realization hit her with an almost physical blow. Oh hell—dehydration. Heatstroke. Bree had warned her about it more than once, had insisted that they keep drinking water all the time they were out irrigating. Now and then they'd even drenched themselves with water between tank runs. Heatstroke was serious. How long had Seth been cooped up here, without any water? Since early morning?

She laid a hand on his shoulder and shook him, noting that his shirt was stiff with dried sweat. Even his arm felt hot. She fought to keep her panic under control. "Seth? Wake up!" *Please, please, wake up.*

His eyes opened slowly, and it took him a moment to focus, first on Max, who was still licking his face. Then his gaze turned slowly to her. "Meg?"

Relief hit her in a wave. "Yes, it's me. Let me get this stuff off you." She cursed the fact that she didn't have a knife or anything useful with her. Of course there wasn't anything in the shed that could be used to cut—someone had wanted him to stay here, not figure out a way to escape with a handy sharp tool. For how long? Until he died? In the end she had no choice but to laboriously unwind the tape that circled his body with excessive thoroughness. She tried hard not to acknowledge that even with his hands free, he wasn't making much of an effort to help himself. She pulled the sticky lengths of tape away and threw them across the small room in sheer frustration. "Seth, can you sit up?"

He regarded her blankly, as though she was speaking a foreign language. If he couldn't sit, then he couldn't stand or walk, and how the hell would she get him out of here? Was whoever had done this planning to come back? She pulled on his near arm until he was in a more or less up-right position, leaning against the interior wall of the shed. "Seth, what happened? Why are you here?"

Maybe moving had helped get his blood flowing again,

because his eyes finally focused. "I . . . I'm not sure. I was looking for something—oh, right, following the electric line—and I came to this cabin and the . . . I think somebody knocked me out. Is anyone around?"

Why was it that he took it upon himself to investigate every problem this blasted town had? Was he really the only person in Granford who could look for electricity thieves? Meg shook her head. "Not right now. So you've been here since this morning?"

"I think so. What time is it?"

So he could have been here all day, cooped up in the heat. Not good. "Past six. Whose property is this?"

"The town's. Nobody's lived here for years."

"Can you stand?"

"I . . . don't know." He struggled to get his feet under him, but when he tried to stand upright, he wavered and then dropped back to the floor. "Damn, my head hurts." He leaned his head back and shut his eyes.

Things were going from bad to worse. Walking back to her car or the road would apparently be out of the question for him, Meg could see quickly. What were the alternatives? She pulled out her cell phone and called Art. He answered with another abrupt "What?"

Meg said quickly, "I've found Seth, but I think he's extremely dehydrated."

"Where are you?" Art demanded.

"I'd guess about a mile from where the van is, straight back in the woods. There's a building here, kind of a rough cabin, and that's where I found him."

"Can he walk out?"

"I don't think so. Can you send someone?"

"No can do. We're fully engaged here and the fire's probably headed in your direction."

Could things get any worse? "Can you send the ambulance?"

"Sorry—I had to ship a couple of guys to the hospital with burns. It's bad here."

She had to get Seth moved, but he couldn't move. No way was she leaving him here, when whoever had done this to him might be coming back, and a forest fire might be headed in this direction. "Okay, what's the treatment for heatstroke?"

"Symptoms?"

"High temperature, no sweat. Headache. Can't stand up, much less walk."

"Damn, damn, damn. Okay, look, the most important thing is to get some water into him, and get his body temperature down. Is there water there?"

"I don't know. I haven't checked out the cabin, but if it has power it might have water."

"Power?" Art said.

"Yes. Seth said he was following the electric line this morning."

"So there's probably water. Like I said, get water into him, but not too much at once. He'll probably need electrolytes, too, but we can worry about that once you get him out of there. Dump cold water on him. If there's a hose, spray him down. You've got to get him mobile. I'll try to alert the medics, but I can't promise anything. Gotta go. Let me know once you get moving and I'll try to find someone to meet you." He hung up.

Meg looked back at Seth. His eyes were open and he was

watching her, but without much comprehension. She knelt by him again. "Seth, I need to find water, in the house. I'll be right back. Max, stay." Max obediently sat down next to Seth, pleased that he'd done his job of finding his master— and unaware that it wasn't over yet.

Meg hurried around to the front of the main building. There was a shallow porch across the front, and while the corners were dusty, the central part leading to the door wasn't, suggesting that someone had been using it regularly. The door was flanked by grimy windows. She peered into the nearer one and was surprised to see what looked like scientific equipment rather than ordinary furniture. Even more surprising was the sight of a window-unit air conditioner on the far side of the single room—and she could hear it humming. Who the hell would cool a cabin in the middle of the woods?

She turned to examine the door. Damn, this one had a real dead bolt lock, so a rock wouldn't help her much. She'd have to break a window to get inside. She jumped off the low porch and went back around the side to get the rock she had used before, but when she returned to the front, someone else was there, approaching from the other side. She stiffened, until she realized that she recognized him: Gabe Aubuchon. She felt a stab of relief.

"Gabe? What are you doing here?"

He looked startled. "I could ask you the same thing."

That wasn't the reaction she had expected, but it didn't matter. "Look, I really need your help."

"Why are you here?" he asked again.

Gabe was acting very oddly, Meg thought. "Do you know this place?" she asked.

"You're trespassing," Gabe said.

Now she was getting seriously concerned. If she was trespassing, so was he: Seth had said the property belonged to the town. Was Gabe here on an innocent bug-hunting trip, or was there something else going on?

Stay calm, she told herself, although that did little for the pounding of her heart. She knew how far away she was from other people, so she was on her own. Maybe Art knew where she was, but he was kind of busy right now. Gabe had always seemed cheerful and helpful. Christopher had hired him, which should mean something. But nothing explained his odd demeanor at the moment.

Wait—was *he* the one who had stuffed Seth into a hot, dark place where he could have died in the heat? Still could, if Meg didn't get him help? If Gabe was the one who locked up Seth, maybe he didn't know she'd found him. Gabe had approached from the other side of the building, so he probably wouldn't know that Meg had broken open the door. Maybe she could spin this out until she knew a little more. "I was looking for Seth Chapin. He hasn't been seen around town today, and his van is parked on the road not far from here."

"Why would he be here?" Gabe asked, without inflection, giving nothing away.

"I don't know," Meg said. "I followed the road from where his van was, and this seems to be the closest building. Maybe he was looking for something." When that brought no reaction from Gabe, she pressed on. "Is this your place?"

"I don't live here, if that's what you're asking."

"Does this have something to do with your research for the university?" she countered. What was this, Twenty

Questions? She didn't have time to waste. "Look, do you know if there's any running water here? Like, inside?"

Maybe she'd given too much away. As she watched, Gabe's expression shifted, then shifted again, although she had no idea what he was thinking. "You found him," he said flatly.

So much for pretense. Meg squared her shoulders. "Yes, I did. Did you lock him in there?"

Gabe nodded, without taking his eyes from her face. "He was snooping around."

"And you had to stop him?"

"Yes. He was going to spoil everything."

Spoil what? she wondered. Not that she cared. Whatever Gabe had been doing here in seclusion, it had nothing to do with her. She had only one thing to worry about right now: moving Seth to somewhere he could get help. "Gabe, all I want is to help Seth. If he doesn't get some water, get cooled down, he could die. I need your help."

Gabe looked blankly at her. "What are you talking about?"

"Hyperthermia. You get too hot, you die."

"I didn't know. I'm from Maine—never gets that hot there." Now he looked stricken. "This wasn't supposed to happen . . . I didn't mean . . . Look, Meg, I'm not a bad person. Really, I'm not. But things kinda got out of hand, and I don't see how I can fix it without making it a lot worse."

"Gabe, I don't know what you mean," Meg said carefully, not that she cared—she needed to worry about Seth first. "Just tell me, is there water inside?"

"If I let you inside, you'll know what I mean. All of it."

She struggled to keep her voice level, calm. "Gabe, I need water, and I need it now. There's a fire to the west of us, and it may be headed this way. And unless you help me, Seth will end up dead."

Gabe's body sagged. "He showed up and I didn't know what to do, so I stuck him back there until I could figure it out." Gabe's mouth twitched. "I can't let someone else die."

That made no sense to Meg, unless . . . "Gabe, are you talking about David Clapp? The logger?"

He nodded and looked down at his feet. "That was an accident."

But why would Gabe have killed that logger, accidentally or otherwise? Meg's brain seemed to be working too slowly, probably because of the panic she was trying hard to suppress. And then she made the connection. "Gabe, if I look inside this building, will I find beetles?"

Gabe's head came up, and he looked almost relieved. "Yes."

"That's what all the equipment is for? You're rearing your own? And seeding them in the forests around here?"

He nodded. "That logger guy caught me in the act at Nash's place—I was putting some where people would be sure to find them, because nobody had noticed them yet. But I swear, he tripped. I never touched him."

But you hid the body so you could go on doing what you were doing, Meg added to herself, but now was not the time to split hairs. It was time to go for broke. "Gabe, you found Seth Chapin snooping around here this morning, and you wanted to stop him, so somehow you managed to lock him into the shed, right?"

Gabe nodded. "He asked me if I was the one stealing power and told me I was trespassing. I couldn't let him shut me down—my beetles would die."

Gabe hadn't figured out yet that the game was up. First the logger had found him, and then Seth, and now her. He couldn't keep silencing everyone. Surely he must see that? "But you didn't plan to hurt him, did you?"

Gabe shook his head vehemently. "No! I needed time to think. I mean, I'm not a killer. I couldn't look him in the eye and just . . . do it."

Thank heavens for that. But a corner of Meg's mind wondered, *But he could tie him up and let Seth die from heatstroke?* Seth wasn't a violent person; how would he fare against someone who was trying to cover up a murder, not to mention a number of other crimes? They were probably evenly matched, physically. How had Gabe managed it?

And hadn't he figured out that heat could kill?

Meg sniffed and smelled smoke, stronger than before. She had to act fast. Meg said carefully, "Gabe, I'm pretty sure that Seth is suffering from heatstroke, and that's serious. He needs water. He needs to get cooled down. I don't think you are a killer, Gabe, but if you don't help me help Seth, he *will* die. Is that what you want?"

Gabe looked close to tears. "This is so screwed up. I never wanted to hurt anyone."

Should she play one more card? Did she have anything to lose? "Gabe, Art Preston, Granford's police chief, knows where we are. He's going to come here as soon as this fire is under control. He'll find us, because Seth is his friend and he won't stop looking until he does. No matter what you've been doing, whatever happened along the way, this will only get worse if you let Seth die." *And you'll have to take me out, too, because I'm not going to let that happen.* Meg managed not to say that out loud.

Gabe's anguish was clear on his face, and Meg all but

held her breath. Then his expression shifted to one of res-
ignation: he'd given up the fight.

He nodded once, decisively. "All right, let's get him inside. I'll crank up the AC and open up the refrigeration
units—that should help. And there's water."

26

"Gabe, I'm going to need help getting Seth inside—he can't stand."

"Oh. Sorry. Let's go, then." But when they reached the lean-to, Gabe was greeted by a growl from Max, standing guard over the still-prostrate Seth.

"Whoa," Gabe said, backing away.

Good judge of character, Max, Meg thought. Out loud she said, "It's okay, Max. Friend. Come here." Max stepped out of the lean-to reluctantly and moved next to Meg, alternately watching Gabe and Seth. Gabe stepped into the shed. "Sorry, man," he said to Seth, as he reached down to pull him up. The two of them almost toppled when Seth couldn't maintain his balance. There was not enough room for Meg to help, but in the end Gabe managed to gain control. "We're going inside now, okay? It's cooler there, and there's water." He backed out and got Seth turned in the right direction, and together they somehow lurched around the building to the front. Meg trailed behind, trying to restrain Max, who was eager to help.

When Gabe shoved open the door, blessedly cool air rushed out. Meg followed Gabe and Seth and closed the door behind her. Max had followed them in, and she said sternly, "Sit." He did, but he remained watchful. Meg scanned the room for a chair or stool for Seth, but the room was crammed with a mini version of the lab she had seen at the university. Gabe seemed to recognize her predicament. "There's a desk chair in the next room."

Meg went through a door to what appeared to be the only other room in the place, although she spotted a basic bathroom in the corner. There was a cot and a table that served as a desk, piled high with papers, with the chair in front of it. She rolled it back quickly into the lab room, and Gabe maneuvered Seth into it. "Can you get some water, Gabe?" she said. Then she knelt in front of Seth and waited until he focused on her. "How you doing?" She laid her hand over his on the arm of the chair: still too hot.

"Not good," he said.

Gabe shoved a plastic bottle of water in front of Seth's face. "Drink this. It's just water, honest."

Seth was having trouble holding the container, so Meg guided it to his mouth and held it while he drank. "Easy, Seth—not too much, or too fast. You have ice, Gabe?" She pulled the bottle away from Seth to slow him down; he was taking huge gulps.

"No. The refrigeration units were for the insects, but I never needed ice. You want to cool him down?"

"Yes, as fast as possible. Just fill a bucket or something and dump it over him," Meg said, watching Seth's face.

Gabe went back to a sink Meg hadn't noticed in the corner, stopping first to adjust the setting on the air conditioner
she had seen through the window. He pulled out a plastic
bucket from under the sink and filled it from the tap, then
hauled it back to where Seth sat. "Ready?"

"Go." Meg didn't move; getting wet was the least of her
worries.

Gabe raised the bucket and dumped it over Seth's head. He
jerked spasmodically, and for a moment Meg wondered if he
was going to have a seizure, but then he swiped a hand across
his face, wiping the water away. "Damn, that felt good."

Meg looked up at Gabe, waiting with the bucket.
"Again." She handed the plastic bottle back to Seth. "Here,
drink some more. Slowly." He complied, but she took it
away from him again before he'd drained it.

Gabe returned with another filled bucket and repeated
the process of drenching Seth, though gently.

Meg nodded, then stepped back. Now that she was wet,
too, the chilled air in the room was exaggerated, and she
shivered. But Seth was looking better, or at least taking in
his surroundings. She approached him again and laid her
hand on his neck: definitely cooler. He looked up at her,
then twisted around to look at Gabe. "Who's he?"

Gabe put down the bucket and came around to face
Seth. "I'm Gabe Aubuchon—I work at UMass, for Christopher Ramsdell. Meg knows me."

Seth looked confused, and this time Meg didn't think it
was due to dehydration. Gabe must have hit him from behind. She glanced at Gabe, silently asking permission to fill
Seth in. Gabe shrugged.

"Seth, Gabe does research on Asian longhorned beetles
at the university," Meg began. "I'm guessing he set up this

place so he could rear his own. He's the one who's been scattering them in the local forests. Have I got that right, Gabe?"

"Yeah, more or less."

"You're the guy who hit me?" Seth asked.

"Sorry about that. I panicked. I didn't want you to see what I was doing here. I didn't mean to hurt you, but I needed time to work out what to do. And I didn't know about the heatstroke thing, I swear. Guess it really doesn't matter anymore," he muttered.

Meg took stock. Seth was looking better, but she didn't think he'd be up to trekking the mile or so through the woods back to the road—yet. Maybe he'd have to eventually, but right now he needed some more time to stabilize. Gabe didn't seem to be a threat—even Max had relaxed on the floor, although he was keeping an eye on the least familiar person. Maybe it was time to get a few answers.

"Gabe, *why* were you planting bugs in the woods around here?" Meg asked.

He turned to her. "To save my job."

That was the last thing she expected to hear. "At the university? What's the problem?"

"Government funding. The government gives, and the government takes away. The university lab funding for ALB isn't in next year's budget, which makes me expendable."

"But isn't the Worcester project still going on?"

"Yes and no. That's a big deal—something like a hundred people, if you count all the inspectors and the office folk. Kind of a showcase for the state and the Feds. Thing is, they've done a good job—came in, sweet-talked the homeowners, cut down tens of thousands of trees—and it's more or less worked. There've been only a couple of new sightings there this year. Big success, right? Everybody's happy. So there's no pressure to keep up the research end of things, and they cut back on lab funding. Besides, USDA and their buddies have moved on to other, sexier critters."

Meg leaned against one of the counters and wrapped her arms around herself. She was actually getting chilled, which was an unusual sensation these days. Seth looked more alert, although he wasn't jumping into the conversation. "So, let me guess: you figured if there was another infestation, the program would be extended?"

"Right," Gabe said. "You know, it takes only one confirmed sighting to set the whole thing in motion? One damn bug, and everybody mobilizes. I figured they'd find the money someplace."

Meg debated telling him that the experts had tagged the Granford infestations as nonnatural, but she decided against it. She doubted that Christopher would have told anyone else. "Was that what you were doing at Nash's? Putting an insect where someone was bound to see it?"

"Yeah. I mean, I started putting the ALBs out two years ago, and so far nobody had noticed. I had to put it right under their noses, but then this logger guy comes along and asks me what I'm doing. He kinda caught me with my pants down. Plus he wasn't some curious hiker—he recognized what it was right away."

"Then what happened?" Seth said suddenly.

"I didn't hit the guy, if that's what you're asking. I'm sorry I had to hit you, man, but it was only to knock you out so I'd buy time. But that logger—I mean, maybe I took a step forward and he thought I might take a swing at him, but I swear, I never touched him! He tripped over a log, and fell backward and hit his head, and it was over, just like that."

"But then you hid the body," Meg prompted.

"Well, kind of. I know—that was dumb. I just dragged him out of sight. I figured somebody would find him soon enough, but I wanted somebody to find the beetle first, and I thought that if they found the body first it wouldn't happen."

"But that's more or less what happened," Meg said. "I saw the beetle and didn't think anything about it, but then I smelled the body, and when I found it and the authorities took over, the beetle got shoved aside and lost. If I hadn't mentioned it to Christopher by chance, and he hadn't told me that it might be important, nothing would have happened."

"I know, because he told me. I was going to go back and leave another one, or maybe I would have given it to Jonas Nash and told him I found it, but then I didn't have to, thanks to you."

Meg remained skeptical. Gabe's planning had been haphazard at best, except for the construction of the lab where they now sat. Was he telling the whole truth? Right now it didn't really matter, because Meg's primary mission was to win his help to get Seth out of there. They could sort out the rest later.

"If David Clapp's death really was an accident, you could have reported it, you know," Seth said. "No one would have pointed at you, if you'd said you just happened to find him."

"I realized that later. I wasn't thinking too straight. I freaked, okay? The whole thing was stupid."

Desperate people do desperate things, Meg thought— not that that excused Gabe's actions. She handed Seth the water bottle again. "Keep drinking, a little at a time. How're you feeling?"

"About ten percent better than the last time you asked me. Why'd you come looking for me?"

"Because I couldn't find you." Meg was startled to find herself near tears, and this was not the time for that. "Donald called this morning and wondered where you were. I tried all the obvious places, and you weren't at any of them. I called your mother to see if you'd mentioned any change of plans. I even talked to Sandy at town hall to see if you'd told her anything. And finally I called Art, who, by the way, is busy putting out fires all over Granford, and he happened to see your van off the road near here, and he called me and told me where to find it." And had it not been for that, Seth could have died. Meg shut her eyes, hoping to hold back the tears.

"So you came looking for me?" he said, with something like wonder in his voice.

"Well, I stopped at your house and saw that Max was there, outside, and I was pretty sure that you wouldn't have just gone off and left him like that in this heat, so I knew something had to be wrong, and I brought him home with me. And then I realized that he could help me find you. Which he did." Now she could feel the tears running down her face. Okay, maybe this whole thing wasn't over yet, but this was so, so much better than that awful gnawing uncertainty when Seth was nowhere to be found. She'd been right: he'd been in trouble, and she had been the only person who could do anything about it, and she had done it, and now at least they had a chance to get out of this. If Gabe helped.

"You two are together, huh?" Gabe interrupted. "I didn't realize that. Course, I didn't know him." Gabe nodded at

Seth. "He just showed up, nosing around, and all I could see was everything falling apart. Glad you aren't dead, man."

No thanks to you, Meg thought. She wasn't about to forgive him so easily. And he faced a world of trouble now— murder, or maybe manslaughter; kidnapping; and she couldn't even begin to put a name to whatever crime planting illegal insects might be. An act of terrorism? She wasn't even sure how many different authorities Gabe would face, but she was pretty sure it would be more than one. Still, he'd brought it all on himself, and she wasn't going to pity him.

She approached Seth and knelt in front of his chair again, reaching for his face. Definitely cooler, if not yet normal. This time he reached up to cover her hand with his own. "Thank you," he said softly.

"Did you really think no one would miss you?"

"I didn't think about it. But I'm glad it was you."

"Hey, guys, I hate to interrupt your lovefest, but I think we have a problem," Gabe said urgently.

Meg stood up and followed his gaze out the window. She'd been so focused on Seth that she hadn't noticed that outside the air had thickened with smoke, and as she watched, a single flaming spark drifted down, landing on the ground—and a tongue of fire sprang up immediately. Her eyes sought Gabe's. "We've got to move."

"You got that right. Which way's the fire?"

"Art said it's coming from the west—he was over by Route 202 when I talked to him."

Suddenly Gabe was all business. "Then we'd better move fast. Hey, you—Seth, is it?—can you walk out of here?"

"If I have to," Seth said grimly. Meg was not reassured.

"Okay, then everybody take water," she said with more authority than she felt. "We'll soak our clothes now, just in case. I'll soak Max, too. Find something to cover your mouth. The smoke will get us before the fire does. Is that lane back to the road the only way out of here?"

"It's the fastest," Gabe said.

"Let me check and see what's happening." Meg pulled out her phone and hit Redial. This time it took longer for Art to pick up.

"Meg? What's the story? How's Seth?"

"Better, but it looks like the fire's heading this way, so we're going to try to walk out."

"You're right about the fire. You'll be cutting it pretty close. Can he make it?"

"I don't know," Meg said, "but I don't see a lot of choice. This building is old, and it'll go up fast. Can you get someone to meet us back at the van?"

"I'll do my best. You want EMTs?"

"I think so."

"Good luck, Meg. Tell Seth to get his sorry ass out of there."

"Will do." Meg turned back to Seth. "Art says to get your sorry ass moving."

"I'm on it." He stood up and wavered again. He was in no shape to trek through a burning forest—but as she'd told Art, they had no choice.

"Then drink up, wet down, and let's get moving," Meg said firmly.

27

Once they were all thoroughly wet, and carrying plastic bottles of water, Meg helped Seth to the door. Max kept winding anxiously around their legs, which didn't help Seth's stability.

When Gabe pulled open the door, however, Meg knew they were in trouble. The air was brownish, and there were now a number of little flickering patches of fire. Max cringed, torn between sticking with Seth and hiding from the strangely altered world outside. "Come on," Gabe said, leading the way. Meg and Seth followed more slowly, and Max chose to stay with him.

It was beginning to get dark out, the evening dimness compounded by the smoke. At least the path was clear before them. Gabe was standing some ten feet away, bouncing impatiently. "Move! This brush is going to go up fast, any minute now," he said.

Meg draped Seth's arm over her shoulders and wrapped her own around his waist. "We can do this," she said. To him or to herself?

He looked down at her and nodded. "Meg . . . you can go ahead."

"You idiot, this is not the time to get all noble on me. Let's just go!"

Their faces shielded by damp cloths—which didn't stay damp very long—they began a hellish march back toward the road. All Meg could think was that they were too slow. She kept her mind busy by trying to calculate rates and distances. Say it was a mile. Say a normal walking pace was maybe four miles an hour. Their pace was nowhere near normal—more like two miles an hour. At that rate it would take half an hour to reach the road and the cars. Was the fire going to wait that long?

It looked like the answer was no. Meg could hear the fire now. She had no way of gauging how far they'd come, but evidently it wasn't far enough. Gabe stopped and took a critical look at them, then came back and said, "Look, let me take him—we'll move faster."

Meg hesitated, but Gabe had to be stronger than she was. She unloaded Seth, then looked around for Max—Seth would never forgive her if she lost him. Unless, of course, they all ended up dead, but then it wouldn't matter, would it? She swallowed a sob. Luckily Max was still sticking close to Seth, so she grabbed his collar and reattached the leash she had stuffed in her pocket. Gabe had already moved down the lane with Seth, and she hurried to catch up. At least now they were moving faster.

Behind her she heard what sounded like an explosion. "What was that?" she gasped.

"Probably a compressor on one of the fridges. Doesn't matter," Gabe replied. "Keep moving."

Max was getting increasingly anxious, tugging on his lead, and Meg had trouble keeping her grip on him. Would this blasted forest never end? It was definitely getting dark now, although the darkness was punctuated with glowing orange patches of moving flame. There was a stir of wind, bringing hotter air with it, and it was getting harder to breathe.

Gabe stopped, and Meg nearly bumped into him. "We should drink now, right?"

"Yes, and pour the rest over us," Meg said, coughing. "If we don't get out soon, it won't matter that the water's gone." Gabe parked Seth against a tree and opened up his own water bottle and drank half of it down, then poured the rest over his head. Meg followed suit.

Seth's eyes were closed, and his breathing was labored— but then, so was hers. She opened his bottle and shoved it at him. "Drink. Now."

He opened his eyes, then raised a shaky hand to take it. "Meg . . ."

"Don't you dare start again. We're going to get out of here. Drink."

He gave her what might be a faint smile and did. She opened her bottle and drenched him with what was left. Not enough.

"Homestretch," Meg said.

Gabe hauled Seth upright again. "Not far now. Looks like there's a welcoming committee."

Meg looked down the lane. At first she couldn't see anything different, and then she realized that some of the flickering lights were not the orange of fire, but rather red and blue—police, emergency services, it didn't matter. It was hard to tell how far away they were, but they were definitely there. Art had come through for them. "Let's go."

The next stretch seemed to take forever. Meg kept glancing between the flashing lights—they were getting closer, weren't they?—and Gabe and Seth. She stumbled over tree roots and her own feet and tried to keep Max from toppling her. Finally, she saw a break in the tree line ahead, and the road beyond, thick with emergency vehicles. She didn't see her car or Seth's van, but maybe some intelligent officer had moved them out of harm's way. All they needed now was to lose their vehicles to a fire—the insurance costs would go through the roof.

Irrelevant, Meg! Her mind was drifting, until Gabe stopped abruptly and took in the gathered forces at the end of the lane. He turned back to her and thrust Seth into her arms. "You take him the rest of the way."

"But, wait . . ." she protested, trying to keep Seth standing—he wasn't helping much, and when had he gotten so heavy?

Gabe faced her squarely. "I can't go through all that. I'm sorry." He turned away and headed back the way they had come, leaving Meg with mouth agape.

Seth sagged against her. She hitched his arm over her shoulder again. "Come on, we're almost there. If you give up now, I'll never forgive you."

If he heard, he didn't say anything, but somehow she and Seth and Max managed to bumble their way forward until they could make out figures moving through the smoke-haze. Art Preston emerged from the murk.

"Jeez, you two took your sweet time. Chapin, you do the damndest things to get attention." Art's words were humorous, but he looked worried. "I'll take him to the EMTs," he said to Meg.

Relieved of the burden of Seth, Meg felt suddenly lighter, and she had to catch herself from falling when Max pulled her forward, eager to stay with Seth. She managed to hang on to him and followed Art to the road, where the Granford ambulance was waiting, along with a couple of police cruisers and two fire trucks.

Art handed Seth off to a pair of EMTs, and Meg followed. "What's the story?" one of them asked.

"Heatstroke. I got him cooled down and got some water into him, but then we had to walk out."

They went into what looked like a well-rehearsed dance, checking vital signs. Seth was conscious, but he sat, dazed, on the back of the ambulance. "Seth Chapin, right?" one of the EMTs asked. Seth nodded. "We need to get you to the hospital, get your electrolytes stabilized."

"No," he said. "No hospital." Seth was looking at Meg.

"Seth, don't be stupid. Let them do whatever it takes," Meg said.

"I'm okay, Meg, really. I'd go if I wasn't."

Meg looked at the med techs, then took one aside. "Can he do this?"

The tech shrugged. "Probably. Keep pushing liquids and keep him down for a while. Can you handle that?"

After what she had just done, that would be a walk in the park. "No problem."

When she got back to the ambulance, the other tech had already set up an IV drip in Seth's arm, with a bag of clear fluid suspended above him. She sat down next to him and took his other hand.

Art materialized in front of them. "You two had us worried. Seth, what the hell happened?"

Meg spoke before Seth could answer. "Art, can it wait until morning? Right now I know I'm exhausted, and I can't imagine how Seth must be feeling. We'll both be a lot more coherent tomorrow. Come by for breakfast—say, eight." *Why didn't you mention Gabe, Meg? Do you want him to escape?* She was surprised to realize that maybe she did. She wasn't about to judge what had happened with David Clapp, but she knew that without Gabe's help, she and Seth would probably be dead. For that she was willing to give him a chance, however slim.

Art gave her a searching look, but in the end he nodded. "Fair enough. It's not like I don't have enough to keep me busy."

"How're the fires going?"

"Most have burned out—this is the last patch. No homes damaged, thank God. It's been a hell of a day."

"Tell me about it," Meg said.

"I'll see you in the morning, then. Take care of him, will you?" Art nodded toward Seth.

"I plan to," Meg said, and watched Art walk away.

Seth spoke suddenly in her ear. "You didn't tell him about . . ."

She turned to him and said in a low voice, so the EMTs couldn't hear, "Gabe? I wanted time to think about what happened here. Gabe told me some things . . . I don't think he was a bad person, but he got caught up . . . I just want to get my head clear before I tell the authorities anything. And talk to you about it, and now is definitely not the time for that."

"What, I'm not my usual levelheaded self?" he said with a more authentic smile.

"Not exactly. But you're here." Meg couldn't think of anything more to say, so she just leaned against him, and Max settled himself at their feet. They sat like that for a while, until the fire crew declared the last fire under control and all but one of the trucks departed.

Art came back one last time. "We shifted your vehicles in case the fire came this way—they're down the road a bit. Meg, why don't you take Seth's van, and I'll get someone to bring your car back?"

"Thanks, Art. For everything."

"Just doin' my job, ma'am. Although I may have to add a few things to that official job description. See you in the morning."

The EMTs took a whole new batch of readings, then unhooked Seth from his IV. One of them said, "I won't say I approve, but I think you're good to go. Here—take a couple of these, and make sure you drink them tonight."

Meg looked at the bottles that he held out. "Gatorade?"

"It's got electrolytes—it'll do the job."

Seth stood up, and he seemed steadier than before, Meg noted. "Thanks, guys. Good job."

"You still have your keys?" Meg asked. "No way I'm letting you drive."

"No argument." He fished a key ring out of his pocket and handed it to her.

They found their vehicles down the road, as promised. Meg let Max in the back of the van, and Seth climbed into the passenger seat, sat back, and closed his eyes. Meg started the van and drove cautiously home, fighting a sense of unreality. What had happened today? She'd told Art that she didn't want to talk about it until she'd had time to think—but there was a lot to think about, and it was going to take time

to process. Tomorrow morning might not be time enough,
but they had to start somewhere. And she had a feeling that
she needed to include Christopher in the conversation.

But there were still things to do. She pulled into her
driveway and parked the van as close as she could get to the
kitchen door. She nudged Seth. "We're home." Even as she
said it, she realized she had never stopped to question what
he had meant by "home." She'd come straight here.

He opened his eyes and smiled. "I know." She climbed
down and came around to help him out on his side, but he
seemed steady enough and managed the steps into the
house. Bree was sitting at the kitchen table. She took one
look at them and said, "What the hell?"

"I'll explain, but first could you get Max out of the van?
Oh, and there're some bottles of Gatorade on the floor in
front—bring those in, too, please."

"Right," she said dubiously, but she went out the back
door.

Meg stood in the midst of her brightly lit kitchen, leaning against Seth. Or was he leaning against her? It didn't
matter much. They were alive, and they were safe. That was
what mattered. It took her half a minute to say, "You need
to lie down and drink that stuff."

He nodded. "Can I get a shower in?"

"I think that would be okay. But I'd better be there in
case you feel weak. Wouldn't want you to pass out and fall
down now, would we?" They leaned together for a few
more seconds. "Are you hungry?"

"Nope."

Bree returned, Max in tow. "I let him do his business.
You said something about an explanation?"

"I think that's going to have to wait until tomorrow

morning. By the way, Art's coming by for breakfast. Hand me those bottles, will you?"

With a puzzled expression, Bree handed over the bottles.

"We're going upstairs. See you in the morning."

The stairs seemed endless, and Meg was beginning to feel each and every muscle. And here she'd been thinking she was in pretty good shape. She guided Seth toward the bathroom and sat him down on the commode. When she caught a glimpse of herself in the mirror she nearly burst out laughing: Bree had shown admirable restraint, because between the sweat, soot, and, yes, even a few small burns from cinders that she hadn't even felt, Meg looked like she'd been through a war. Seth looked worse.

She handed him a bottle. "Here, drink this. Then shower." When Seth had drained the bottle, she had to help him out of his boots and unbutton his shirt, and somehow together they managed to get him undressed and under the tepid shower. She leaned against the wall, her eyes shut.

"God, that felt good," he said afterward, finally drying himself off.

Meg laid her hands on his chest—his temperature felt almost normal. He wrapped his arms around her and pulled her close, and she found she was fighting off sobs.

"Are you crying?" Seth said into her hair.

"I don't know. Maybe. Probably. Oh, Seth, I was so scared, and I couldn't even admit it to myself, because then I couldn't have done anything at all, and I knew I had to do something . . ." She was babbling against his wet neck.

"Shh, shh . . ." he murmured.

She fell silent. Who was comforting whom here? And did it really matter? Somehow they'd survived, and here they were.

"Can you make it to the bedroom?" she said finally.

"I think I can handle that."

"Then go. I need a shower."

By the time Meg was clean and dry, Seth was sound asleep, and Max was lying on the floor keeping an eye on him. She lay down next to Seth and was out.

28

Meg woke at first light and hovered in that lovely place between asleep and awake. Could she sneak in a little more sleep, if she didn't open her eyes?

And then reality came slamming in, as she recalled all that had happened the day before. Her eyes flew open and sought the clock—six thirty. It seemed dark for that hour. She rolled over to find Seth awake and watching her, and she reached out to touch his face.

"How're you feeling?"

"Tired. Sad, too, I guess."

"I know what you mean. What a mess. You should call your mother. I don't think I alarmed her, but just in case, it would be good to touch base." He was still watching her. "What is it?"

"Meg, marry me."

For a few long seconds she couldn't say a word, a

kaleidoscope of emotions whirling through her. And then she found her voice. "Yes. *Yes!* Of course. Wait—is this because of what happened yesterday?"

"You mean when I almost died? In part, I guess. I did have some time to think, before things got woozy, and I knew that if I didn't make it out of there, the thing I'd regret most was not telling you how I felt. I love you. I want you. I want to share your life. I want to be part of it every day, not just when we happen to have the time."

"Oh, Seth," Meg said helplessly. She laid her head on his shoulder. "I was so terrified when I couldn't find you yesterday, and it made me realize how much a part of my life you are now. I can't imagine living here without you. And I want the whole package, including kids."

"Me too. It's not a deal-breaker, but I'm glad you feel that way."

They smiled gleefully at each other. Suddenly Meg heard a noise and stilled: she'd realized why it seemed so dark. "Seth," she said, in a hushed whisper, "I think it's raining!"

He raised his head to listen. "I think you're right. That's good, isn't it?"

"That's very good. Definitely."

It was close to an hour later when they managed to get down the stairs, where they found Bree in the kitchen.

"It's raining, right?" Meg asked cheerfully. "I mean, it's been so long since I've seen rain, maybe I don't remember what it looks like."

"Yes, ma'am, that is rain. I would have told you about the forecast last night, but you two seemed a little, uh, preoccupied. You gonna fill me in?"

"Of course, but I want to say it only once, and Art should be here soon, and I want to call Christopher."

Bree looked bewildered. "Why?"

"You'll see when we explain—it's complicated. Can you make a fresh batch of coffee while I make that call? And, Seth, can you see if we have anything that resembles breakfast?"

"Of course."

Meg found her cell phone and went into the dining room. At this early hour Christopher should still be at home.

He answered quickly, sounding chipper. "Meg, my dear, to what do I owe the honor of this early call?"

"I'm sorry to bother you so early, but there's something important that we need to discuss in person. Could you possibly come over here?"

"You mean, right now?"

"Yes, and Art Preston will be here, too, if that tells you anything. Again, I apologize for the abruptness of this, but you'll understand soon enough."

"Give me half an hour."

Back in the kitchen Meg announced, "Christopher will be here in half an hour. Have you talked to Art this morning, Seth?"

"Not yet," he said, mixing what looked like a coffee cake batter.

She came up behind him and hugged him. "Afraid of what we might hear?" she asked softly.

"About Gabe, you mean?" He kept stirring. "Maybe. But I don't want to face bad news on an empty stomach."

"Hey, you guys, you're creeping me out," Bree said. "What'd I miss?"

"A lot. Be patient." Meg's landline rang, saving her the need to answer Bree's question. She wasn't surprised to see Lydia's number. "Morning, Lydia."

"Have you seen Seth?" Lydia said immediately.

"Yes. He's right here—I'll put him on." She held out the phone to Seth, mouthing "your mother."

He took the phone from her. "Hey, Mom. Sorry about yesterday—Meg told me she called you. Hope you didn't worry. I was moving around a lot, but Meg and I connected late in the afternoon. I forgot to call you." He paused. "Yes, everything's fine—couldn't be better. Maybe we can get together later today?" Another pause. "Sure, great. Call you later." He handed the phone back to Meg and resumed mixing.

Bree was watching them both with something like amusement. "Uh, you know, guys, you didn't look exactly 'fine'"—she made air quotes—"when you stumbled in and crashed last night. Although I gotta say, you're looking a lot more fine this morning."

"Oh, we are," Meg said. "Definitely fine. Seth, you want me to grease the pan? And you did turn on the oven, didn't you?"

"Done and done. Don't worry. Time?"

"Quarter to eight. Art should be here any minute, right?"

"Come on, you guys—what do you need Art for?" Bree protested. "Does it have to do with that dead guy you found?"

"That's where it started, but there's a lot more. Just hang in there a little longer. At least there'll be breakfast. So, tell me, what will this rain change?"

Bree gave Meg a disgusted look at her abrupt change of

topic. "Depends on how long it lasts. Obviously longer is better. But the forecast says this is the real deal, not just a passing shower. I'll have to keep an eye on the soil saturation numbers, and watch the water level in the well, but I think we can take a breather, for at least a few days. Oh, Seth—that pal of yours, Donald what's-his-name, called at least three times yesterday. I stopped answering after the second call. But for the record, I have now passed the messages on to you—you deal with him."

"I will." Seth slid the pan into the oven and set the timer.

Meg reached past him to refill her coffee cup and somehow ended up in Seth's arms, which was fine with her. "It'll work out—you'll see," he said quietly.

"I hope so. We haven't had time to talk about any of this. How much do we tell them?"

"I think we have to lay it all out and then figure out what to do. I trust Art—let him decide what he passes on. And I have a feeling Christopher may have additional information we need. Let's just play it by ear."

"I'm not going to lie to either of them. I only wondered if maybe we should kind of omit a few details." Funny, she was still in his arms. It felt good.

Bree's voice interrupted their quiet exchange. "Guys, I'd tell you to get a room, but I think you already have one. Is there something I need to know?"

Meg looked at Seth before answering. "Yes. We're getting married."

"Well, congratulations! It's about time you two got it together. Everybody's been expecting it."

A knock at the back door announced Art's arrival, effectively shutting down Bree's commentary. And he came in carrying a box of donuts, which Bree seized from him. "You're welcome," Art said, as she dove into the box.

"These guys cook too slowly. I'm a growing girl," she said around a mouthful of glazed donut.

Art turned to take a closer look at Meg and Seth. "You two look a couple of hundred percent better than you did yesterday, not that that would be hard. You feeling all right, Seth? Because last night you looked like . . . well, I won't try to describe it with tender young ears listening."

Bree snorted.

"I'm good," Seth said, "thanks to you. And Meg, of course. But I'll admit it was a close thing."

"It was," Art agreed. "As for my end, the fires are out, and this rain is a big help—I don't think they'll pop up again. I was getting a bit worried at the end of the day—we were stretched pretty thin. Sorry I couldn't do more to track you down."

"You did enough, and Meg did the rest. Uh, about that property where you picked us up—did you happen to find anything, or anyone?"

Bree looked up when she heard Seth's question but kept quiet. Art said, "No, but once we got the fire out it was full night and nobody felt like hanging around. Why?"

Seth glanced at Meg. "I think we have to tell this story in the right order. Let's wait for Christopher."

Now Art looked perplexed. "Christopher? Why is he coming?"

"You'll see, Art," Meg answered. "Coffee?"

"Well, if you're going to clam up about whatever this big mystery is, maybe there's something else you want to tell Art?" Bree challenged.

"If I tell Art before I tell Mom, she'll disown me," Seth said.

"So I should save my congratulations?" Art said, smiling.

"Told you so," Bree said. "They're the last to know, right, Chief?"

The timer went off just as Christopher rapped at the screen door. Bree went to let him in while Seth extricated the coffee cake from the oven. Meg placed the full coffee carafe and mugs in the center of the kitchen table. How odd this all felt, she thought: refreshments for a discussion about murder and more than one kind of mayhem. Granford was not the peaceful little town she had once thought it was.

Once everyone was settled around the table and supplied with food, Meg realized she didn't know where to start. She looked at Seth, sitting next to her. "Do we begin at the beginning, or the other way around?" she asked.

"I think we need to lay out some ground rules first. Art, we're going to be talking about more than one crime here, but I'm not sure what they all are or who's supposed to have jurisdiction. I know it's a lot to ask, but can you listen as a friend rather than a police officer?"

Art gave Seth a long look. "I think so. As long as you aren't asking me to do anything illegal."

"I hope it doesn't come to that. But there are some rather gray areas in all this. You'll see."

"Excuse me for interrupting," Christopher said, "but I'm not quite sure why you asked me to be here. How is it that I am involved?"

"Again, you'll see. Meg, maybe you should start."

Meg took a deep breath. "As you all know, two weeks ago I found the body of David Clapp on Jonas Nash's land.

And I also found a dead Asian longhorned beetle at the same time."

"And you have determined that these two events are linked?" Christopher asked.

"They are, and through someone you know: Gabe Aubuchon."

29

Christopher was clearly startled. "Gabe, from the rearing lab?"

"Yes, that Gabe," Meg said. "Christopher, you told me that the state agency thought there was something unusual about the distribution of the insects they found in Granford?"

Art looked blank. "What are you talking about?"

Christopher explained how the state agencies had noticed the local beetle infestations seemed too consistent to be natural. "It was suggested, albeit cautiously, that somehow the insects had been planted in several places at the same time."

"What the heck does that mean?" Art demanded. "Is it illegal?"

"It is, although under what laws is something that has not been tested, as far as I know. I've heard of one case in which a commercial nursery knowingly shipped infested trees beyond the quarantine area, and they were prosecuted and fined. They could find no example of an individual acting independently to perpetrate such a thing." Christopher turned back to Meg. "My dear, are you saying that Gabe Aubuchon is behind this? How do you know?"

Meg looked at Seth, who took her hand. "Do you want to tell this part?"

"I'll do it. I'll admit I wasn't paying much attention to the science side," Seth said. "All I knew was that an invasive pest had been found in Granford, and suddenly I had all these government agencies showing up and demanding things from the town. I recognize that there are official protocols to follow, though, and the state agency asked me to act on behalf of the town to keep the public informed. It's my understanding that they're going to have to cut down a lot of trees, particularly maples, on our public land, which will affect our recreational areas, but there's not much we can do about it."

"Hey, Seth, could we move this along?" Art asked. "I've got a job to go to, and there's follow-up to all the fires. Do you know what happened to Clapp?"

"I'm getting there. At the same time, Sandy at town hall had pointed out that there was an unusual power drain over the past year or two—more than a simple household would account for. It turned out to be an old line running to an abandoned house on the north end of town, which was suddenly drawing power. I decided to stop by and check it out, on my way to a job site, yesterday morning. That's why my van was parked up there, Art."

"And then you went missing for the rest of the day," Art said, "and Meg called me, and I told her when I saw the van, and the next thing I know, the two of you come stumbling out from the middle of a forest fire. What the hell happened?"

Meg looked at the people around the table, who were all watching her. "I can tell you what happened, and there are some things that are clearly illegal, but there may be more to it. Can you reserve judgment until you know the whole story? And can we keep this information in this room until we've all had time to consider?"

"You mean me, as a law enforcement officer, I assume," Art said. "You know I can't make any promises, but I'm listening."

"Just hear me out first. Yesterday afternoon when I went looking for Seth, I took Max along. I found the van where you told me it would be, and then Max led me into the woods for a mile or so, where we came across that old house Seth mentioned. It was clear that somebody had been using it. Anyway, Max led me around the house to a kind of shed attached to the side of the house. It was locked, so I had to bash the lock off, and that's where I found Seth trussed up with duct tape."

She had to swallow hard, as the memory of that awful moment came back with full force. Seth's hand tightened on hers. "I . . . thought he was dead, for a moment. Obviously he wasn't, but he was way too hot and kind of disoriented, and I knew he was in trouble. You do the math—he'd been stuck in there all day, and the temperature had to be over a hundred. That's when I called you again, Art."

"Right, and you asked about heatstroke."

Meg nodded. "And you told me I needed to find water and get him cooled off, so I went looking around the building, but it was locked. I could see equipment and stuff inside, and an air conditioner. I was getting ready to break into the house when Gabe Aubuchon appeared." When Art started to say something, Meg held up a hand to stop him. "At first I thought maybe he was just wandering through the woods looking for more insect sites, but he made it pretty clear that he was the one who'd been using the place."

"Whatever for?" Christopher exclaimed.

Now Art looked angry. "What're you saying, Meg? Did this guy Aubuchon kidnap and lock Seth up to die? Seth, what do you know?"

"Not much, Art. Like I said, I followed the electric line in and I found the house, and then there's a big blank. I don't remember anything until I kind of came to inside the house, with the two of them dumping water over me and shoving water bottles in my face, and then we had to get out of there because the fire was getting close."

"Great witness you make," Art muttered. He turned back to Meg. "So what happened?"

Meg faced him squarely. "Art, right then Gabe had a choice. He could have overpowered me quite easily and locked us both up to die. He could have walked away and disappeared, and I don't know if I could have gotten Seth out of there on my own. Instead, he helped us. Gabe let us into the building, we got Seth cooled off enough to function, more or less, and then when we saw how close the fire was, Gabe more or less carried him out, back to the road. Seth could very well have died without Gabe's help."

Everyone fell silent for a moment. Then Art said slowly, "I never saw anyone else—just you and Seth, when you came through the smoke. There could have been an army back there, and I wouldn't have known. What did Aubuchon do?"

"When we got close enough to the road to see that you all were there, he said 'sorry' then turned and disappeared into the woods."

"Why don't you two ever make things easy?" Art leaned back in his chair and stared at the ceiling. "So right up front you've got Aubuchon committing kidnapping and assault, and maybe attempted murder. Seth, how do you feel about that?"

"I . . . don't know. I don't remember a whole lot. If he did all that, I'm angry, of course, but in the end he got us out of there. Meg's right—I couldn't have made it without his help."

Art turned to Meg. "You said David Clapp's death was connected. How?"

"Gabe told me it was an accident. The guy found him planting a bug on Nash's land where someone was sure to find it and confronted him, but somehow he tripped and hit his head—at least, that's what Gabe said happened. You'd know more about the cause of death than we do. Gabe did admit to concealing the body because he wanted the bug found first, but he said he didn't kill him."

"Okay, we'll keep that one on the back burner. What about this whole bug-planting scheme? Is that illegal? Christopher, can you help us out with that?"

Christopher was clearly troubled. "Oh dear—what a mess. Perhaps I should go back a bit and fill in the background, which may help you understand. Gabe Aubuchon was hired to work in the insect-rearing facility at the university, the one you visited, Meg."

Meg nodded. "Yes, and it was Gabe who gave me the tour. I recognized some of the same equipment at the old house, although on a much smaller scale."

"Gabe appeared to be a bright and personable young man. His academic record was not stellar, but he made up for that in enthusiasm and dedication. As I worked with him, I learned that he had overcome considerable obstacles to attend college at all—he came from a very small town up near the Canadian border, and he was the first in his family to do so. It was a financial hardship for him, but he scraped by. He truly wished to improve himself, and he was a model employee. Very thorough and conscientious. He always covered the lab on weekends—insects need to be fed no matter what the calendar says, and data collected. He never complained. Nor did he ever mention anything about his life outside the lab—I'm not sure he had any other interests, or any personal relationships.

"But then the government announced it planned to cut the funding for that particular project, and there were no other openings under my purview. I would have been happy to give him an outstanding recommendation, but he seemed particularly upset about leaving the university."

"Christopher," Meg said, "he admitted to spreading the insects, but he told me it was to save his job."

Christopher stared into space for a moment. "Then I would surmise that he believed that by creating more infested sites here, the government would be persuaded to extend the project."

"Hey, guys, this is way out of my league," Art protested. "You're saying he grew his own bugs out there in the woods and turned 'em loose in the forest, so official people would think there was more work to be done and he'd get to keep his job?"

"In a nutshell," Meg replied.

"He was a skilled technician, so he would have had no

trouble rearing them himself. Obtaining the live insects would be difficult for most people, since they are carefully controlled, but I would guess he took enough from the lab to start his own colony," said Christopher. "I don't believe he removed any significant numbers from the lab, nor did he help himself to any equipment."

"But you'd guess he stole at least a few from the lab?" Art asked.

"Yes, which would also be a crime, of some sort. I can't even tell you if it's a federal or a state issue. They are kept under strict quarantine. But it would not have taken many to establish his first colony. Still, I wonder—" Christopher paused. "None of the infestations discovered were very large, but reports suggested that they started at least two years ago."

"So Gabe was planning ahead? He saw the writing on the wall that far in advance?"

"Perhaps. He knew when I hired him that his position was not a permanent one, but he must have harbored hope that it would be extended. When that looked unlikely, apparently he took action to ensure it."

The assembled group digested that information for a moment.

"Well, before we do anything else, we've got to find the guy," Art said grimly. "Meg, you said he was on foot when you first saw him?"

"That's right. I didn't hear any vehicle, but I wasn't exactly paying attention."

"What was in that building?"

She was beginning to see what he was getting at. "A lot of equipment—including a couple of fairly good-sized refrigerators, and that air conditioner. More than he could have carried in by hand. So it's likely there's another access road?"

"Probably. We'll look. As of this moment, we don't know whether Aubuchon made a clean getaway in an unknown vehicle, or on foot, or didn't get away at all."

"Who's going to go looking?" Bree said, speaking for the first time. "You? The staties? The Feds? Heck, what about Homeland Security? Terrorism by bug?"

"Good question, Bree," Art replied, "and I don't have an answer. Not yet, anyway. I'd bet it's going to be a real dogfight if all the interested parties start arguing about who gets to go first."

"What about Detective Marcus, Art?" Meg asked. "What are you going to tell him?"

"About Clapp's death? I don't know. Marcus's office has already written this off as an accident, and you've given me no new evidence to override that. Maybe Gabe made some kind of confession to you, but the facts haven't changed. As for the bug thing, our scenario is based largely on guesswork, and it would be hard to prove—or maybe harder to convince government authorities."

Art turned to Seth. "Seth, you're the one with the greatest personal stake in this, at least for yesterday's events. Do you want to press charges?"

"I'm not really sure. Yes, technically he kidnapped me, or at least restrained me against my will. I don't know if he meant to kill me—he just overreacted when I showed up unexpectedly. Maybe he was coming back to let me go— we don't know. But he did end up helping Meg and me in the end, so I'd say that's a wash."

"Will the lab suffer, Christopher?" Meg asked.

"Oh dear, I hadn't even thought of that," he said. "It will

not reflect well upon our quarantine procedures, although no one could expect us to keep a head count of our insects. Theft has never been a consideration."

"Let me see if I've got this right," Meg said. "David Clapp's death—it's already on the books as a likely accident in the eyes of the state police. Seth's kidnapping—he and I are the only witnesses. Art, you and the fire crews saw only the two of us. If we say nothing, there is no crime. And he saved our lives. As for the bug-planting? Christopher, can that be proved?"

"I'm afraid not. Either way, the official eradication process has already begun. The authorities aren't as concerned about the source as they are about stopping the spread."

Meg pressed on. "So it's possible that none of these events will be acknowledged as crimes? And nobody would go hunting for Gabe Aubuchon?"

"It's possible, but I'm not sure it's legal, Meg," Art said.

"I know, Art. I just wanted to get it out on the table."

"So what happens next?" Bree asked. "I mean, doesn't somebody have to do *something*?"

Art stood up. "I have to get to work. In answer to your question, Bree, I want to take some time to think about this, and all the possible outcomes. And you all think about your positions, too. We'll talk again tonight. I think this'll keep that long. If Aubuchon is lying somewhere in the burnt-out part of the forest, he's not going anywhere. If he's on the run, he's long gone."

And Gabe will be a day farther away, if he's running, Meg added to herself.

Seth stood up as well. "I'll walk you out. I'd like to remind myself what rain feels like."

The two men went out the back door, leaving Meg, Bree, and Christopher sitting around the table.

"Boy, you sure know how to find messes, Meg," Bree said. "You might have mentioned that you almost died yesterday. This is not a good time to go job hunting."

"I was a little preoccupied. Thank you for your concern, though—I'm touched."

"Sorry," Bree said, contrite. "You know I don't mean it, right?"

"I do." Meg summoned up a smile. "And I was never really at risk. Seth was. I don't know if I can forgive Gabe for that, even though he came through in the end. I don't suppose he's a bad person at heart, but he didn't consider the consequences of his actions."

"I am so sorry, Meg," Christopher said. "I never suspected."

"Why should you?" Meg asked. "He seemed like a nice person. Shows us how little we know about other people. But I suppose in some backhanded way I ought to thank Gabe, because he finally forced me to realize how important Seth is to me. If I'd lost Seth . . ." She couldn't finish that thought. "He asked me to marry him, this morning. And I said yes."

Christopher beamed. "That, my dear, is wonderful news, although I won't say I'm surprised." He laid his hand over hers. "Don't dwell on what might have been. It didn't happen. I'd like to comfort myself with the notion that Gabe tried to do the right thing in the end, else you and Seth might not be here now. I think we all need time to come to terms with these events." He glanced at his watch. "My word, I have an appointment with the contractor for the new building, so I must go. We'll talk later today."

He too went out the back door, and Meg noticed that he didn't bother with an umbrella. Nor had Art or Seth. But she understood: this rain was very welcome, and getting wet was a happy change. Meg watched as Christopher stopped for a moment to talk with Art and Seth, then returned to his car and pulled out, followed quickly by Art. Seth waved them off, then came back. Inside the door he wrapped his arms around Meg and they just stood there. Meg relished the feeling of his rain-wet, now cool body against hers. If things had turned out differently . . . no, she wasn't going to go there.

"Yo, guys, I'm still in the room. Want me to leave?" Bree called out.

Reluctantly Meg peeled herself away from Seth. "No, not just yet. Is there anything we have to do today? I mean, in the orchard?"

"You mean, something less than life or death? Actually I think we've all earned a day off, and it looks like the rain will keep up for the rest of the day. You two can go do, uh, whatever."

They went.

30

They made it upstairs, but the events of the past few days had clearly taken a toll, and sleep trumped romance. As she drifted off, Meg relished the rare feeling that there was nothing she had to do right that minute, and that a lot of problems had somehow resolved themselves, or at least crept closer to resolution, and she was exactly where she wanted to be . . . She slept, with Seth's arm around her.

It was a few hours later when she woke up again. It was still raining, a nice, steady rain. She could imagine her apples sucking it in and swelling by the moment. Not too fast, she hoped, or they would split. But that was beyond her control, and lots of rain was better than no rain.

Was she ready to work through the whole Gabe situation in her mind? Art and Christopher had something to lose, whether it was their legal standing or their professional reputation. What would they choose to do? Or maybe more important for all of them, what was the *right* thing to do? Not the correct legal thing, but the moral human thing? That was trickier. She kind of hoped that her own answer would become clear to her, but it hadn't yet.

She'd rather think of happier things, like Seth, warm and solid next to her. Seth wanted to marry her. They'd been drifting in that direction for a while now, but putting it in words took it to a whole other level. He'd been letting her find her own way, she knew. It wasn't that she'd been reluctant to commit to him; she'd just had so much on her plate since they'd met. To her, marriage wasn't something you just did because it was convenient and you had a little spare time. If she was going to get married, she wanted to *stay* married, for the long haul. There was nobody else she could imagine marrying, and there never had been. Seth was pretty close to Mr. Perfect, apart from his tendency to think of everybody and anybody else before himself. Should she make it her project to make him more selfish? Interesting idea, but probably hopeless.

He wanted children; he'd been up-front about that. She had always tabled that discussion in her own mind, too, mainly because there had been no one in her life that she could imagine having children with. She wasn't the type of woman who would have a baby on her own, although she had to admire the women who did—the ones who knew their own minds and just went for it, despite all the challenges. But having children with Seth? That was a whole different matter. She'd seen him with Rachel's kids and he was great—sincerely engaged with them, not just going through the motions. For the first time, she could visualize a fuller life for herself, with Seth, with a family, with work that she loved, with a place in the community . . .

As if reading her mind, Seth stirred and pulled her closer. "You're thinking again."

"Hey, at least now I'm thinking about *you*."

"That's progress. Bree said you could play hooky today, right?"

"She did. Do you think she approves?"

"Of us? Mushy, romantic Bree? Got me. Does it matter?"

"Not really, but it helps if I'm going to keep working with her—I don't want you two sniping at each other over who gets more of my time and attention."

"We can share." Another warm, fuzzy interval followed.

"We should go talk to your mother," Meg finally said. "She'll be happy, won't she?"

"Of course she will. She likes you. You like her, right?"

"I do. She's got her head on straight." In spite of Lydia's own less-than-perfect marriage, Meg reminded herself. But Seth wasn't his father, and he'd emerged from that troubled household a good man. "Should we ask her over for dinner? She's home today, right? I have a vague recollection that this is Saturday."

"I think so. Your call, as long as we do it together. I'm surprised Donald hasn't called this morning."

"It's Saturday!" Meg protested.

"That doesn't seem to matter to Donald. Especially since as far as he's concerned, I skipped work yesterday."

"Maybe Bree turned the phone off. Have you checked yours lately?"

"Battery's dead."

"Ah, blessed peace." Suddenly energized, Meg swung

her legs over the edge of the bed. "Let's go talk to your mother in person. We can walk over in the rain."

Seth smiled. "Romantic but soggy. All right." Then he added, "Art wanted to talk again later."

"So let's invite your mom and them all to dinner," Meg replied.

"Deal."

Meg dressed quickly, then went downstairs to call Christopher, who was pleased to accept the invitation, while Seth called Art on the landline.

"Art says his wife won't be back until tomorrow and he'd love another free meal," Seth reported after hanging up. "Nothing else new. He'll be here at five. Let's find Max and go up the hill."

Meg found a rain slicker covered with dust—she hadn't worn it for weeks. Max was sitting outside on a long lead, under the roof of the connecting space, and jumped up eagerly, his tail wagging furiously, when he saw Seth. "His loyalties are certainly clear," Meg said, as dog and master exchanged enthusiastic greetings. "Good thing, too."

Seth gathered up Max's leash, and together they walked up the hill, angling northward. Meg turned her face to the sky, relishing the feel of the rain, oblivious to her soaked hair. They stopped when they came to the newly planted section of orchard that bridged their properties. Meg regarded it critically.

"Problems?" Seth asked.

"Like I'd know? Their leaves are green, mostly, and the trees are still standing. That's about the extent of my expertise. Bree tells me I should be worrying about their root systems this year. At this moment I don't feel like worrying about anything."

"I second that." Seth pulled her close, joining her in contemplation of the orchard. "Do you want me to give this land to you outright?"

"I do not! We have a business agreement, remember? I don't know if this is a community property state or whatever, but I want to keep business and personal separate. Unless you want me poking around in your business, commenting on how much you paid for your last miter saw, and couldn't you buy your supplies in bulk and get a better rate?"

"Point taken!" Seth held up his hands in surrender. "But you'll agree that this is ours?"

"This orchard? Yes, it is—our first joint effort. Sappy, aren't we? Standing here in the rain admiring a bunch of spindly little trees?"

"But happy, right?"

"Oh yes. Very. Let's go see your mother before we get distracted again."

They were both thoroughly soaked by the time they reached Lydia's back door. She pulled it open and said, "What on earth? Come in, come in, you two. Whatever possessed you . . ." Then she took a closer look at them, holding hands and beaming foolishly. "No, you didn't? You did! I don't know who to hug first—Seth for finally figuring things out, or you, Meg, for saying yes. I'm assuming it was yes?"

"Of course it was. I'll take a hug."

It didn't take much persuading. "I'm so happy for you both," Lydia whispered to Meg as she held her. Then she stepped back and said to her son, "Do you know how many times I wanted to give you a kick in the butt? You may be my offspring, but I have no idea what you were waiting for. Come in and dry off."

"Actually we just came over to invite you to dinner, but we wanted you to know before the news went viral."

"Who else have . . . No, I don't want to know. Thank you. I'd love to be there. I'll even bring champagne. What time?"

"Say, six? I don't think we'll be grilling outside tonight, with this weather."

"And isn't that welcome news? All right, six, with bells on. Have you told Rachel?"

"No, not yet," Seth answered.

"Can I do it?" Lydia asked eagerly. "Or would you rather?"

"You look like you're going to burst if you don't tell someone. You go ahead," Seth said.

"And tell her 'thank you' from me," Meg added. When Lydia looked confused, she said, "She'll understand."

They made their farewells, and Meg and Seth, with a dripping, frisking Max, turned toward Meg's house. "Now you have to tell *your* parents," Seth reminded Meg.

"I'll call as soon as I get back. This is all my mother's fault, you know—she's the one who sent me here. Or maybe she was just channeling all our ancestors who lived here— they seem to want me to stay. Should we go thank them, too?"

"Mother first. The others can wait. They aren't going anywhere."

"True. Look at the time! Art and Christopher will be showing up in a couple of hours and I have no idea if I have any food to offer them."

"We'll improvise," Seth said calmly. "It's not the food, it's the company."

"Easy for you to say . . . I think I froze something, and I've still got plenty of vegetables . . ."

Meg managed to scrounge together a lasagna from what she had among her supplies, including a batch of fresh tomatoes that demanded to be used sooner rather than later. Bree volunteered to go out and buy bread, and she came back not only with the bread but also carrying a cake. Seth set the table in the dining room, complete with candles to offset the overcast sky outside, where it was still raining lightly.

When Art and Christopher arrived within minutes of each other, Meg convened a brief meeting around the kitchen table. Meg led off. "Art, do you know anything more?"

He shook his head. "If you're asking if we've found Gabe Aubuchon, no. Look, if I asked my people to do a search, they'd want to know why. So I went back into the woods myself and found the building, or what's left of it—looks like a propane tank exploded, so right now it's mostly splinters and ashes. I doubt that anyone could identify whatever was going on in there. If anyone finds it, I can say it might have been a meth lab. Which means you, Meg, are the only person who really knows what was in there, because you saw it. I won't count Seth, because he wasn't exactly paying attention. As for Gabe Aubuchon? As I said, no sign of him. But there *was* another road in, and he did have a car registered in his name, which I found abandoned halfway to Amherst."

"So he's gone? Art . . ."—Meg hesitated before putting the most important question into words—"are you willing to just let him go?"

Art looked at Seth for a long moment before answering. "I think I am."

"Christopher," Meg went on, "does anything change if

he's found and he tells the state agency about his role in the insect infestation?"

"Not really. However they came to be here, the insects *are* here now, and the procedures would be the same. There is no way to stop the process."

"So Gabe's actions would have no bearing on what they do?"

"No, I'm afraid not."

"What about you? Do you have any liability, if what he did is discovered?"

"My lab may come under scrutiny as a potential source for the insects—they can do DNA analyses now and match the ones they found in Granford with the ones that have been distributed legally. I hope it doesn't come to that, and it seems unlikely—we're close enough to Worcester to make this infestation credible. I would not be comfortable making an effort to deflect such an investigation, because that would compound the problem, but if it does not arise, I won't say anything."

"How will you explain his sudden disappearance from the lab?"

Christopher shook his head. "I will profess to be clueless about his whereabouts, which is no less than the truth."

"I am truly sorry to put you in this position, Christopher," Meg said, then turned to Seth.

"And you?" She knew his answer, but it was important that the others hear it, too.

"I don't plan to press charges. Gabe could have let me die, and he didn't. He could have killed you, too, Meg. He made the choice not to. I think we have enough—what do you call it? Plausible deniability—to say nothing."

Meg nodded. "I feel like I owe him, for both of us. So

we all agree? Let Gabe Aubuchon go on his way, without taking any official action?" Meg scanned the faces around the table. "You realize we're probably breaking a few laws by doing this."

"I'll take the heat, if it comes to that," Art said. "But I don't think it will."

Meg looked past them to where Bree was standing. "Bree, if you go along with us, that makes you an accomplice. Are you okay with that?"

Bree shrugged. "I'd say it's for the greater good, as long as none of you guys gets in trouble for it. If you do, I'm going to pretend I'm real stupid and didn't know a thing."

"Then we're done. Thank you all."

Lydia timed her arrival perfectly, pulling in a few minutes later, clutching two bottles of chilled champagne. She was welcomed warmly. "I take it you all know the news?"

"You mean about Meg and Seth?" Art asked. "Heck, we had an office pool going about how long it would take him to ask."

"You did not!" Meg protested.

"Maybe." Art winked at her.

"Small-town living," Meg muttered to herself. Louder she said, "Food's ready—we just need to get it to the table in the dining room."

Meg looked around her candlelit dining room, filled with happy people. She and Seth sat at one end, simultaneously hosts and guests of honor; they were holding hands under the table. Bree had agreed to deal with serving and clearing, with as much grace as she could muster. Meg's phone call with her parents had gone well, with Elizabeth Corey promising to visit soon and to not interfere with Meg's necessary harvest activities, which was as much as Meg could hope for.

Gabe Aubuchon had been pardoned, at least within their inner circle. It felt right, and whatever the legalities, she would always be grateful to him.

It was a perfect evening . . . until someone started pounding at the screen door in the kitchen. "Hello? Is anyone there?"

It sounded suspiciously like Donald Butterfield. "You want me to get rid of him?" Bree offered.

Seth stood up. "Let me take care of it." He strode off to the kitchen, and Meg could hear the rumble of voices, Seth's lower, Donald's querulous. How would Seth manage to explain his conspicuous absence the last couple of days?

Meg was surprised to see him return quickly—with Donald in tow. "I told Donald that he was welcome to join our celebration. Will someone please find him a glass?"

Donald looked both mortified and touched to be included. "I'm sorry to barge in . . . I had no idea . . . I completely understand now . . ." He paused when Bree thrust a glass of champagne into his hand. Donald took a deep breath and straightened his back. "My heartfelt congratulations to Meg and Seth. May their union endure as long as the houses that shelter them."

Recipes

Raspberry Shrub

The drink called "shrub" has a long history. In the Colonial era in America it was a soft drink, also known as "drinking vinegar," because it included vinegar that had been steeped with fruit or herbs for up to several days. (Vinegar is actually less acidic than lemon juice—and a lot easier to obtain in Colonial America.) Strained and sweetened, it would be reduced to a syrup and added to water or carbonated water. The sugar in the fruit plus the added sugar smooth out the acidity of the vinegar.

At her restaurant Gran's in Granford, Nicky Czarnecki has been experimenting with a version that can be served with or without alcohol. Either way, it's a cool drink for a hot evening.

Here is a simple recipe from a half-century ago:

> 5 quarts ripe raspberries
> 1 quart mild vinegar (any kind)
> Sugar (to taste)

Crush the berries and add the vinegar. Let it stand for 24 hours, then strain. Measure the liquid and add one-half pound of sugar for each quart of juice. Heat to just boiling then put in jars or bottles.

When ready to serve, dilute this with three parts cold water to one part syrup, and serve in tall glasses with plenty of ice.

Of course you may add white rum or brandy, and you may vary the fruits depending on what is ripe.

Here's a more modern recipe:

Select very ripe fruit. Chop or mash it, then weigh it. In a bowl, combine equal parts of the fruit and sugar, and cover. Let the mixture sit for anywhere from a few hours to a few days, while the sugar draws all the liquid from the fruit. Then add an equal amount of vinegar and stir. Strain it and bottle it. It is ready to use right away, but it will also age well.

Spatchcocked Chicken

If you've never heard the term, "spatchcocked" means flattened. Remove the backbone and the breastbone from your whole chicken, then press it flat so you can cook it on the grill or broil it. Flattening it will make it cook more evenly.

If you're grilling the chicken outside, it will definitely benefit from a marinade. This one is simple and tasty.

> The thinly peeled rind of 2 lemons
> 2–3 thin slices fresh ginger
> 2 tablespoons soy sauce
> 4 tablespoons olive oil
> 1 teaspoon sesame oil
> 2–4 cloves garlic (pressed or finely minced)
> Thyme (fresh if possible)
> Freshly ground pepper

If you love to julienne, make slivers of the lemon peel and the ginger. If you're in a hurry, grate the ginger and even the lemon rind. Use fresh thyme if you have it, but dried is fine too.

Mix everything together and massage the chicken with it. If you don't want your hands to smell like garlic and sesame oil for the rest of the day, wear latex gloves or paint the marinade on with a brush.

And grill away!

Puffed Apple Pancake

Sometimes this recipe is called "Apple Dutch Baby" but Dutch baby is usually more like a flat pancake. In contrast, this one puffs up and the top becomes crisp. It resembles Toad in the Hole, a savory pub dish with sausages in England, but this recipe is sweet.

Preheat the oven to 400 degrees F.

APPLES:

> 2 tablespoons salted butter
> 3 medium cooking apples (like Cortlands), peeled,
>   cored, and sliced thickly
> 2 tablespoons sugar

Melt the butter in a 9" cast-iron skillet, then add the apples and sauté on medium-high heat until they begin to brown just a bit. Sprinkle the sugar over them and continue cooking for a couple more minutes. (If the mixture looks too soupy, drain some of the liquid off so the batter won't become soggy.)

When the apples are just about ready, make the batter.

BATTER:

> 1 cup whole milk
> 2 eggs
> 1 cup white flour
> 2 tablespoons sugar
> ½ teaspoon ground cinnamon
> ½ teaspoon salt
> 2 tablespoons vanilla extract
> 1 tablespoon melted butter

Combine all the ingredients in a blender or food processor, then blend for a minute (a full minute—this is important, so time it), right before you're ready to bake.

While the apples are still over the heat on the stove, pour the batter over them (the batter should sizzle around the edges) and immediately place the skillet into the preheated oven. Bake for 30 minutes. If all goes well, the batter will puff up and turn golden and crisp.

This is a dish that should be served as quickly as possible, while it's still warm, maybe with a sprinkle of powdered sugar.

Apple orchard owner Meg Corey is about to find herself in a whole herd of trouble.

FROM NATIONAL BESTSELLING AUTHOR
Sheila Connolly

SOUR APPLES
• *An Orchard Mystery* •

Meg is finally feeling settled into her new life in Granford when her old Boston coworker Lauren Converse comes barreling into town, running the congressional campaign for a former hometown football hero. But Meg doesn't have time to worry about why her boyfriend, Seth, seems reluctant to back Lauren's campaign when her neighbor, local dairy farmer Joyce Truesdell, is found dead from an apparent kick to the head from one of her cows.

When an autopsy shows that the fatal blow actually came from a weapon, Meg is even more troubled. Popular opinion points to Joyce's husband as the culprit, but Meg can't help wondering if someone wanted the outspoken dairy farmer out of the way—but why? She'll have to find out who had a beef with the victim, before she's the next one to get creamed . . .

Includes Delicious Recipes!

sheilaconnolly.com
facebook.com/SheilaConnollyWriter
facebook.com/TheCrimeSceneBooks
penguin.com

M1185T0912